# What Peo[

MW00526198

"This novel has as many twists and turns as the roads leading to Minerva." *~David J. Shivers, President of the Salem Historical Society*

"*pieces* is a remarkable piece of fiction. The story of the boys' journey from the innocence of youth to tragic maturity is a riveting and engrossing tale. The journey is one of greed, mayhem and murder and takes place in the unexpected and unfortunate world of the very young. *pieces* is a "must read" for all lovers of mystery as well as lovers of good fiction." *~Karen J. Common, author of Held in Heaven's Arms*

"*pieces* is a book that you will become absorbed in from the first page to the last. You will not just read but fall into the excitement, suspense and intrigue. It just may be the book you will want to read in one sitting. The surprising pieces illustrated on the cover just keep coming through the pages. I love the creativity presented by Karen Biery in this beautifully imagined book."~ *Carol Minteer, retired teacher*

"Think of your most cherished childhood memory of adventure shared with your best friend. Karen Biery's *pieces* takes the reader through these memories and weaves a sordid tale that spirals out of control from one bad decision. This gripping, page-turning story moves the reader through a stack of moral decisions and their consequences that will end in self-reflection. A great novel for Book Club discussions!" ~ *Sandy Copeland, Sandra's Gardening Services*

"A real page turner. Karen Biery takes the reader from the simple innocence of two young boys' accidental discovery of pieces of historical artifacts with special powers, through a complex evolution of moral dilemmas among many intertwined characters sharing small town life. Full of suspenseful action and vivid imagery, the fantasy makes the reader question his or her own moral choices when it comes to ambitions, wants and needs." ~ *Gwen Eastlake-DeCrow, Freelance Writer*

# Karen Biery

**River Road Press**
**Branson, Missouri**

Published by **River Road Press**

COPYRIGHT © 2011 by Karen Biery

Library of Congress Control Number: 2010936439

pieces Soft Cover: 978-0-9827923-2-2

Edited by Pat McGrath Avery

Printed in the United States of America

To those crippled
by envy
and greed.

# ACKNOWLEDGEMENTS

It has been only one year since my first novel's release. After the launch of *believe* my life has changed forever and it is difficult to pin point the special people who have supported this new effort. But I will try….

Special gratitude is sent out to my husband, Jeff for believing in me when I did not believe in myself and for the countless hours of listening. Thank you to my parents, Max and Evelyn Newton, who have been two of my leading advocates. Props to you, Dad for helping me with the inspiration to draw the "pieces." To my in-laws, Bob and Laura Biery, for their support and blessings. To my step children, Anne and Adam Biery (and Brian Cushman) for their excited support and smiles. Thank you to my Aunt Carol for her enthusiasm and witty support.

I am especially grateful for my group of readers (you know who you are) who had a tough assignment and did a remarkable job. A constant grateful mindset is extended to Dr. Craig Paulenich for encouraging the voice of poetry to scream in my head. Thank you to the grammar king and queen, Bill and Jean Esposito for their suggestions and help. To my eagle eye word "fixer", Sue Stitle for her willingness to read countless times with enthusiasm. To my anxious grinning supporter, Barb Biery for her kindness, excitement, and most of all help and a big thank you to Gwen for her friendship, encouragement, knowledge and genuine interest. I'm proud to call all of you friends.

A much delayed thanks, as well as recognition, to the woman who has the amazing ability to create not one, but two pieces of jewelry from a verbal description and a two-dimensional drawing. Barbara Gillis you are a remarkable and gifted artist.

Thank you to the people of the area who have enthusiastically supported and followed my work. And a heartfelt thanks to those who have given me the opportunity to view history untouched and unearthed. Your graciousness will never be forgotten.

# BEYOND HER SHADOW
*for the Adena Indian princess, and those who came before her*

## I. The Great Trail
Innocence runs
Past Whispering Trees
And Dead Man's Lookout.
It's a race to the top.
I am the Victor.

Stolen breath,
Lifeless limbs.
One hundred degrees
Welcomes a summer shower.

A new world comes into view
From the top of the stones
Set in a ring,
Their purpose kept hidden.

A jealous lunge
From slick minerals
Gives way to darkness.
Falling, falling...
Stop.

## II. Discovery
Cold,
Blind,
Silent,
And breathless.
Am I dead?

Wandering fingers
Reel from morbid thoughts.
Her bones embrace metal and stone,
Of pieces long forgotten.

Beads of teaching,
Purpose, and knowledge
Form the crafted necklace
That calls to the Helper.

Imagined beauty
Of aged days
Brings life to bones,
And energy to souls,
From a lowered stance.

### III. Ruin
Secret curiosity
Pulls him to Indian Hill.
Noiseless battles
Conquer a twisted heart.
His sticky fingers gain.

Resisted desires
Warp the coveted power,
And turn honor to greed
That twirls unrestrained.

Whispers that stir,
Backwards glances,
Callous laughter,
Warn the mind of threats.

Cold stares and
Obsessive fingers
Grasp for her ultimate gift.
Only suffering and death
Brings her peace.

### IV. Redemption
Sleepless appeals
Spoken in dreams
Are performed in honor,
Debt, fear,
And query.

Her cry of praise
Spools from the depths,
And tickles the skin
Pricked with fright.

Held breath
Stolen by nerves
Is restored by reflections
Of embraced loss.

Her radiant stare
Melts his riveted dread.
Kindness from her eyes
Warms the air
And relaxes the force.

### V. Free
The gathering wind
Throws death's confetti
Around the closure.
A psalm of avowal
Sent by design.

Upturned faces
Color the sky.
Red wilts to orange,
Pink ensues.

Veiled by dusk
Transparency reigns.
Life's voice snuffed still,
Resonating memories
Spiral...

# 1

"I don't wanna go fishin'."

"Ah, come on."

"It's raining. Fish don't bite good in the rain."

"Says who? Ah, come on. It'll be fun."

"I don't feel like it."

"You *never* feel like it."

Anger flashed in Collin's eyes. It was true. Fishing was the most painful memory since Mark Sims' death.

Collin's father had been an avid fisherman most of his life. His collection of fishing lures overflowed into six tackle boxes. One special box was filled with unfinished pieces begging to be a part of the sportsman folklore. Bits of feathers and string made up many of the half-finished ties. They hadn't been touched for eight months.

After a brief silence, Collin offered a compromise, "How about riding bikes?" He tried to sound enthusiastic.

"Nah," Jesse replied automatically.

"Swimming?"

"It's raining, remember?"

"You're a jerk, Jesse." Collin started to walk away.

"I'm just kiddin', Collin. Don't be so stupid."

Collin faked a smile. Most of the time Jesse knew just how to get under his skin. He wasn't in the mood today. He had walked out of the kitchen door this morning while his mother held her head in her hands. She had a huge pile of papers from the bank that covered the surface of the table. He recalled the conversation.

"What's wrong, Mom?"

She didn't answer. She never looked up. Collin tried a lighter approach.

"Looks like it's gonna rain." Still, she didn't respond.

He walked up to his mother and put his hand on her shoulder. He tried to be grown up. He even lowered his voice when he spoke. That brought a smile to his mother's face.

"Are you okay, Mom?'

She roughed up his hair. "Collin Robert Sims. You have grown up so fast."

He smiled at his mother's kindness. He tried to help out as much as possible with the chores around the house. He took on a paper route to help out with the family's finances. He thought about adding a second route. He never asked for money. He knew there wasn't enough, so most of the time he went without. He did the best he could for an eleven-year-old.

If he admitted the truth, he was scared to death. He had a hard time thinking of himself as the man of the household. Waves of anger clouded his thoughts of his father. In those insecure moments, he sought his mother's approval. Today was one of those days.

She put her arm around his thin frame and squeezed him. "Did I ever tell you how proud I am of you?"

"Not today," he responded, enjoying the change in his mother's mood.

"Well, buddy, I am very proud of you. I want you to know how much I appreciate all you do for me," she pulled him closer, "...for us."

"It's just my job, ma'am." He lowered his voice again.

She laughed. "Go on outside and play, before it gets too wet."

"No, I can stay and help." He motioned toward the pile of papers.

"I'm fine. I just have to read all this stuff. It will take me a while."

"I can help." He tried to sound convincing.

Again she smiled at his effort. She marveled at how lucky she was to have a kind son. She whispered a silent prayer of thanksgiving.

"I appreciate that, but this is something I have to sift through. Why don't you come back in an hour or so to make sure I haven't been swallowed up by the paper monster?" They both giggled.

Her smile was convincing enough. "Okay, Mom. I'll see you in a little bit."

He walked over to the kitchen door and just before he walked out, he turned back to her and said, "I love you, Mom." He blew a kiss in her direction.

She looked up from the papers in front of her. Her eyes flooded with tears. Her hand followed the old ritual of pretending to grab the kiss in mid-air. She pulled the symbolic kiss to her heart and quickly responded, "I love you more." He walked out of the door.

The weather had been strange for northern Ohio. Normally, the days were sweltering hot and humid, but this year June and July were wet and cool. In the early mornings, warmth came from a sweatshirt, but not today; the air was thick. The clouds hung low leaving the sky shadowed by a thick haze. Collin stared at the darkening vapor as it slid toward the earth.

"Collin? Hello...Earth to Collin." Jesse smirked.

3

"Shut up, Jesse," he snapped. "I was just thinking."

"Thinking about what?"

"About what to do." Collin's thoughts drifted toward home.

"Come on, Collin, let's do something. I'm tired of standing around. It's been such a boring summer." Agitation filled Jesse's voice.

Excitement lit Collin's face. "Hey! I've got an idea. Let's go to Indian Hill."

"That's a great idea!"

The two boys raced through a small section of houses to an old warehouse parking lot. Their legs brushed through the overgrown weeds in the abandoned pavement until they broke through the green jungle to the railroad tracks, just beyond the property line. They stopped for barely a second as they listened for the sound of a train. With the air empty of sound, they crossed the tracks and climbed the embankment on the opposite side. The hill was steep, but their repeated trips marked the trail well. They knew from experience where not to step.

Their youthful legs carried them through an unmarked path until it intersected with *The Great Trail*. The innocence and excitement of the two boys kept them from the significance of this historic place. They rarely thought about the folklore that has been part of local whispers for more than two hundred years.

Collin's breathing was labored first. "Slow down, Jesse! I can't breathe." His body was doubled over with his hands on his knees. He tried to take in as many deep breaths as possible.

Jesse threw himself on the ground beside him. His body sprawled out like a bird in flight. "Ah, c'mon!" he whined. "We're almost there."

4

"I know! Just relax, will ya? I can't breathe."

Jesse mocked Collin by playing dead. With his body still on the hardened trail, he hung his tongue out of his mouth and crossed his eyes. Collin kicked the bottom of his shoes.

"Last one there is a rotten egg." He sprinted away from him.

Jesse jumped to his feet, but Collin had the lead. Jesse followed Collin up the path through 'Whispering Trees' so named because of the sound the wind made as it rushed through their branches. He trailed Collin through 'Dead Man's Lookout', a cliff that overlooked *The Great Trail* on Old Man Crafter's farm.

Collin used his last spurt of energy and ran hard to 'Indian Hill'. He fell on the ground and clutched his side to soothe the pain. Jesse's face hit the ground with a dull thud. They panted for air side by side.

"I guess I won," Collin chided.

"You did," Jesse answered sarcastically. "You usually do."

The rain clouds skirted their faces as they faced the sky. A sporadic raindrop reminded them of the coming threat. With renewed strength from the mile uphill sprint, they faced each other with their knees drawn to their chests and talked.

"How many did you find last time?" Jesse asked.

"Nine," Collin responded proudly.

"I wonder how many are here."

"None, as long as we sit here." Collin jumped to his feet and started to search the ground for arrowheads.

They walked slowly, first in parallel position and then separated to opposing directions. Jesse was the first one to shout with excitement.

"Wow! Look at this one!"

He clasped his tight fist and ran toward Collin. When he opened his hand, Collin gasped. Carved from white flint, the arrowhead held a pale pink cast. Its serrated edges were still sharp. When Jesse ran his fingers over the edge, a small piece fell to the ground. They dropped to their knees, but were unable to find it.

"It's okay, Jesse." Collin tried to comfort him, "It is a beautiful arrowhead. I've never found one that color." Jesse smiled at the gesture.

Of all of his friends, Collin was by far the kindest. Jesse was a decent kid, but he had a tough life. His mother was a drug addict and spent more time in rehab than at home. The empty promise of going straight was long dismissed. His hard-working father spent too much money on booze and cigarettes. Jesse, like Collin, had grown up too fast, but Jesse's eyes reflected his mother's wildness. Collin had a calming effect on him. More than anything, he wished he could be more like Collin, but the sarcasm in his voice usually won over the sweetness. As hard as he tried, he just couldn't rid himself of that trait.

Jesse pointed to the top of the field and said, "Let's go up there. We usually do pretty good up there."

He pointed to an unusual mound in the middle of the field. Most of the surrounding ground was flat, almost abnormally so for this area. It seemed as if it was intentional. Perfect farming ground many folks said and truth be told, this property was the envy of many for its rich soil. The mound seemed displaced but was accepted as part of the terrain.

Mr. Crafter, the landowner, did not like intruders. He usually fired a few shots in the air to warn off the trespassers, but Collin's father had been a good friend to Bob and the old man didn't mind Collin looking for arrowheads. He didn't care for his troublemaker friend, but he tolerated Jesse as long as he was with Collin. Only once did he shoot into the air to warn Jesse. He never returned to 'Indian Hill' alone.

They climbed to the top of the knob. "It never looks this high until you get up here," marveled Collin.

"It's higher up here," Jesse answered as he scrambled to the top of a large boulder. "Look!" he yelled. "I can see your house!"

Collin quickly scrambled on top of the rock beside Jesse. It was true.

"I never noticed that before," Collin said with surprise. Jesse didn't respond.

At the very top of the hill sat a group of rocks. All were oversized and placed in a circle. Each rock was separated by equal distance. The top of each boulder was flat and measured about four feet wide. There were eight of them.

When Collin's father and Bob Crafter brought him to this place the first time, he remembered lying on one of the rocks. He stretched his hands and feet and barely touched the edges. Now, when he placed his head on the edge, his feet hung over the other.

Jesse jumped from rock to rock, taking great pleasure in the distance he was able to jump. Collin mimicked him. They made their way around the ring of stones once, but before they started their second round, the clouds burst open with a loud clap of thunder. Within seconds, rain soaked their clothes.

"At least it's a warm rain," Collin yelled over the pounding rain.

Jesse cupped his hand over his ear. "What?" He pointed to a tree. "Let's get under that!" He motioned for Collin to follow.

7

They scrambled to a maple tree, which had rooted itself on the steepest part of the mound. Jesse slid past the tree on the wet ground. They both laughed.

Collin stared into the falling rain. He held out his palm to catch the drops. "Looks like it's letting up already."

"Let's wait just a little longer. It's gonna quit."

They stood under the tree until the rain softened to a light sprinkle. Carefully they climbed back to the top of the hill. After losing their footing several times, they finally scrambled to the top.

"The rain should help the flint stand out better," Collin said without hesitation.

"I swear, Collin, you come up with the weirdest stuff. Where did you hear that?"

"Dad told me."

Jesse's eyes dropped to the ground. All he could manage was, "Oh."

Within a few minutes, they each had two more arrowheads. Collin wanted to make a point about his earlier statement, but Jesse was too excited to listen. They sat down together on a rock to compare their treasures.

"I found the prettiest one," Jesse said with pride as he held up a pink serrated arrowhead.

"Oh yeah! Well, I found the biggest one." Collin quickly added.

"Let me see."

Jesse snatched the dark grey arrowhead from Collin's open palm. The edges were cut with a row of deep chisel marks, and the point was still sharp. A vein of white flint ran diagonally through the arrowhead. The bottom was carved with two notches to bind it to an arrow. Its size was much larger than normal.

"It's really cool, Collin. Can I keep it?"

"No. I found it."

Jesse made a motion like he was going to put it in his pocket.

"Give it back, Jesse." Collin demanded.

Jesse stood and jumped across the top of the flattened rocks. "Catch me if you can," he taunted.

"Jesse! Give it back!

Jesse used the extra length in his legs to gain an advantage over Collin. Within a few leaps, he was several feet ahead of him. He lifted the arrowhead in the air and taunted his friend.

"Jesse! You're a jerk. Give it...."

Collin jumped off the front of the rock toward the center of the ring to intercept Jesse. His shoe caught the edge of the rock and he lost his balance. The surface was too slippery to recover. He hit the ground with a thud and disappeared.

Jesse screamed, "Collin!" No reply came.

When Collin woke, all he found was darkness. His first instinct was to feel for his eyes. He rubbed his hands over them and forced himself to breathe. He looked up and saw a faint patch of light. Slowly he realized he had fallen.

Jesse's cries were coming louder, more strained. Collin tried to speak, but couldn't. He patted the ground. It was damp. He felt something slide over his hand. He found his voice.

"Ahh!" He shook his hand free of slimy thoughts.

He yelled up to Jesse, "I'm...ok...I think."

The echo started as a whisper and became more agitated at the disturbance. Collin swallowed the rest of his comments. He jumped at the sound of Jesse's voice.

"Oh my God, I thought you were dead! Did you break anything?"

The true concern in Jesse's voice comforted Collin. He slowly moved each part of his body. He pulled his legs under him. He winced from the jolt of the fall. Even his teeth were sore.

"Nothing's broken," he responded.

"Can you stand?"

"Yep." Collin tilted his head to listen to the echo soften.

"Are you bleeding?"

"I don't think so. I can't see a thing down here!"

"What the hell happened?"

"I don't know. I just jumped off the edge of the rock and fell down...here."

"How far down are you?"

"I don't know. Quite a ways, I guess."

"Can you see me?" Jesse waved his hand through the opening in the grass.

Collin looked toward the ceiling, "Barely." His head swooned.

"Are you on solid ground?"

"I think so." Collin knelt to the dark ground and felt for another opening. He was careful not to move his feet.

"For God's sake, don't move!" Jesse's voice rose. "You may be on a ledge or something. You must have fallen into a secret cave." Jesse's voice echoed loudly. "Can you see anything?"

"No. It's completely dark. I think...."

Collin screamed. His hands brushed something smooth, cool, and sharp. He patted the soft earth and felt a group of slender objects. They felt like bones from a rib cage. He stood in a panic.

"Jesse! Get me out of here!" His strained voice cracked.

"How?"

"Go get a rope from the barn."

10

"What rope?"

"In the barn!" He yelled with disgust. "Get the longest one you can find."

"How am I gonna get you out?"

"I...I don't know, we'll figure it out!" Fear closed his throat. "Just get me out of here!" His words came in short panicked bursts. "Hurry!"

Jesse heard Collin's muffled voice, "Don't tell Mom!"

With Jesse gone and Collin standing alone in the dark, the place started to crawl with life. Collin heard things as they moved around him. The strange noises echoed against the black walls. His imagination worked overtime. He muttered to himself to stay calm. He could feel his heart race in his throat. His mouth was dry.

He whispered to himself, "Don't panic...just breathe...that's it...breathe... one...two...three...fo...."

Suddenly, a rock fell from the opening. It crashed to the ground at his feet. He covered his head to shield himself. A large clump of dirt followed. A mound of grass soon followed. With all of the rain and flash floods of late, the saturated ground was very soft. Another clump of dirt fell, followed by a spatter of small gravel. It echoed wildly around him, like spitting firecrackers.

After a few moments, it was quiet. The sound of moving things surrounded him again. He tried to focus but he couldn't see his hand as he waved it in front of his face. He tried to calm his nerves by taking deep breaths, but he caught himself holding it more often than not. The slithering sound throbbed in his ears. He covered them in defiance.

Suddenly the ground above him slid into action. Echoing debris resonated through the room. He almost welcomed the noise as it drowned out his panic, except the clumps came hard and fast. He dodged dirt and rocks as they

11

pounded the floor around him. He covered his head with his hands and crouched to the ground. He dared to move his feet in the darkness. He thought if Jesse didn't get him out soon, he would be buried alive. All he could do was pray.

# 2

Jesse's lungs burned as he ran down the hill. He slid more than he ran, but nonetheless, he stayed upright. He rushed through the trail in the woods, taking many shortcuts along the way. Several trees had fallen in the past few weeks blocking his hurried movement. He jumped over each one with the skill of a hurdler.

Down over the railroad embankment he slid. He never stopped to look for a train. He leapt across the double tracks in four strides. The prickled thistles mixed with the sting of nettles slapped his bare legs as he rushed through the abandoned parking lot. He didn't notice the tiny streams of blood racing down his wet legs. His breathing came in short, labored gasps.

He never heard the call of his friend Keaton as he ducked through the small cluster of houses. He ran down the alley to the end of the street, up over Mrs. Henderson's rose fence, ripped his shorts on the thorns and landed in the field, which led him to Collin's barn. Fresh cow pies littered the pasture but he made no attempt to dodge them. Slop covered his legs. His eyes were fixed on the barn.

By the time he swung the door open, his limbs were sapped of all energy. His eyes darted around the room scanning for a rope. He found one hanging on a nail by the door, but it was too short. He saw a wire cable wound around a tire rim. He tried to pick it up, but knew there was no way he would make it carrying the weight. He started to panic, and then his eyes found a long rope tied around a beam in the haymow.

He climbed the wooden ladder to the top and swung his body over the beam. Moving as quickly as possible, he untied the knots. He shimmied over to the second knot. His balance never failed even though he was deathly afraid of heights. His friend needed to be rescued, and he was the only one who could do it.

He flung the rope from his right shoulder down around his left hip. He moved quickly until the end knot caught on a nail. The rope jerked tight and Jesse lost his balance. He dangled on the ladder by his left hand. Sweat poured down his face and burned his eyes. He stretched his feet until he felt the next rung. His other hand rested on a flashlight that stuck out of the hay. He shoved it into his pocket. After a deep breath, he shook the rope free and ran out the door.

The cows in the field gave no thought to this panicked young boy as he ran past them. His feet splattered through the soiled grass. He retraced his same jump over the fence, but this time he avoided the thorns. Keaton yelled again as

14

he ran past for the second time. He followed him, but Jesse's assertive 'NO!' kept him from continuing.

When Jesse reached the top of 'Indian Hill', he couldn't speak. He quickly tied the flashlight to the end of his rope and lowered it down the hole. The hard bump of the flashlight on Collin's head was the welcomed announcement of Jesse's arrival. He was too happy to be irritated.

He felt the end of the rope and recognized the flashlight. Quickly he fumbled for the switch and turned it on. The light bounced around the walls in an erratic swing. He was too hurried to notice the skill with which the walls had been formed. He freed the flashlight and tied the rope around his waist.

"Take the end to the maple tree, wrap the rope around it, and pull like hell!" he yelled to Jesse.

Jesse grunted in response and followed Collin's orders. Collin hoped his ordeal would soon be over. He shined the light over the walls. The intentional curves of the ceiling left no doubt in Collin's mind that this was not a natural cavern. At the center of the dome was the opening Collin had fallen through. His heart began to beat faster as he realized he was standing in some sort of a chamber.

He moved the light down the wall in front of him. He turned in a circle and kept the light on the walls tracing where they met the floor. There were no other openings, no other way out, but up. He moved his feet and kicked something. Instinctively he moved the beam of light to his feet.

He felt a slight tug around his waist. Jesse must have wrapped the rope around the tree. Soon he would be out of there. Another shower of small pebbles started to fall around him from the movement of the rope. He held his breath. A few more tugs and he would start to rise. He felt the rope squeeze tighter. He positioned it under his arms and held on tight. His feet began to lift from the floor.

The movement was slow. He heard Jesse calling from the distance, yet his eyes were drawn to the floor. Slowly he ascended.

Suddenly, the rope fell limp. Collin's body tumbled. He braced himself for a hard fall, but instead the rope caught and stopped him a few feet from the floor. His body swung wildly. The flashlight plunged toward the floor. With the final burst of light, Collin thought he saw a skeleton. He strained his eyes to see, but darkness covered them.

Jesse wrapped the rope around the tree and pulled. He was surprised how easy the heavy weight moved. He felt he was gaining momentum when he slipped on the wet ground. The rope slid from his hands. He scrambled to grab it. With his hand wedged between the rope and the tree, he screamed in pain.

With thoughts of Collin's rescue, he wrapped the rope around his hips. He twirled his body until his hand worked free. He refused to look at his mangled fingers. He knew if he stopped so would the rescue. From depths unexplored, he pulled with what strength he had left. It worked. Collin began to rise toward the light of the opening.

As Collin approached the gap, he noticed the ceiling narrowed drastically. He guessed it couldn't be noticed from the floor. His movement upward was slow but steady and gave him plenty of opportunity to study the structure. For the final ten feet, he moved through a narrowed opening. It looked like some sort of a chute. The walls had stones that protruded from the sides and were strategically placed. He placed his hands and feet on these stones and helped to scale himself to freedom. It seemed effortless.

Finally his hands touched the wet grass. He remembered breathing for the first time in what seemed like hours. He yelled to Jesse.

"I'm up!" Jesse continued to pull with the rope wrapped several times around his waist. "Jesse!"

Jesse looked up from the ground. He wouldn't allow his concentration to be broken. He had to help his friend.

"Are you okay?"

"I think so."

"Can I let go?"

"Let me get away from this hole first."

Collin scrambled across the wet grass until he was sitting on top of a rock. He couldn't shake the vision he thought he saw. He turned to look for Jesse and saw him lying on the ground.

Jesse held his hand to his chest. Something about that looked strangely familiar, but Collin quickly dismissed his thought and ran to him. He found Jesse panting erratically as he coddled his hand tight against his chest.

"What happened?"

"I smashed my hand."

"Let me see."

"No, it hurts."

"Did you break it?"

"I don't know." He looked at Collin with tears in his eyes. "It really hurts."

"Let me see."

Jesse slowly moved his hand to reveal the one that was hurt. His fingers were swollen like sausages, and their color looked abnormal.

"It's throbbing like crazy," Jesse said pathetically.

"We gotta get you to the hospital. It don't look good."

17

Collin helped Jesse to his feet. Together they began their way back.

When they arrived at the railroad tracks, they both stopped and looked down the embankment. Collin knew Jesse would have a difficult time trying to climb down the steep slope.

"Let's go over to the main steps. I know it's quite a bit farther, but it will be easier, I think."

"I can do it," Jesse committed through the pain.

Without hesitation, Jesse started down the hill. The first few feet, he did fine, but the ground was so wet, it didn't take long to lose his footing. He rolled to the bottom of the hill and hit his head on the rail. He didn't move.

Collin's eyes were wide. He watched his friend fall in slow motion, yet it happened in a second. He slid down the hill on his heels and knelt beside Jesse. He was out cold.

Collin pulled Jesse away from the train tracks. Jesse moaned with each movement. A train whistle sounded from the distance. Collin moved Jesse a little farther off the tracks and ran for help.

The closest place to go for help was the barbershop. The barber, Jack Hilbert, was a strange fellow, but he knew Jesse's father well and would know how to get in touch with him. He ran until he saw the still red, blue and white pole. He burst through the door as if he had been thrown. His face was flushed red.

"Jesse's...hurt...by...tracks..." His words were fragmented and labored.

The barbershop was filled with old men waiting to have their hair cut and beards shaved. No one spoke a word. The only movement was from Jack. He walked to the phone and dialed an ambulance.

He held his hand over the receiver, "Where did you say he was, boy?"

"By the tracks," Collin was breathing easier now. Help was coming.

"Where by the tracks?"

"Beside the old factory parking lot."

"Okay...hang on a minute. Boy, is he breathing?" Jack's tone was unmoved.

"Yea...he hurt his hand...and maybe his head...he hit it on the tracks...."

Jack wasn't listening to Collin's tale, he spoke into the receiver, "Yep, he's alive...Okay...I'll tell him...."

Collin was busy explaining his tale to his captivated audience. He completely left out the story of falling into the hole. He picked up with a rope crushing his hand.

One gentleman asked, "What was he pulling?"

Collin stuttered at this question. He opened his mouth to answer, but Jack interrupted just in time.

"Hey, boy...help is coming." He went back to the phone, "Yeah, Bill Williams' boy, Jesse. He works at Jenkins' place downtown...you want me to call him? Okay...I'll tell him." He hung up. "They're coming," he tossed his words to Collin. He picked up his razor and went back to work.

Collin rushed out of the door thankful for the help. He ran back across the parking lot to where he left Jesse. He could see him from a distance. He was sitting up. Collin was relieved.

"You okay?' Collin asked as he sat beside his ragged friend.

"What happened?"

"You slipped down the hill and smashed your head on the rail."

"God!"

Jesse looked a mess. His legs were scratched and covered in dried blood beads. His right hand was twice the size of his left and his head had a bump that puffed up so quickly, it split his skin. He was bleeding quite a bit. Collin took off his t-shirt, turned it inside out, and wadded it into a ball.

He handed it to Jesse, "Put this on your head." Jesse was silent.

Within a few minutes, they heard the ambulance siren. The two boys sat quietly as the back door burst open and out jumped two paramedics. They knelt beside Jesse and checked his blood pressure.

"I think he's in shock," one said to the other.

"His blood pressure is dropping."

"I figured as much."

Gently the young man lifted his hand. "Looks like you did it up good," he spoke to Jesse. He didn't respond. His only sound was a slight moan. Pain warped his face.

"We'll have to get you to the hospital for some x-rays. What's your name, son?"

"Jesse."

"Jesse what?"

"Jesse Williams."

"Where do you live, Jesse Williams?"

"Fourth Street."

"How old are you?"

"Eleven. I'll be twelve in August."

The young man looked at his colleague, "His head's okay. The laceration is from expansion."

They lifted him onto a gurney. After strapping him tightly, they wheeled him over to the door of the ambulance. With a quick shake, the legs underneath the stretcher collapsed and Jesse disappeared from Collin's sight. The final glimpse of his friend was the bottom of Jesse's shoes.

One of the soles had been torn away. His sock protruded and was twisted into a muddy ball. Collin was thankful for his friend's loyalty and sacrifice, and he was sorry Jesse was hurt.

As the ambulance screamed from the parking lot, Collin wondered how his friend would explain the accident. He realized he better go home and tell his mother before someone else did. He shoved his hands into his pockets.

Something sharp pierced his skin under his fingernail, "Ow!" Quickly he withdrew his hand. Fresh blood rimmed his fingernail. He shook his hand.

Slowly he placed his hand back in his pocket and felt a smooth spiral object. The sharp tip tore his pocket lining.

"Cripes!" he exclaimed, disgusted.

What he held in his hand, he had never seen before. He had no idea where it came from and how it got into his pocket. The open spiral was fashioned from some sort of ivory he thought. It was white in color with a slight pearled appearance. It was about three inches long, smooth and hand-carved by someone very skillful. The base of the spiral was wide and it gradually wound itself to a narrow point. At the tip was a tiny open ring. Collin tried to hold the piece by the ring, but it was too small for his fingers to grasp. It slipped to the ground.

When it settled to a stop, the color changed. It took on a pastel rainbow hue. When the shadow of his body covered it, the color changed again to silver. Curious about this strange object, Collin gingerly gathered it in his hand. The side that rested on the ground was slightly flattened compared to the front.

It felt smooth and cool in the palm of his hand. It was then he remembered that feeling in the darkness after he fell. He knew it came from that place, but he didn't remember picking it up. Perplexed, he placed it back in his pocket, being careful not to poke his finger again.

He turned to walk home.

# 3

Bill Williams ran through the emergency doors. His body of six-foot-three and 230 pounds could not be halted. Nerves reddened his face. His hair dripped with sweat. His t-shirt was filthy, and his hands were black from ground-in grease. He ran past the nurse's desk, ignoring her warnings.

"Sir...You cannot go in there," she ran after him as he burst through the emergency room doors. "Sir...."

He spun around to face her. He gritted his teeth. "My son has just been brought here."

Her tone immediately changed, "Well, why didn't you say so, instead of just barging through the doors?"

In his mind her question was not worth answering. "Where is he?' he asked, still irritated.

"He's over here in three," she tried to sound sweet, but his abrasive tone was a reminder of what waited for her at home. Trying to shake the similarities between Bill Williams and her husband Frank was too much for Janey Hemple to handle at this moment.

Her sweet, yet guarded tone continued as she ushered him to bed number three, "He's doing fine, Mr. Williams. He's just a bit shaken. There was a train coming, you know?"

Bill had heard enough from this meaningless woman. Without a thought, he shoved her to the side as soon as she opened the curtain divider. Janey lost her balance and fell into an empty chair. She was stunned and angered at his assertiveness. She started to speak, but when she saw Bill's tender side, her anger subsided and she slipped out behind the curtain. "Just a bit different than..." she muttered under her breath as she walked back to the nurse's station.

Bill placed his hand on Jesse's leg. "Hey slugger. Who hit ya?" It was the only thing he could think of to say.

Jesse's eyes turned to flooding pools, "I'm okay, Dad." He tried to sound brave as he wiped his eyes with his left hand.

"What the hell happened?" The gruffness in the voice returned.

Jesse felt a flash of hot nerves run through his body. He hadn't thought about what he was going to say, but for some reason he felt he should keep the cave a secret. The morning scene played like a mini-movie in his mind as he remembered the run to the barn, the flashlight, and crunching of bones when the rope tightened. The sound nauseated him, not to mention the pain.

"Jesse? Are you okay?"

"Yeah. I'm just rattled I guess."

"Well, what happened? I heard a train was coming."

'Oh thank God,' Jesse thought. 'That was his out.' Quickly he added, "And I hit my head."

"Were you stuck on the tracks?"

"No, I slid down the hill and fell I guess. I knocked myself out." Bill anxiously waited for the story. "I was with Collin. We were walking on *The Great Trail* and took our secret shortcut, but on the way back, the ground was slippery because of the rain." His eyes flew open wide and his voice burst with excitement, "It came down in buckets, Dad!"

"Yea, we got quite a bit in a short time. Go on...."

"Well, anyway, I lost my footing coming down the hill and rolled out onto the tracks and hit my head." He hesitated and added, "I guess I smashed my hand somewhere in all of that." His father believed his lie.

Their conversation was interrupted by a nurse, "X-ray is ready for you, Jesse."

He could hardly answer for the lump that appeared in his throat. "Okay..." his voice cracked.

She looked toward Bill, "You can wait in the waiting room. We'll tell you when we're finished." She rattled the side of the stretcher, flipped the brake off the wheels and down the hall they disappeared to x-ray.

It seemed an eternity while the machine moved over Jesse's head and hand. He had not seen the inside of a hospital and did not like the smell. He fought waves of nausea until it was finished.

Bill sat patiently in the waiting room. He analyzed his role as a father and decided he hadn't done a very good job. He spent too much time with his friends and not enough time with his son. As Jesse told his story, Bill realized that he had no idea what he was talking about when he mentioned their secret shortcut. He didn't even know Jesse

25

knew anything about *The Great Trail*, and for the life of him, he could not recall what Collin looked like. He made a promise to himself that he would be more involved in his son's life. After all, Jesse was his sole responsibility. His mother had been gone for nearly two weeks, and Bill had no idea where she was or if she would ever return. No kid deserved to grow up like that. He felt ashamed of himself.

"Don't look so glum," said a frail old woman who sat beside him. "Everything will be fine."

He wanted to ask how the hell she knew, but instead he forced a smile and said, "I hope so."

The woman patted his knee, "I know so."

There was something in her eyes that made Bill not question her statement. Her small round face shone from the light in her eyes. Her smile seemed to cover her whole face. Those were the only words they spoke.

A nurse appeared from around the corner, "Mr. Williams?"

Bill stood, "Yes?"

"Your son is back in three." She disappeared as quickly as she came.

"I guess that's my cue," Bill said as he glanced toward the empty chair beside him. He looked around the room and saw a mother with a young boy, a woman probably in her thirties sitting alone, and himself. Not another soul was in the room. He felt a rush of nerves run hot through his body as he hesitated. Their eyes followed him from the room.

Jesse's nerves finally calmed, thanks to the medication he had been given. He counted the ceiling tiles in the room. He saw a clear bag with his personal belongings hanging on the wall hook. A label had been written in black magic marker: Williams, Jesse. A clipboard covered in scribbles rested on a shelf below the bag. His clothes were folded on a small stainless steel table beside his bed. He didn't recall any of this before. It seemed hours before his father walked back through the curtain.

"How ya doin', slugger?"

"Better."

Conversation had never been their strong suit. They sat in silence for a long time until Jesse finally spoke.

"Dad?"

"Yeah?"

"Have you told Mom?"

Bill stuttered, "I...I don't know where she is." The strain in his voice was obvious.

"But...I thought she was in the hospital?"

Bill sighed and stared at the floor, "I lied to you, Jesse." He never looked up. "She's been gone almost two weeks this time. I don't know where she is or if she's coming back."

Jesse fought the tears for the second time. He had suspected his father was lying, but he didn't expect him to admit it. Somehow seeing the pain reflected in his dad's eyes made it worse. He opened his mouth to speak but found no words.

A nurse reappeared to take Jesse's blood pressure. She grabbed the chart and scribbled the results on it. Before she left, Bill started to speak.

"How long will it be?"

"Just a little longer. The doctor is reading the x-rays now." She patted Bill gently on the shoulder, "He'll be in soon. Then you two can get out of here." She chuckled as she left. No one else laughed.

Jesse watched the clock move from one o'clock to one-thirteen without the doctor. The silence was killing him, but he couldn't think of anything to talk to his father about. Finally he got a bright idea.

"How's work?"

"It's work." After a long pause, he added, "Pays the bills."

That was not the response Jesse wanted. More than anything, he wanted to be able to talk to his father like Collin used to talk to his. They used to make fishing lures together and compare how they worked. They had an ongoing contest about which lure caught the biggest fish. Collin's mom packed them a snack and they would be gone for hours. Sometimes they drove to the local fishing lake, but mostly they walked to their secret fishing hole. Jesse went with them a few times. It was hard to not feel jealous of their relationship, and the longer he thought about that, the angrier he got.

Finally in frustration he spit, "Damn it, Dad. Why can't we talk?"

"What did I tell you about your mouth, boy?" Bill's voice was elevated and his hand frozen in striking position.

The doctor entered the room and shot a disapproving glance at Bill. The silent stare lasted for fifteen seconds. Jesse watched the second hand on the clock. It was 1:23 p.m.

Finally the doctor spoke to Jesse, "Well, I have some good news, young man." Jesse sighed with relief. "Your head is fine. You have a nasty bump that will need to be tended to with dressings and ointment, but there is no concussion." He paused for a brief minute, "Now your hand will take a bit longer to heal. You broke your index finger and your ring finger. You have some ligament damage to your middle finger as well, but the good news is none of these fractures are compound and they will heal quickly with proper rest." He shot another disapproving glance to his father. "I'm going to splint the three fingers and bind them together. It will be difficult to move them, so don't try, okay?"

"Okay," Jesse said quietly.

"You will need to see your doctor next week to check on your healing process, but you are a young, strong man and you will be fine in no time." He scribbled something on a pad of paper and handed it to his father. "Here is a prescription for some pain medicine. Get it filled on your way home. It will help him rest more comfortably." He smiled at Jesse, "Any questions?"

Jesse looked at his father for help, but Bill was staring at the prescription. "I...guess not."

"Okay, I'll be back in a second to get you ready." He looked at his father, "You can wait in the waiting room. We'll find you when we are finished." Bill walked from the cloaked room as if he had been scolded.

After a few minutes, the doctor returned with a nurse beside him. Within a minute of their entrance, a woman dressed in a suit joined them. She sat in the empty chair beside Jesse's bed.

She laid her hand on Jesse's shoulder. "What happened, Jesse?"

Jesse sized her up. He knew she was from Children's Services. He had seen them before. They all looked the same. Grey suits, hair pulled back, briefcase in hand, and a tape recorder in their pocket.

"I fell down a bank and hit my head on the railroad tracks!"

The woman glanced at the doctor. She squinted with disbelief. Sarcasm and anger were all she heard. She opened her mouth to speak several times before any words were audible.

"Where?"

"Down by the abandoned warehouse."

"Were you alone?"

"No." Jesse was steamed by this point. He wanted to make this accusatory bitch work for it.

She stared at him with disbelief. Her distaste for this young boy was obvious in her eyes and her body language. She crossed her legs and arms and pushed her chair away from the bed with each response. Her dangling foot tapped the air with impatience. Jesse had gotten the best of her and he knew it.

"Who were you with?" she asked trying to disguise her irritation.

"A friend."

"Does this friend have a name?" she asked through gritted teeth.

"Yep."

She threw her hands up in surrender. Jesse tried to hide his smirk. He sat in silence waiting for the next question. She slid the chair from under her and walked out through the curtain. Jesse was alone with the doctor.

"That wasn't very nice," he spoke with a gentle tone.

"Shit, she must be new. That's not how it's supposed to be done."

"And how would that be?" the doctor asked calmly.

He sat and listened to Jesse explain how many times Children's Services had been called to intervene with his small family. He explained his mother's addiction and his father's work ethic. He left out the part about his father's drinking, just in case the woman was listening from the other side of the curtain, which indeed she was.

"I am alone quite a bit, but I spend a lot of time with my good friend, Collin Sims."

"I know Collin," the doctor interjected. "I was on duty the night his father came into the emergency room." He paused for a moment, "They were a nice family." As he said those words, he wondered how the two boys could be friends. In his mind, they were polar opposites.

"Was Collin with you today?"

"Yes, he's the one who ran to the barber shop for help. Old Man Hilbert called for the ambulance.

"Where was your father?"

"At work. He works at Jenkins' garage. The hospital called him at work."

"How did you hurt your hand, Jesse?"

A rush of nerves ran through his body. His face flushed and his neck broke out in blotches. The doctor waited patiently.

"I...I...don't know. I guess in the fall somehow. Maybe I caught it on a root or something. All I know is everything went black when I hit my head. Collin said he pulled me off the tracks, as far off as he could, `cause a train was coming. He ran for help. When I woke up, I was alone and my head and hand was killing me."

"Where was Collin?"

"He hadn't got back yet. I was only alone for a few minutes when I saw him running through the weedy parking lot. We both looked like hell."

When Jesse finished speaking, he heard the tap of high heels walk away from the curtain. He was right. She was listening. He knew she wouldn't have left.

The doctor finished wrapping his broken fingers. The metal splints protruded from the end of his finger. The three fingers were taped tightly together and his pinky had a few pieces of tape around it as well.

The doctor pointed to his fingers, "You must be very careful. Do not try to use them. Keep them dry and elevated." He placed a sling over his shoulder and carefully placed his hand inside the fabric. "Is that comfortable?"

"This thing comfortable? Hardly."

The doctor smiled at his candid comment. "Jesse, this is very important. You must be careful with these fingers or your baseball days are over."

"How did you know I played…."

"I know many things. Just remember what I said, dry and elevated. No cheating for ten days. Go see your doctor next week. Your healing process will be quick."

Jesse's father appeared from behind the curtain. The two men exchanged stares. Finally, the doctor spoke.

"Did you get all of that?"

"Loud and clear," Jesse answered.

"Get this prescription filled on your way home. His medication will begin to wear off soon. He'll need it to rest comfortably." Bill nodded, but did not speak.

He turned back to Jesse. "I want you to go home and rest. You have been through quite an ordeal today, Jesse. Your body needs a chance to recuperate. And remember dry and…."

"Elevated. I got it."

"No cheating."

"No cheating." As the doctor turned to walk out, Jesse added, "Thanks, doc."

"You're welcome." Just as he slipped out beyond the curtain, he said, "And Jesse, no swimming either."

"Aw…" Jesse responded with disgust.

They followed the nurse out of the curtained area. She gathered an information pack and placed them in a bag with some additional bandages.

Jesse turned to his dad, "Can we stop for ice cream? I'm starving."

He ran his hand through his son's hair. "Sure thing, slugger, but we have to stop at the drugstore first. You heard the doctor. You need this to help you rest." He shook the prescription paper in the air. They both laughed.

# 4

Collin burst through the kitchen door. Before he had a chance to say a word, he noticed two men in suits sitting at the table with his mother. The papers were arranged in neat piles. His mother was signing the last one. Her eyes were rimmed in red. Collin knew she had been crying.

Without a word, he slid to her side. His thin arm wrapped around his mother's shoulders. She pulled a nettle leaf from his hair. They were banded together in silence as the bankers stood from the table.

"I believe we have all in order, Mrs. Sims. If you have any questions, give us a call." He held out his hand with a business card in it. She took it and shoved it in her pocket. "We'll be in touch."

She nodded in response. She couldn't bring herself to form any words. The lump of sadness closed her throat until she thought she couldn't breathe. Only the sight of her son coming through the door brought a smile to her face.

When the door closed behind the last man, Collin asked, "Bankers?"

"Yes."

"I told you I would take a second paper route. We can do it, mom."

This was one of the things she loved the most about her son. It reminded her of her late husband. They both were optimists. She couldn't bring herself to talk about it right now. Her emotions were too raw.

She began unconsciously picking things out of Collin's hair and off his pants as she searched for the words to tell him they were about to lose the farm. As she touched his bare back, she asked, "Where have you been, young man? And where is your shirt?"

"Mom! Jesse fell down the hill and smacked his head on the railroad tracks!" Excitement elevated his voice. "There was a train coming, so I pulled him off as far as I could and ran to Hilbert's barber shop. He called the ambulance. His head was bleeding pretty bad, so I put my t-shirt on it."

"Is he okay?"

"I don't know. I hope so."

"Was he awake?"

"By the time I got back from the barber shop, he was sitting up. I waited until the ambulance left for the hospital and came home."

"We should call to see if he is okay, don't you think?'

"Yep." He watched as his mother ran her fingers through the telephone book. His mind stalled for time and words.

Sharon dialed the number. She whispered to Collin with her hand over the receiver, "I'm getting the answering machine. They must still be at the hospital."

After a brief pause, she said, "Bill, this is Sharon Sims. Collin just told me about Jesse. We were calling to find out how he is feeling. Please call us back with the news. Thank you. Collin is worried about Jesse. We hope he is okay. Thank you." She hung up.

She turned to Collin, "What is his favorite cookie?"

"Chocolate chip."

"Let's make a double batch. We'll keep a few for us. Is that bad?"

"No, that sounds good to me."

Sharon pulled the mason jar down from the third shelf. The jar looked pathetic with its meager contents. She fished for the last of the bills and counted out four dollars in loose coins. The jar jingled with the final layer of coins barely covering the bottom. Sharon placed it on the shelf. Collin's stomach flipped.

"Mom, let's just do a single batch." He eyed up the empty jar, "We don't need any cookies."

"Nonsense." Sharon forced a smile. "It will do us both some good. Besides, chocolate chip cookies sound wonderful to me."

She placed the money in her purse. "Ready?"

"Yep."

They walked together to the car. She fumbled for the keys. She started the engine, but before she put it in reverse, she glanced at the gas tank reading. It was in the red zone. She quickly turned off the engine and looked at Collin.

"On second thought, let's walk. It's a beautiful day for a walk, don't you think?"

Collin smiled at his mother's not-so-clever disguise. "Sounds good to me." He didn't want to tell her how sore he was and how his legs burned from his episode this morning. He only wanted to make it easier for his mother, so like her, he put on his brave face.

"A walk to the grocery store it is." She knew he could see straight through her, but she was glowing with pride at his reaction.

They talked the entire trip. Collin did his best to suppress his limp. Occasionally, he caught himself as he stroked the carved spiral in his pocket. He didn't mention it to his mother, but he felt a strange urge to keep it a secret, and he didn't know why.

They bought the groceries needed to make the cookies as well as some milk and a loaf of day-old bread. As they walked out the door, a man wearing sunglasses, a dirty muscle shirt, and many tattoos nearly knocked them down as he hurried past them. Collin dropped his bag on the sidewalk. He quickly opened it to check the contents.

"Don't worry. I have the eggs," his mother chuckled.

They each carried a bag as they walked home. Collin carried the bag with the milk. His mom carried the rest of the groceries.

When they walked in the back door, Collin set his bag on the counter. He sat in one of the kitchen chairs as his mother emptied the bags. He needed to get off of his feet. His legs felt like overstuffed sausages ready to burst.

"Are you tired, honey?" Sharon asked full of concern.

"I just ran a lot this morning. My legs are aching."

"Why don't you lie down for a minute and prop your feet up. I'll call you when...."

Sharon stared into the grocery bag. She couldn't believe what she saw. She had pulled out the loaf of bread and set it on the counter. When she had reached for the carton of eggs, she stopped in mid-sentence and stared into the bag.

"Mom?" Collin walked to her side.

She said not a word but held the bag open for Collin to see. Lying on top of the carton of eggs was a fifty-dollar bill.

"How in the world did that get in there?" Collin asked.

"I have no idea," she responded with question in her voice. "Do you think I should call the store?'

"And say what? Hey, I found a fifty. Is it yours? Like that's gonna work." As soon as he said it, he realized he sounded just like Jesse. The look on his mother's face confirmed his fears. She didn't need to say a word. Her eyes spoke volumes.

"I'm sorry." He threw his arms around her. She gently stroked his shoulders. His apology was enough. She walked over to the telephone and dialed the store.

"Hi. This is Mrs. Sims. I was just in there a few minutes ago. When I came home I found some money in my bag. If you are short tonight, call me and I will return it."

She listened as the voice on the other end spoke.

"No. I don't know where it came from. It was in my bag under the loaf of bread I bought."

She listened again.

She picked up the money and looked at it. "No, it looks real."

Again she listened.

"Okay, I will, but in the meantime if you are out of balance, please call me." She hung up.

"What did they say?"

"She told me to take it to the bank to be sure it wasn't counterfeit."

"What? How could that be?"

"I don't know. She told me that maybe someone was playing a bad trick on me." Collin didn't respond.

"We'll take it by the bank on the way over to Jesse's with the cookies."

Collin still didn't respond. He was standing with both hands in his pocket. His spiral was gone. All he felt was the hole in which it slipped through.

Jesse and his father climbed out of the pickup truck at the ice cream shop. The medication had begun to wear off, but Jesse was determined to enjoy his ice cream. His hand throbbed and his head felt light as he stood at the window.

"What'll it be?" came a voice from inside.

"We'll have two cones, one medium twist and one medium chocolate."

"Coming right up."

Bill looked at Jesse and realized he was hurting. Why don't you sit over there?" he pointed to the table under the umbrella. "I'll run next door to get your medication." He leaned into the window, "Hey, bud?"

The young man who was making the cone said, "Yeah?"

"Just make the chocolate cone. I'm gonna pass on the twist."

"Okay. Whatever." He handed the chocolate cone to Jesse, "Here ya go, kid. Enjoy." He closed the sliding window.

Jesse walked over to the table and sat down. He was starting to feel faint, but he was determined to eat his ice cream. He couldn't remember the last time his father bought him ice cream.

The sun burned with intensity. Mixed with the morning's shower, the heat index rose. Even under the umbrella Jesse felt worse. He walked over to the neighboring parking lot in search of his dad's truck. All he wanted to do was lie down. He tripped over a parking stop and lost his cone to the pavement. Disgusted he kicked it into the grass. He saw the truck and walked toward it.

His world began to narrow. Nausea gripped him. He leaned over the edge of the parking lot and gave up all that filled his stomach. He felt worse.

He lost his balance and fell to his knees on the soiled grass. His hand fell on something sharp, but he was too dizzy to notice. He thought it would be forever before his father would find him.

As he walked out of the drugstore, Bill heard Jesse's moans. He ran to his son, picked him up in his arms, and carried him to the truck. He did not mention the foul smell. He just wanted to get his son home.

The notion of losing the spiral consumed Collin's thoughts as his mother baked the chocolate chip cookies. He retraced every step in his mind. He remembered touching it when they got out of the car. He also remembered how it felt as they walked past the barbershop. He felt it in his pocket inside the grocery store. He recalled it feeling cool to the touch as they walked past his mother's favorite dress shop and again past the cheese factory, but that was the last time he touched it. He held the bag in one hand and his mother's hand in the other. He decided he would have to look for it, but he wasn't sure how to tell his mother. Her voice interrupted his thoughts.

"What are you thinking about?"

"Jesse," he lied. He hated lying to his mom.

"He'll be fine. He'll love these…" The telephone rang.

There wasn't much that struck fear into his mother's heart, but the sound of a telephone ring. It had brought so much bad news for the past several months. She answered it when the hospital called with the news about his father. She had been standing in the same place she was now. Bill collectors called all hours of the day. It rang four times and she didn't move. Collin walked over to the phone.

"Hello?"

"Collin?"

"Yes."

"This is Bill Williams."

Collin's voice cracked from excitement, "How's Jesse?"

"Well, he'll be okay, but the medication has made him sick. He's resting right now."

"What did the doctor say?"

"He broke two fingers and has some ligament damage on the middle one. His head is fine, but he's got a nasty bump. He'll probably end up with a black eye before all the healing is done."

"Oh, a trophy!"

Bill laughed, "Yep, a trophy." He laughed again, "And no one even hit him."

Collin laughed too. "We're gonna bring over a surprise for him when he wakes up. Don't tell him, okay?"

"Okay, but you don't have to do that."

"We want to, Mr. Williams. Jesse's my friend."

The tender moment touched the hard crust known as Bill Williams. He wiped the moisture from his eyes. "We'll be here. Come over when you want."

"Okay. We'll see you in a bit. Bye."

"Bye." He hung up the phone and cried.

Collin set the receiver down. "How soon will we be ready?'

"About fifteen, twenty minutes, why?"

"I gotta do something. Don't leave without me." He didn't give his mother a chance to respond.

He ran to the last spot he remembered feeling the spiral. Slowly he walked looking only to the left of the sidewalk. His fingers were wiggling in his pocket and making the hole larger.

"Please, please, please, find it," he muttered to himself as he searched the grass.

He walked past several businesses in the downtown area without any sign of his treasure. He walked past the bicycle shop without peering in the window. His eyes were fixed on the ground. He didn't allow the thought of not finding it to enter his mind.

He approached the drugstore and started to feel a bit panicked. He walked through the paved lot until it met the grass. He slowed his pace. His throat was dry, but he didn't give up.

Just as he was about to enter the ice cream lot, he saw it. He was so excited that he hardly noticed it was lying in a pool of vomit. He picked it up, shook it off, and sprinted for home. His mother pulled the last cookie sheet from the oven as he ran through the back door.

"I'll help. I just have to wash my hands," he yelled as he brushed past his mother and closed the bathroom door.

He pulled the spiral from his pocket. The light from the window reflected its iridescent hues. He rolled it around under the running water. He was afraid soap would spoil its beauty, so he set it beside the sink while he washed his hands. He stopped before he put it back in his soiled pocket. The thought of putting it back in there with remnants of the vomit made him wrinkle his nose. He opened the door and burst upstairs.

"I gotta change my shorts," he yelled down to his mother.

When he bounced down the steps, his hair was wet, and he was dressed in different shorts and a clean t-shirt. His mother smiled at his appearance. He shoved both hands in his pockets.

"My, my, aren't you handsome?" she said as she handed him a warm cookie. "Where did you go?"

"I lost something," he said without thinking.

"Did you find it?'

"Yep!' he beamed proudly.

"What was it?' she questioned.

He dropped his eyes to the floor. The only thing he could think to say was, "Money."

# 5

Bill Williams answered the door with a smile on his face. He could smell the cookies through the broken screen door. His mouth watered. He tried to remember the last time he ate homemade chocolate chip cookies.

"Come on in." He said, "Sorry for the mess. I'm not much of a housekeeper."

"You know, I could do that for you, if you want. It's what I do. I've been looking for some extra clients."

"Well, um…."

"No pressure, Bill. Think about it. How's Jesse?"

"He's still resting, but those cookies smell great!" He couldn't control himself any longer.

Sharon giggled and handed him the plate of cookies, "Help yourself. They are for you both."

44

He took a cookie for each hand, and when he had finished the first, he took another. Sharon smiled at his actions. It reminded her of a child.

"Where's my manners? Have a seat. I'll tell you what the doctor said." He gathered the two shirts, three pair of dirty pants, and quite a few pair of socks from under the kitchen table. Embarrassed, he quickly threw them in a nearby closet. Sharon noticed a lot of dirty laundry piled up in that narrow space.

"Bill, why don't you let me take those?" she pointed toward the closed door.

"I...I don't know what to say. Liza usually does the laundry, but she's been gone for...," his voice fell silent.

Sharon felt pity for this man. She knew a bit of what he had gone through. She decided to take charge.

"Fetch me a few bags, Bill. I'll gather them up and toss them in the car."

He obeyed without question. He grabbed two black plastic garbage bags and jammed all of the clothes from the closet into them. By the time he had gathered each piece of dirty laundry the two bags were stuffed.

"I'll take them out. They're heavy."

Sharon followed him out to the car and opened the trunk. They laughed a bit as he closed the lid. Collin watched from the screened door. By the time they reentered the house Sharon had another customer.

"It's gonna take you some extra doin' the first time."

"It's okay, Bill. I've seen worse." The truth was, she hadn't.

They sat around the kitchen table as Bill told his story about the hospital, the doctor and the woman in the grey suit. Sharon was appalled. She knew of Bill Williams' reputation, but to treat him that way disgusted her and she told him so.

"Oh, I suppose they are just doing their job," he responded to her comments. "They have to dig sometimes to get the truth."

The room fell quiet for a few minutes as they all pondered the story. It was Bill who broke the silence first.

"Collin?"

"Yes, sir?"

"Tell me about this secret way to *The Great Trail*."

This was the conversation he was dreading. He had no idea what Jesse told his father and the doctors, but he was determined to keep the morning a secret if he could. He made a conscious effort to only answer the questions. Volunteering information was where he always got into trouble. 'Too much information...' was the conversation he had many times with Jesse. He prepared himself for the next wave of tough questions.

"Secret way?"

"Yea, Jesse said you went the secret way to *The Great Trail*."

"Oh, he meant our back way. We made a little path on our own down by the old warehouse. The hill is quite steep, but it cuts off a lot of walking down to the steps."

"Steps?"

Collin thought, 'Oh here we go, Collin, too much information...just answer his questions.' He gathered his thoughts and said, "The steps the state put in to lead up to *The Great Trail*. You know, by the parking lot."

"I don't understand."

"Why? Is it important?"

Bill stammered, "No...not really. It's just that...," he lowered his head. "When Jesse was telling me about what

46

happened, he mentioned this secret way and it made me wonder, that's all." He sat in silence staring at the floor. Finally he looked up and said, "I was so scared when I got the call from the hospital. I thought, not my little boy! I have been too wrapped up in my own problems to pay much attention to his. I was ashamed to admit to myself that I don't know much about my boy's life." His voice cracked, "I made a promise to myself to be better."

Sharon put her hand on top of his as it lay on the table. His hands were trembling. She knew he was struggling to hold in his emotions.

"You love your son very much to come to that conclusion," she whispered softly.

There was a creak at the bottom of the stairs. They turned to see Jesse standing there in only his underwear. His arms hung limp at his sides.

"Where's your sling, buddy?" Bill jumped to his son's aid.

"I dunno," he rubbed his eyes with his fist.

Sharon stood, "Jesse, it's good to see you. How are you feeling?"

He didn't answer. He only stared.

"Bill," Sharon said, "I think we need to be going. We'll let Jesse get some rest." She put her hand on Collin's shoulder as a signal to stand. "Say goodbye, Collin."

"I'll talk to you tomorrow, Jesse."

"O...kay." He stared emotionless into the kitchen.

Sharon and Collin walked to the screen door. Bill came up quickly to open it for them.

"This handle is broken. I've got to fix it. I've got to do a lot around here." He smiled at Sharon. "Thanks for the cookies."

47

"You're welcome." She turned to Jesse, "Feel better." He still gave no response. They walked out to the car.

After the doors were closed, Collin said, "Man, Jesse was out of it!"

"It's the pain medication, honey. Remember how it affected your dad?"

Collin thought about that question. He remembered his dad staring out of the window for what seemed like hours. Normally they would have great conversations, but near the end, he was pretty quiet. He muttered to himself a lot. His words were hard to understand.

"Yeah, I remember." They rode to the bank in silence.

Sharon opened the door and said, "I'll be right back."

Collin sat in the car alone. He thought about the spiral as he closed his hand around it. He prayed the fifty-dollar bill was real and that the cashier at the grocery store was not out of balance. They could use that money. Mom needed gas to get to work. She couldn't carry all of her cleaning supplies on her shoulders.

She walked out of the bank with a smile on her face. "It's real," she said as she slammed the car door closed. "Let's go call the grocery store."

After a brief conversation with the manager, she hung up the phone.

Collin waited anxiously for the news.

"Well, the cashier was not out of balance." She had a spring in her voice. "I told the manager if anyone reported missing money, I would return it. I didn't tell him how much, so that has to be our secret."

"Okay!" Collin responded with a snap in his voice. "Let's celebrate with a peanut butter sandwich!"

She smiled, "That sounds good to me."

Collin grabbed the peanut butter from the cupboard. There was enough left for about four sandwiches if he spread it thin enough. He pulled the loaf of bread from the drawer. He made two sandwiches and put them on two plates. He filled two glasses half-full of milk and set the table.

Sharon had separated all of Bill and Jesse's laundry and had placed the first load in the washing machine. Their whites were so dingy that she put extra bleach in the water. She filled the machine to the top with hot water and let the clothes soak. She walked back into the kitchen.

"I've got to get some more bl...." She dropped the jug on the floor.

Collin held three fifty-dollar bills in a fan shape.

"Where did they...."

"They were stuck to the bottom of the bread bag." Collin's voice squealed, "Mom! We have four of them! Two hundred dollars, stuck to the day-old bread bag!"

She rushed to Collin's side and knelt on the floor. He handed her the money and shoved his hands in his pocket. She pulled the fourth bill from her purse and examined them. She started to cry.

"Collin, it's a miracle!" Through her tears, she whispered as she stared at the gift which had come their way, "A miracle!"

# 6

Collin couldn't sleep. He kept thinking about his fall that morning. His legs jumped from fatigue and his mind raced. He replayed the final scene over and over again in his mind. He could not shake his vision of the skull. He had himself convinced that's what he saw. The idea of lowering himself back down into the hole alone scared him, but he knew there was no other way to get answers. He had always been an inquisitive child. This was no exception, fearful or not.

The last time he looked at the clock was 3:13 a.m. He had wrestled his next step through the night, but with his final decision to visit the site in the morning, he fell asleep. He didn't dream.

When he woke, the sunlight was strong and high in the sky. He looked at the clock. It was nearly ten o'clock. He threw the covers off and ran down the stairs. His mother was folding Bill's clothes on the table. The piles were high. She hummed to herself.

"Good morning, sleepyhead," she said.

"Why did you let me sleep in?"

"Now you sound like your father," she teased. "Because you needed it."

"I couldn't sleep last night."

"Me neither."

"Why?"

"I don't know. I was thinking about the money, where it came from, how it got there, and how lucky we were to find it."

"Lucky? Maybe we should play the lottery?"

She scolded Collin with her eyes, "You know that is just a waste of money."

"I was just kiddin'." They both laughed. "What are you gonna do with it, Mom?"

"Well, I already filled my gas tank this morning and bought the cleaning supplies I needed to clean Bill's house and finish his laundry."

Collin wrinkled his nose. This was not the response he wanted to hear, but he knew how conservative his mother was and he wasn't surprised.

"Yeah, and...," he motioned for her to continue.

"Yeah, what?"

"Why don't you buy yourself something from that dress shop?"

"I would love to, but this money would be better used to make more. Don't you agree?" She knew how the mind of

51

an eleven-year-old worked. She was trying to teach him a valuable life lesson.

Collin hung his head as if he had been scolded, "Yes, Ma'am." He walked over to the loaf of bread and looked at the bottom one last time.

His mother chuckled, "I already looked this morning."

Jesse woke with a terrible headache. His hand throbbed. His stomach felt queasy, yet he was hungry. He slowly sat up in his bed. He inched to the side and dangled his legs until they touched the floor. His sling lay beside the bed. He bent to pick it up. All went black.

Bill woke to a thud. He rushed into his son's room and found him lying on the floor. Carefully he picked him up and laid him back on his bed. He sat beside him and stroked his hair. It was 5:30 a.m.

The bump on his head was stitched with four tiny sutures. It started to take on a black tinge, although it didn't appear to be as swollen. He looked carefully at his eye, but he couldn't see any signs of a black eye, yet. He knew it would come. He whispered a prayer of thanks for his son's safety.

He walked down the narrow staircase as quietly as he could. He turned on the light in the kitchen and started a pot of coffee. He opened the refrigerator door and pulled out the carton of eggs. Within a few minutes, he had scrambled six eggs and toasted four slices of bread. He smelled the carton of orange juice and decided to dump it down the drain. He poured a glass of milk instead. With the plate piled high with scrambled eggs and toast, he carried it upstairs.

Jesse was sitting on his bed when Bill walked into the room. He had placed his sling over his shoulder and laid his swollen hand in its comfort.

"Are you up for some breakfast?"

"I'm not sure."

"How do you feel?"

"Like hell." Bill let it slide. He knew he'd said worse.

"How's your stomach feel?"

"Empty." He placed his hand on his belly, "and funny."

"That's from the medication. You need to eat something if you can." Bill held out the plate for him to take.

"Don't tell your friends you were served breakfast in bed. They might get the wrong idea about me." He laughed at his own joke, but Jesse sat expressionless. "I'll go get you some jelly."

"Okay."

Jesse sat with the plate on his lap. He drank a swig of milk and waited for a reaction. He took a bite of toast and then another. By the time his father returned with the jelly, he had finished both pieces of toast. His eggs hadn't been touched.

"Eggs don't sound good to you."

"Not really." Jesse tried to sound cheerful.

"Do you want some more toast?"

"No."

After a long pause, Bill asked, "Do you want anything else?"

Jesse stared at the floor. Medication exaggerated his emotions. He felt depressed. His hand hurt and his head ached. He felt sorry for himself. The only thing that felt better was his stomach.

"I...want mom." His flooded eyes looked to his father for comfort.

Bill froze with the comment. Anger flashed in his eyes. He wanted to scream, 'I don't know where she is! How the hell can I find her? She's a dope head! She's screwed up! I'm screwed up...we're all screwed up!' His eyes burned from frustration. He opened his mouth to speak, but thought better of it. Jesse's comment had pissed him off, and he had to cool down before he could talk. He walked out of the room shaking his head.

Jesse sat on his bed and cried.

# 7

Collin helped his mother carry the clean laundry to her car. After four trips each the back seat was full. The stacks of Bill's clothes outnumbered Jesse's. The fresh smell of the laundry detergent and fabric softener filled the car. Sharon jumped in the front seat.

"I'll be back in a few hours. I'm going to start Bill's house this morning."

"That's gonna take days!"

Sharon laughed at her son's innocence, "It won't take as long as you think, but it will take a lot of effort in the beginning."

"Do you want me to help?"

"Now, Collin, how do you think it would make them feel if you cleaned their house and they didn't?"

Collin shrugged his shoulders. "Not very good, I think."

"Let's rendezvous here at noon. We'll have lunch and I'll fill you in on how it's going."

"Sounds good to me." Collin jumped at the freedom of time before lunch.

"See you at noon."

"Bye." Collin waved to his mother, "I love you."

"I love you more," she responded with the ritual. She blew him a kiss and drove out of the driveway.

Collin watched the car until it disappeared around the corner. He stared at the space between his neighbor's bushes until he spotted the car driving down the street. He headed toward the barn.

He climbed the ladder into the haymow. Wrapped on a nail in the corner was a rope his father had made. It had a series of knots tied in it for 'better gripping'. They used to use it when they went swimming. It was the perfect rope swing. Today was the first time Collin held it in his hands since his father died. He felt a lump in his throat and climbed out of the loft.

He walked over to his father's workbench. The tools were well organized. Each hung on its own hook on the pegboard. His dad's hammer was the only tool lying on the bench. Collin picked it up and placed it in its designated spot on the wall. He brushed the cobwebs off with his hands.

"There ya go, Dad." He said proudly, "It looks better now."

He pulled the large flashlight from the pegboard hook. He turned it on. The beam was strong and wide, just what Collin needed. He tied it to the bottom of the rope.

He scanned the pegboard for anything else that would be of use. His eyes settled on a hunting knife. There were seven notches in the leather case. Each notch had a date written in pen next to it: Oct 17 '04, Nov 6 '05, Oct 22 '06, Oct 13 '07, Nov 13 '08, and Oct 30 '09, all marking the annual deer his father had shot with a crossbow. The final notch, Nov 1 '09-Collin, was for his own deer that he had shot this past November, ten days before his father's death.

His dad felt the only way to hunt was with a bow. He liked to go to the woods in early season while the deer were still traveling their common paths. He said their routine didn't change until the doe went into heat. During rut, the bucks were so preoccupied with the scent of a doe that they could be caught off guard.

As Collin got older, he hunted with his father. They washed their camouflage coveralls and masks in a special laundry detergent to rid them of any human scent. They hung them outside for days until it was time. If it rained on the gear, it was better, for then they truly smelled like the outdoors.

Collin had received his own crossbow the Christmas of 2008. Sharon thought he was a bit young, but Mark insisted. She gave in. She always did. She enjoyed watching their relationship grow, and hunting was one way to do it.

They made a deer stand together in August of 2008. Mark felt he needed a new vantage point. The deer he had shot the year prior was a bit smaller than his usual size. He prided himself on killing one of the county's largest every year. He always saved the rack, but could not afford to have one mounted.

His largest buck was a twelve point, sporting a 22 1/2" spread. It scored 160 on Boone & Crockett scale and took third place in the county. Second place beat the spread by barely a ¼", and first place that year was a non-typical with 37 points and a 38" spread. The left side of the antlers grew straight out from its skull, causing the spread to measure abnormally wide. It was a big deer, but not a pretty one to mount. Anyway, Mark was pleased with third place. He received a large gift certificate from the local archery store, a case of arrows, and a free mount from the local expert. The picture in the paper was icing on the cake.

Collin sat proudly beside his father to pick up his mount when it was finished the following spring. The taxidermist had won several awards for prize mounts and the trophies hung on the wall beside all the spoil. Collin had never seen so many different animals stuffed before. There were squirrels, raccoons, minks, ducks, pheasants perched and flying, turkey sporting their rut colors, and hundreds of deer. He used competition eyes on his father's deer. The veins in the eyes surrounding a colored iris looked so life-like. The mount looked fantastic. He remembered the pleasure in his father's eyes. He hung it in the living room above the couch against Sharon's wishes. She never moved it.

Collin slid the memories and the knife into his pocket. He patted his other pocket for the spiral. It was still there. He left with his exploration gear in tow, anxious for what he may find.

He felt apprehensive as he walked up Indian Hill. He stopped periodically to shake his trembling hands as he fastened the two ropes together. He calculated and re-calculated the length of rope needed to reach the floor of the cave. He needed to be sure he wouldn't be stranded. The last thing he wanted was to get stuck down there, stuck with no way to get out.

He walked to the opening with the end of the rope in his hand. He tied the flashlight to his belt loop and checked it for security. He tugged on the rope several times to assure its stability. He looked one last time toward the tree, which secured the rope. Slowly, he lowered the knotted rope down through the opening until it stopped. He exhaled and drew in another deep breath. Carefully he crawled through the hole.

Gravel pelted him as he lowered himself one knot at a time. The earth smelled damp and he felt the room close in on him. With the light from the opening he could clearly see how the stones had been placed. He wondered why, since the drop from here to the floor was several feet, at least fifteen, he guessed.

He stopped after the narrow passageway opened into the large room. His feet dangled free until he slid to the next knot. He held his breath and strained to hear any sound. It was silent.

He wrapped the rope around his leg as he fumbled for the piece of rope attached to his belt loop. Tied at the end was the flashlight. He gripped the handle and turned on the switch. The brightness of the light blinded him as it lit his face. He closed his eyes and waited for the spots to go away.

Instinctively, he moved the light to the floor. When he opened his eyes, the beam illuminated the skull. He screamed and dropped the flashlight. It swung wildly from the bottom of the rope. The light skirted across the walls in an erratic pattern until it slowed to a rhythmic swing.

"What was that?" Collin exclaimed as he watched the light skim the walls.

He grabbed the rope to steady the beam. He held his breath and fumbled for the flashlight handle. He squeezed his eyes tight and slowly exhaled. He wasn't ready to shine the light onto the floor. Instead he focused on the walls.

As he scanned the light over the walls, he saw drawings of birds, flowers, lizards, mixed with many other odd markings—parallel lines, straight and wavy, arrows, zigzags, circles and many other symbols that he did not recognize. The images were drawn in rows, as if they were acting out a story. There were no breaks, and the drawings were extremely vivid near the top. The last symbol was an arrow that pointed toward the hole into which he had fallen.

The rope jerked. Collin froze in horror. Questions of the rope's security flooded his mind. His body swung from the halted slack. The rope jerked again. He dropped nearly a foot. Collin started to panic. If he hadn't attached the rope securely, he would fall and be stuck down here. No one would ever find him, until it was too late.

"Why did I come?" He cried out loud. The rope slumped again.

Spurred by pure fear, he began to scramble up the knots. He was determined that if he had to die today, he would die trying to escape. He moved up the rope faster than he thought possible. He grabbed the protruding stones in the chute and fumbled to find them with his feet. The rope went limp and slithered through his legs. Supported only by the protruding stones, he was surprised how effortless he climbed the narrow passageway to safety.

He pulled himself out of the hole and lay on his stomach. The grass caressed his face. His body felt weak at the possibilities he had just escaped. His left foot dangled over the hole. He felt nauseated.

He tried to breathe deeply, but dared not to move. He was afraid he would be sucked back through the hole and left there to die, left with the skeleton and whatever else was down there. He started to move his foot away from the opening when he stopped cold. He heard singing, deep from within the earth. It was a soft sweet voice of a young girl.

Collin's throat constricted. He assured himself that place was empty. No one was down there—nothing but a bunch of bones. He jumped to his feet and ran down the hill to the tree. He worked his fingers as fast as he could to untie the remaining rope.

When he had run the length of *The Great Trail* to his secret entrance, he stopped. He bent over and placed his hands on his knees. The rope lay at his side in a heap. His lungs burned from hard, shallow breaths. He didn't know if he was exhausted or terrified. It felt the same.

He tried to calm himself. His hands shook wildly. He paced over the soft moss gathered at his feet. He forced his trembling hands into tight fists and punched at the hot air. He shook them loose and wiped the perspiration from his palms. He plopped himself onto the ground and began to force the rope into loops as he muttered to himself.

"What was that? Maybe I was hearing things...No, you weren't, you heard singing...that's crazy...I must have been hearing things...No one was in there...I saw with my own eyes...with the flashlight...what was I thinking...that was the dumbest thing I've done." He stood with renewed energy and whispered, "I am never going back there again."

He tossed the long rope over his head until it rested on his shoulder. His breathing came more easily with his new resolution. His body felt less fatigued.

He swung his hands free as he slid down the steep bank to the railroad tracks. He looked both ways and ran across the tracks. His mind wandered to Jesse and then to his mother. He glanced at the position of the sun.

"She should be home soon," he said looking toward the sky. "I'll slip into the barn from the back way, just in case she is home. I don't want any questions."

He crossed the parking lot and jumped Mrs. Henderson's fence as Jesse had done the day prior. He leapt with the skill of multiple attempts. The rope obeyed his lead and moved with him through the thorns unscathed. His feet landed firmly on the ground. He ran through the field, careful not to run through the cow's waste. As he threw the barn door closed, it hemmed him into safety with a loud thud.

He felt protected inside his own barn. The smell of hay and manure enveloped him as he transported himself back to the eleven-year-old he should be. He placed the flashlight back on its proper hook on the pegboard and climbed the ladder to the haymow. With the skill of a young farmer, he wrapped the rope twice, secured it together with a slipknot and draped it over a hook.

He jumped past the bottom three rungs of the ladder and hit the floor with a thud. He glanced over to his father's pegboard and smiled. All was in order. His heart felt light as he walked out of the barn. Subconsciously, his hand was in his pocket, wrapped around the spiral piece of history.

# 8

Jesse walked down the stairs after his tears dried. He couldn't help feeling sorry for himself. It was a natural part of being eleven. He just wanted the tenderness of his mother. He needed to be comforted, even if it was only a fantasy in his mind. His mother knew how to be tender, but Jesse hadn't seen much of it. Those emotions were usually directed toward men other than his father.

Jesse recalled a day after his baseball game last spring. He had the winning home run hit. He was elated, though neither parent saw him do it. He had fibbed to them many times about such hits for acceptance and approval, but this one really happened. He hit the back door as if he had been shot from a cannon.

63

"Mom! You'll never believe it!" he shouted as he ran up the steps.

"Mom...I...," his words were stolen from him.

He stood in the doorway of his parents' bedroom as he watched a man he had never seen before struggle to pull on his pants. His body was painted with tattoos. His underwear and his mother's clothes were entangled on the floor. He bent to pick up his shirt and slapped it in the air to shake off the filth. He spoke not a word as he brushed Jesse aside and walked out of the bedroom. His mother bent over to the nightstand and grabbed a cigarette. She made no attempt to cover her nakedness.

She took a long drag and asked, "What do you want?"

Jesse was so crushed by her response he couldn't speak. Tears welled up in his eyes. He ran down the steps and sat on the front porch. He watched the man leave on his motorcycle. His long hair and t-shirt flapped in the wind as he drove from Jesse's sight.

He stood at the bottom of the steps, lost in thought. His father's voice brought him back to the present.

"Come sit down, Jesse." His voice was calmer than he expected.

Bill sat at the kitchen table. Yellow egg yolk was smeared all over the surface of the plate. The only thing left was the crust of a piece of toast and a crumpled cigarette butt. He lit another one. Jesse faked a cough. His father gave him a look of disgust. Jesse didn't try it again. He sat on the opposite side of the table.

"Aren't you going to work today?" Jesse asked.

He blew the smoke from his mouth, "I have to, but I'm going to wait until Sharon gets here."

"Sharon Sims?'

"Yep."

"Why is she coming?'

"To clean for us."

Jesse's heart jumped. If he crawled back into bed, maybe he would get the attention he needed from her.

"She might need your help."

Jesse's heart sunk. The comment made him angry. He wanted to shout to his father about how sick he felt, about how much his hand hurt, about how his head throbbed, but you...you...want me to clean?

His father continued, "She won't know where things go 'round here. If she has any questions, just help her out okay?"

Jesse felt better. "Okay," he answered sheepishly.

"I want you to get some more rest. I'll tell her to be quiet. I'll stop by around lunch and check on you."

"Okay."

"She said it will take her the better part of the day to get things shaped up." He glanced around the house and waved his cigarette in the air, "I think it'll take her a week!" He laughed.

Jesse managed a smile. "Dad?"

"Yeah?"

"Don't be mad about mom. I...just...."

"I know, Jesse. I know...it's hard." His father's voice was soft. "The truth is I don't know where she is or if...," he recovered himself quickly, "when she'll be back."

"Why didn't you tell me?'

"'Cause it was easier to lie to you, then admit the truth, but now you know." His voice was slightly agitated. "I'm sorry."

Jesse didn't respond. His father's slip of 'if' spoke volumes. There was a knock on the door. It was Sharon. Bill opened the door for her and took the load of clean laundry from her hands.

She smiled at Jesse, "Good morning you two. Looks like I'm late for breakfast."

Bill stumbled with the comment, "I...could...."

"I'm kidding. Collin and I already ate." She turned to Jesse and gently placed her hand on his shoulder, "How are you feeling this morning?"

"Okay, I guess."

"It's good to see you up." Jesse smiled at her comment. He liked the feel of her hand on his shoulder and especially the way she caressed his hair as she spoke to him. "Don't you think he should go back to bed, Bill?"

"Yes, I do. C'mon slugger. I'll walk you upstairs."

"Wait one minute," Sharon held up her finger and quickly disappeared out of the door. She came back holding a pile of sheets. She tried to reopen the door but couldn't.

Bill nervously walked to the door and opened it for her, "I gotta fix that thing."

"What size?"

"What?"

"Jesse's sheets, what size are they?"

Bill hesitated, "Uh...twin."

Sharon rummaged through until she found Collin's blue set with super heroes all over them. She looked at Jesse as she held up the sheets, "Maybe these will help you sleep better knowing all these guys are looking out for you." Her smile was wide and genuine.

"Thanks, Mrs. Sims," Jesse said. "I'm ready." His head had started to spin again.

The three of them walked up the stairs. Bill and Sharon changed the sheets while Jesse propped himself in the corner and watched. It felt like a dream, a woman doing housework in his house.

Sharon patted the bed after she fluffed Jesse's pillow, "Come rest, Jesse. Let the medication work its magic." She forced a smile. Those words came too easy but left a bitter taste in her mouth. They were the last words she spoke to her husband.

Jesse wrapped the sheets around his body. The smell of clean laundry was intoxicating. He buried his nose in his pillow. He was asleep before Bill and Sharon left his room.

"Poor thing," Sharon whispered sympathetically.

"Aw, he's tough. He'll be fine."

Sharon shot him a disapproving look, "He could use a bit of tenderness, I believe."

Bill hung his scolded head, "Yes, ma'am." They walked out of the room.

After a few instructions, Bill left for work. Sharon busied herself with the enormous task before her. She washed the breakfast dishes and the other ones in the sink, which from the looks of them had been there for several days. As she opened the cupboard door to put them away, she wrinkled her nose at what she saw—the dishes were actually dusty.

She emptied each cupboard, wiped the shelves, and replaced the dishes as they were washed. She repeated the same with the glasses, pots and pans, and coffee cups. She found a sippy cup, baby bottle, and a pacifier tucked in the far corner of one of the top shelves. They brought a smile to her face.

She took everything off the counter top and placed it on the table. She scrubbed the counter until the color of the Formica could be distinguished. When she placed all the items back in their former position, she polished the table. The refrigerator came next. That took some time and a full garbage bag. She expected the oven to be the same but was surprised when she opened the door. It was spotless, all except for the loaf of moldy bread. She squeezed the loaf into the garbage bag. She tied it and tossed it out the back door, being careful not to let the door close behind her.

She scoured the floor on her hands and knees twice and the third time used only fresh water to finish it. She stood in the doorway to the family room and admired her work. She wagered it never looked so clean. She checked her watch. It was 12:15 p.m.

She heard a car pull into the drive. It was Bill.

She yelled to him, "Don't come in this way. I just scrubbed the floor."

He stood with his nose pressed against the screen. The smell of bleach was pungent. "Wow! What a difference." He looked at Sharon, "Thank you so much."

"You're welcome."

"I...hate to say it, but I have to come this way. The front door is nailed shut."

"Bill Williams, you need to get out your tool belt around here!" she scolded. She covered her forwardness by laughing. He joined her.

"I'll let you in if you take off your shoes."

"You're kind of bossy," he teased. She laughed. She knew he was telling the truth.

"I need to run home for a bit. I have a lunch date with my son."

"Okay."

She picked up her purse and said, "Jesse is still sound asleep. I'll be back in about an hour."

"I'll probably be gone." He glanced around the room, "It sure is nice having a woman's touch around here." He stopped himself and wondered what he was doing. Was he flirting with her? What was he thinking? He was still married and this woman was way out of his class. He hung his head as if she could read his thoughts. "It's…it's…been a while," he stammered.

She touched him on the arm and looked into his eyes, "I know, Bill. She'll be back. Maybe she's getting help."

Her eyes left no doubt that she was concerned, but the concern couldn't be mistaken for interest, as much as Bill would have liked. He placed his hand on top of hers in a gesture of friendship and smiled at her. His eyes filled with tears.

"Thanks," was all he could manage.

He made no attempt to wipe away the tears. Nor did he feel uncomfortable showing his emotion in front of her. There was something about Sharon Sims that calmed him and made him want to be a better person.

He was transported back to his senior year of high school. Bill and Mark Sims were grade school buddies but drifted apart as they grew older. Mark had become quite a baseball player, and Bill watched him play as he sipped on beer poured into a pop can. He always cheered for his old friend. That was when he met Sharon.

She had on a pair of jeans that shadowed her grace. She wore a white tank top under a pink sweater. It hid most of what was underneath, but Bill's imagination could see her shape. He liked what he saw.

He was one of the most popular kids in school when he was younger, but for the past two years, he had started hanging out with a rough crowd. He started smoking, drinking, and cursing. He was a handsome guy until he opened his mouth. His language spoiled his good looks.

Sharon and her parents stood beside the bleachers. He couldn't help staring at her. Her soft brown hair blew in the mid-afternoon breeze. It covered her face, but she made no attempt to push it aside. Her smile was wide. She watched the shortstop as he fielded a ball and threw it while in mid-air to the first baseman.

"Out!" yelled the umpire.

The shortstop brushed the dirt from his pants. A cloud of dust surrounded him.

Bill jumped to his feet, "All right, Sims!"

Mark looked toward his friend, but all he saw was Sharon. He missed the next hit as it whizzed by his head. Trying to recover, he scrambled after it, but the runner had already tagged third. He was disgusted with himself and shook his head as he stared at the ground. Sharon smiled.

"Do you think I can stay for a while?" she asked her mother.

"Sure, honey."

Sharon looked at Bill, "What inning is it?"

Shocked that she spoke to him, he stammered, "Uh...it's...the third." He recovered quickly, "Top of the third."

She smiled at him, "Thank you."

Her father kissed her on the cheek and said, "We'll be back in about an hour."

"Thanks, Dad." She hugged her mother, "See ya later. Thanks."

She stood for a few moments until Bill slid over on the bleacher. "You can sit here, if you like," as he patted the seat next to him.

Sharon smiled and said, "Thanks. That would be great."

He watched her as she sat next to him. The smell of her was intoxicating. She tucked her hair behind her ear and smiled.

"My name is Sharon...Sharon Wells."

Bill extended his hand, "Nice to meet you, Sharon. My name is Bill Williams."

They talked the rest of the game. Bill was funny. He made her laugh. For a few moments, he was the person he thought he could be. He told her everyone's name on the team and a bit about each one, all but Mark. He made her wait for that. It was obvious she was attracted to him. Her eyes followed each move he made. As Mark walked off the field that day, Bill motioned for him to come over. He introduced Sharon to him.

Years later, she was standing in Bill's kitchen. He felt ashamed of how he had lived his life. Her gentle hand on his arm brought back many old memories, a long suppressed attraction. She still had the same effect on him today, even if she did smell more of bleach than lavender.

Her voice ended the sprint down memory lane, "I'll be back after lunch."

"Okay. Maybe I'll see ya."

He choked back the words. He had just told her he would be gone. His face flushed, but she didn't notice. Her back was turned and she was walking out of the door. He wanted to yell to her to stay and talk a while. He wanted to spend some time with her. He wanted to take care of her. He wanted to hold her. Instead, he watched her walk away.

He stuck his hand into his shirt pocket. He pulled out his pack of cigarettes and tapped the top of the new pack. He pulled the cellophane tab from the wrapper and shook out the first cigarette. The white tobacco stick was a stark contrast from the ground-in automobile grease, which accentuated every wrinkle. He looked through the screened door at Sharon as she closed her car door. He broke the cigarette in half, crushed the full pack in his hand and tossed it into the garbage. It echoed in the empty can. He grinned at his decision. He had smoked his last cigarette.

Collin was sitting at the kitchen table eating a chocolate chip cookie when his mother walked in the back door. She was smiling.

"Well...how did it go?" Collin asked in a sarcastic tone.

"Actually not too bad."

She placed her purse on the kitchen counter and grabbed a cookie for herself. "Are we having dessert first?"

"Yep." They both laughed.

# 9

Collin fell into bed exhausted. The past two days had left him feeling spent, like a limp dishrag hanging on a hook. He fell asleep almost immediately.

His legs jerked and woke him. He was damp with sweat. He glanced at the clock. It was 11:22 p.m. He got out of bed and stumbled down the hall for a drink. He opened his bedroom window as wide as it would go. He crawled back in under the sheets. As he was falling asleep, he heard singing, soft and sweet.

His eyes flew open wide. He had fallen again. The singing was louder now, so loud it hurt his ears. He covered his head with his pillow. He closed his eyes tight. He felt as if he were being watched. He wouldn't open his eyes. He whispered softly to himself.

"Breathe…just breathe…that's right. You can do it. One …two … breathe … three…fo…."

The ground started to tumble in through the hole. It quickly covered his feet until he couldn't move. He struggled to work his feet free, but the harder he kicked the deeper he sank. The dirt covered his hands, gluing them to his sides. The voice became louder and closer until it was all he could hear. The gravel and grass clumps hit him on the head. He screamed from the pain, but his voice could not be heard above the singing. There were no words, only sounds, louder and louder they came. He felt hot breath on his skin. He squeezed his eyes tight. He felt as though he were being smothered. The dirt continued to fall. It covered his shoulders and worked its way to his mouth. Soon he would be buried. He struggled to move, but couldn't. His muffled cries could not be heard. His tears were mixed with dirt and sand.

He felt his body go limp from lack of oxygen. His head swooned and swayed. The singing stopped. A hand appeared through the dirt. It uncovered his face and blew breath back into his body. He saw no face, only an outline of a young girl. Her body was frail and thin, yet she managed to pull him from a pile of rubble. She pointed to his pocket. He gasped for air.

His mother sat next to him. "You were having a bad dream," she whispered softly.

He threw his arms around her waist. His eyes found the clock. It was 12:34 a.m. Hot fire ran through his body. That time had always been one of his father's signs. If Mark was thinking about something and happened to glance at a clock and the time read 12:34, he followed through with his thought. Collin knew what he had to do.

# 10

He stood with the rope slung over his shoulder for the second time. He peered down the hole with the flashlight. The beam was not strong enough to reach the bottom. He walked to the tree and tied the rope around it again. He was careful to tie the right knot this time. He only tugged on it once. He patted his pocket for the spiral. He lowered the rope into the hole and began his descent.

He slid down the rope to the bottom. With his feet firmly on the ground, he felt for the handle of the flashlight. His heart pounded, yet he continued. He drew in a deep breath and moved the beam of light across the skeleton.

Promising himself to not let his imagination take control, he moved the light across the bones. It looked as if it had been in some sort of box, which had deteriorated over time.

Only a few shards of wood were left. He was careful not to disturb anything.

The skeleton was lying on its back with its arms crossed over its chest. Clay jars of varied sizes surrounded it. Some were sealed with a waxy substance that oozed over the sides. Collin wanted to touch one of them, but he was afraid. He stared at the skeleton.

He reached into his pocket and withdrew the spiral. In the beam of the flashlight, it looked almost transparent. The colors deep from within shone brilliantly in the light. He twirled it around in his fingers until the color returned to luminous silver.

In his dream last night, a young girl pointed to his pocket. It was as if she was asking for it back. He wanted to keep it. He loved treasure hunting and this was quite a prize, but he knew in his heart he should let it go. For the moment he put it back into his pocket.

Curiosity gained control of his fear. He knelt beside the skeleton. It was then the size of the skeleton became apparent to him. He thought it was about his height. He positioned his body on the ground next to the skeleton with his head lined up parallel to it. The length was the same. He moved his hand to cover the bare bones. It was a perfect match. He crossed his arms over his body in the same position. They fell in the same plane.

"You must have been about my age," he whispered. "I wonder what happened."

He noticed a bracelet wrapped around what would have been the left wrist and another around the upper part of the right arm. Both adornments were made of some sort of metal. He leaned closer to examine them being careful not to touch them. They had markings on them. They looked familiar. He remembered the walls. He moved the flashlight

77

to illuminate the area where he had seen the writings, but they weren't there. That peaked his interest.

"I know I saw them. But...I was up higher." He scanned the light around the room. "Maybe you can only see them from the passageway." He made a mental note to pay attention to that as he left.

He placed his hand over the bones one more time. It was then he noticed several different pieces across the chest area of the skeleton. They were different shapes, some made of stone, some of metal, and some of materials he wasn't certain.

He brought his face closer to the bones. The light played off the images. Some had fallen through the skeleton and were scattered under the rib cage on the ground. Others were teetering on the rib bones themselves. A few were sitting on its hands.

"It must have been a necklace," he said out loud. His voice echoed around the room. Without thinking, he whispered, "Sorry."

The feeling he had in this place was a sense of reverence. It was obvious this place was a tomb. He had heard of burial mounds before but had never seen one. Now he was faced with the responsibility of discovery. He felt he should keep it secret. Why? He wasn't sure. He wasn't worried about himself being quiet. He was worried about Jesse. His reputation for keeping secrets was less than desirable.

"You obviously were very important," he whispered to the carcass. "You must have been wealthy. Maybe you were a king or something. Although I think you were very young, cuz you're my size." He looked at the skull. "Your face is very small." He sat in silence. Finally he whispered, "I think you were a girl." He forced out of his mind the sound of a young girl singing, that sort of thing creeped him out. "I will call you the princess."

He put his hand in his pocket and pulled out the spiral. He looked at the pieces of the necklace again. He wanted to put it back together for her, but he was apprehensive to touch her.

"I don't know what to do," he spoke to the princess.

He wrestled with the thought of leaving the spiral or taking it with him. He fought the urge to gather the pieces and reconstruct the necklace only to return it to the princess of course. He felt a strange power helping him with these decisions, but he struggled against it. He wanted a treasure to remember this experience. Since he promised the princess to keep her tomb a secret, what would it hurt? Against his inner voice, he finally decided to gather the pieces and reconstruct the necklace.

He moved his hand toward the skeleton and was startled by the sound of a loud thud. He jumped and withdrew his hand. He heard the sound of something moving within the tomb. Clawing and scratching noises came from behind him. He spun around to shine the light on his assailant. It was a ground hog, which had fallen through the opening. It struggled until it forced out its final breath with a wheeze. The fall had been too much for it.

Collin breathed a sigh of relief. His heart pounded in his throat. He thought about the necklace reconstruction again and took the death of the ground hog as a sign to abstain. He pulled the spiral from his pocket and placed it on the princess' hand.

"It's yours," he said with surrender in his voice. "I'm sure it means more to you than to me."

He walked over to his rope and tugged on it. He tied his flashlight to his belt loop and the gathered the knotted rope which had fallen the day before. He spit on his hands for friction and began to climb the rope.

After several shimmies, he whispered, "Goodbye, princess."

He stopped for a rest about five feet from the narrowed entrance. He thought it looked like a chute from this angle, wide at the bottom and narrowing as it reached the top.

"The spiral!" He said out loud in confirmation. No echo could be heard. "That's what it is." He was pleased with his discovery.

He felt for the flashlight handle and cast the light back toward the princess. The spiral glowed from a distance. He moved the light to the rounded walls. He looked at the symbols and tried to memorize as many as possible. He found the two he was searching for, the ones carved on the princess's bracelets. He sketched every detail in his mind to draw it later.

The beam of light began to dim. He shook the flashlight for resurgence, but it continued to dim until the images on the wall could no longer be seen. He glanced up toward the opening. His time was over.

Once again he whispered, "Bye."

# 11

Jesse felt better after he woke. It was late afternoon. He woke to the sound of a woman humming. For an instant he thought it was his mother, but only for an instant. He stared at the ceiling and listened to her voice lull him to sleep, but he resisted. He wanted to talk to her.

He slipped down the steps and watched Sharon as she dusted the family room. Through the doorway he could see the work she had done in the kitchen. He could smell something cooking, but nothing was on the stove. He stumbled into the room.

"Well, good morning, or rather good afternoon, Jesse." She smiled at him, "How are you feeling?"

"Better."

"Are you hungry?"

Jesse stammered a bit. He wasn't sure how he was feeling. "Not yet, I guess."

Sharon set the polish and rag on the end table. "Come sit on the sofa and talk to me while I work." Jesse thought she could read his mind. "Do you want something to drink?"

"Yeah."

Sharon walked to the kitchen and pulled one of the freshly washed glasses from inside the cupboard. Jesse followed her into the kitchen. She poured him a glass of milk and handed it to him.

"See if this helps."

Jesse looked around the kitchen. His eyes were wide with amazement. He wondered if it ever looked this good. "Looks great," he said between gulps. "What smells so good?"

"Oh, I put a roast and potatoes in the oven for dinner." She glanced at the clock, "It should be ready in about an hour. Your father said he would be home a bit early today. I told him I would stay with you until he came home."

Jesse barely heard what she said. After he heard the word 'roast', he couldn't think of anything else. His mouth watered. He slurped the last drop of his milk.

"Would you like more?"

"No, thank you." Where did that come from he wondered? This woman made him show his manners. A wave of jealousy passed through him as he thought about Collin. True, he was fatherless, but his mother made up for it, at least in Jesse's mind.

Sharon moved Jesse to the couch. She said she had this last room to vacuum and she was finished. Jesse's eyes followed her as she swept the room. When she turned off the sweeper, she gathered it in her hands and carried it to the closet.

"Well, that just about does it!" she said more to herself than to Jesse. "I'm going to set the table for dinner. Care to come to the kitchen? You can tell me all about your accident if you want."

Jesse sprung from the couch. He was excited to talk about Collin falling into the secret cave and how he rescued him. He had practically forgotten about it. It seemed like weeks ago in his mind. He took a seat at the table and started to tell his tale.

"Well, we were going up to Indian Hill to look for arrowheads. We ran down *The Great Trail* through 'Whispering Winds' to 'Dead Man's Lookout.' We came to Old Man Crafter's field and crossed it to Indian Hill. I found the first arrowhead. Collin said it was the prettiest he had ever seen." He patted his sides for his pocket to see if it was still in there when he realized he was sitting at the table with Collin's mother in his underwear. His face turned red from exposure.

"Go on...," she encouraged.

Jesse gathered his thoughts and continued. His voice was excited and filled with anticipation. Sharon watched with interest. Collin hadn't shared any of this information with her.

"Well, all total we found five. I found three and Collin found two. It was a good day. Then the wildest thing happened...."

Just then the back screen door rattled. A voice came from the other side.

"Hey, Jess. How ya feeling?" It was Collin. He was relieved to see he had arrived at the perfect moment. It was meant to be, he thought, another sign.

"Hey, Collin!" Jesse jumped from the chair to the door and opened it for him. "I was just telling your mom about...."

Collin cut him off, "Wow! What did they do to you?" He pointed toward his bound hand.

The moment was lost. Sharon was held in suspense. It seemed curious to her that Collin would keep something from her. She was determined to find out the answers, but they probably wouldn't come from her son. She listened as Jesse told Collin all about the hospital visit as she set the table for four.

Jesse was still spinning his tale when Bill came home from work. He smiled as he entered the kitchen. The scent of a woman cooking dinner was intoxicating. He had a difficult time containing his excitement.

"How was work?"

"Dad!" Jesse exclaimed as he ran to him and wrapped his arms around his father's waist.

"How are you, slugger?"

"Feeling a lot better."

"Good." He turned to Sharon, "The air smells good enough to eat. What's cooking?"

"Roast and potatoes."

"Smells great."

"Thanks, but it will probably be another twenty minutes or so. You'll have time to shower if you want."

"That sounds good to me," he said while staring at the day's grime tracing every line in his hands. He roughed up Jesse's hair and walked up the stairs.

Jesse and Collin were busy talking about the hospital. Sharon stared in wonder. She had forgotten how wonderful it was to have the house filled with conversation that didn't include her own voice. She sighed and walked into the living room.

Collin took the opportunity to whisper to Jesse. "Hey, don't say anything about the fall."

"Why, what's the big secret?" Jesse asked in his normal voice.

Collin's head snapped around for a glimpse of his mother. She was standing in the front window staring outside.

"Shhhh," he chided with his finger to his lips, "I'll explain later, just do as I say. Don't say anything."

"Why?" Jesse whispered.

"I can't explain it right now except for the fact I promised I would keep her a secret."

"Who?" Jesse leaned into him for details.

Collin's eyes gave away what his words didn't. He rolled his hand around in his empty pocket. 'Too much information' he thought to himself. His mouth was dry from nerves. He looked back at his mother again. She hadn't moved.

"No one."

"Ah come on, Collin. Who?"

"Jesse, I'll explain later. It's our secret." His eyes narrowed at Jesse as he asked, "Right?"

With no hesitation, Jesse replied, "Right. I've told no one. But who are we keeping secret?"

Collin leaned closer to Jesse's ear. His voice was lowered to barely a whisper, "The princess."

Jesse was about to repeat it when Sharon walked into the room, "What are you boys so secretive about?"

The two of them sat still as if they had been slapped. Guilt flushed their faces as hot nerves ran through their veins.

85

"No…thing," they both stammered.

Sharon laughed out loud at their faces. "Well, you look like you're guilty." She set her hands on her hips and spoke in an accusatory tone, "Did you boys get into some trouble?"

"No ma'am," Collin said, "no trouble, Mom. Promise."

His innocent face was riddled with guilt, but Sharon thought she would let it go for now. She would have a talk with him later, or with Jesse. One of those boys would tell her the truth. When she had convinced herself, her shoulders relaxed and she began humming as she took dinner out of the oven.

The boys' eyes were locked onto each other, neither daring to make a sound. Jesse mouthed the word 'princess.' Collin scolded him with his eyes. Finally Collin mouthed the word 'later' and Jesse shrugged his shoulders. His attention swung to the dinner Sharon laid up on the table before them.

"How wonderful that smells!" Bill nearly shouted as he entered the room. He slapped his son lightly on the back, "We are lucky men, Jesse. We've got a clean house and a home-cooked meal…."

The screen door rattled from attempted movement, "…And me to share it with you."

All eyes in the room settled on the woman standing on the other side of the door. No one made a move. Jesse's mother had come home.

# 12

Liza Williams woke to a darkened room. A dim light from the hallway cast an odd shadow across the two men positioned around her. Her knees were pulled to her chest. She struggled to change positions but was stopped by a woman's hand on her back. She moaned.

Liza's head pounded from many days of heroin and crystal meth mixed with cheap liquor. She tried to focus but couldn't. Her head swooned with the slightest movement. She lay still and listened for any other sound. It was silent.

It was difficult to know if it was day or night. A thin whisper of light shone through the boards, which were nailed to cover the windows. The light appeared to change in intensity and clarity as the heavy curtains moved from an unseen source.

Liza tried to lie still, but her position was extremely uncomfortable. She wiggled her way free of the woman behind her and rolled to lie on her back. She sighed from relief as the feeling began to return to her legs and arms. She closed her eyes and tried to fall back to sleep.

She felt the prick of another needle. Her blood rushed hot through her veins warning of abuse. Her vision blurred through her bloodshot eyes and the darkened room began to drift. She squeezed her eyes closed and tried to think of a better place. Soon the drug took effect and she obeyed the required movement of her partners. She lost track of time and quantity.

She opened her eyes to a steady, bright light. It seemed to call to her. It called for release, release from this decrepit place. It called her to home. She heard her own voice utter the word. Home, her body relaxed. Home, she did have one. She smiled at the light and licked her dry lips.

It was finished. Liza watched the light flicker and then vanish. The room was flooded with hushed voices, rustling and settling into silence. Darkness covered their sin. Even the tiny cracks of the boarded windows chastened the outside world. No light could be seen. Life had forgotten her.

Now, several days later and a world apart, she stood on her porch and stared through the door at her own light, which barely clung to the kitchen ceiling. She tried to blink away her recent memories. The broken screen door blocked her entrance.

She tried to remember how she got there. She wrapped her arms around her bare shoulders and gently squeezed her skin. She wore clothing that was not hers. Her feet were bare and stained with filth, which camouflaged the needle tracks. She rattled the door, wordlessly begging for acceptance. Bill pushed himself away from the table to open the door, silently cursing her return.

# 13

By the end of July, Jesse's hand showed much improvement. With the start of school still a distant thought, he grew restless. He wished he could say he was happy his mother came home, but the truth was not much had changed.

She had walked through the screen door that day dressed in a pair of men's pants. A knotted rope at the waist kept them from sliding off her hips. Her white tank top was stained to grey and had permanent sweat stains under the arms. It had worn so thin the color of her pale skin showed through. As usual, she didn't wear a bra. The circles under her eyes were so dark they looked like applied make-up. She stood in a daze. Her only movement was the constant scratching at her skin.

Today, as most days, Jesse woke to talk to his father before he left for work. They sat together at the breakfast table while Liza slept off her hangover. She usually didn't stir until noon. Today was no exception.

"Your hand looks good, Jesse." Bill smiled at his son. His promise to himself about being a better father was still fresh in his mind. "Does it feel normal?"

"Yep, pretty much," Jesse announced proudly. His rolled his hand over and over inspecting it. He giggled when he wiggled his fingers.

"Now, don't use it too much. Remember what the doctor said yesterday. It will be weaker. You need to ease into using it."

Jesse stared at his father and winked at his concern with his words, "I thought about going mountain climbing today. What do ya think?"

Bill laughed, "I think you should practice with your Game Boy first."

Sharon opened the screen door without any hindrance. Bill had repaired it the previous week. "Good morning, you two."

"Good morning," they smiled in unison. It was Wednesday, the day Sharon cleaned for them. "Am I too late for breakfast?"

"Yep," Jesse said as he wiggled his fingers in front of her face.

"Well, Jesse Williams! Look at you. No more splint." She gave him a hug.

The smell of her had the same effect on both men. They seemed to take deep breaths to drink in as much of the fresh pear scent as they could. The scent transported them back a few weeks ago, back before Liza had returned home. Bill sat with his eyes closed.

91

Sharon leaned closer to him. "Boo!" she teased.

He laughed at her gesture. In his mind, he picked her up and twirled her around the room. He kissed her passionately and they had long talks as they ate breakfast together. He loved Wednesdays. His fantasies carried him through the rest of the week.

"How's the smoking going, Bill?"

"Great! I haven't had one in over two weeks."

She patted his shoulder, "I'm proud of you."

"So am I, Dad. It's nice not to have that stinky smell around here. Now if we could only get Mom to...."

He had to do it. He had to mention her name. At that moment the fantasy broke under an oppressing weight, landing on their shoulders with a thud. Their voices seemed strained as they spoke her name.

"Is she sleeping?" Sharon asked.

Bill hung his head in shame. He was so disgusted with his life. Liza wrapped herself around him like a boa constrictor. She swallowed all that was good and choked out his very soul. He hated her and his demeanor showed it.

"Maybe she'll get help this time."

Sharon tried to sound convincing, but it was obvious Bill was finished discussing the subject. He grabbed his work shirt with his name label on it and walked out the door. He damned Liza for stealing into every minute detail of his life without being present. With the toss of the shirt into the front seat beside him, he pulled out of the driveway.

At the stop sign, his fist pounded the steering wheel until it groaned from abuse. His eyes teared. He reached for his shirt to wipe his eyes. His mood softened from the scent of fresh laundry. The last person to touch it was Sharon. He looked at the sleeve that had been smeared with grease. It was gone. He smiled and whispered a thank you to Sharon for taking care of him. He was still smiling when he got out of his car.

Jesse felt uncomfortable from the abrupt departure of his father. He made small talk with Sharon as she cleaned the kitchen. When she had finished, he slipped on his shoes and walked out the back door. He looked back through the screen and listened until she began to hum to herself. He had come to know the tune well. It was one only Sharon knew, her internal life song, which Jesse held dear. He jumped off the back porch bypassing the steps and walked to Collin's house.

"Any one home?" he yelled through the open door. "Hey Collin, you here?"

No reply came. He yelled again. Silence greeted him. He shrugged his shoulders and began to walk, paying no attention to where he was going. Before he knew it, he was heading toward *The Great Trail*.

His mind carried him the long way around. He walked to the main entrance of *The Great Trail*. He stood before the large metal sign and read the words for the first time in his life.

The Great Trail
Of Colonial Times, passed this way. It was the
main route between the French Forts Duquesne
and Detroit. It was also called the Tuscarawas
Trail, since it crossed the Tuscarawas River
at the old Indian town of Tuscarawas, near
present day Bolivar. The grade of the original
trail is visible from this spot.
Col. Henry Bouquet's army passed here in 1764
enroute to Coshocton to parley with the
Indians. Col. Lachlan MacIntosh's army passed

here in 1778 enroute to building Fort Laurens
by the Tuscarawas. The legendary "Treasure of
The Tuscarawas Trail" amounting to sixteen
packhorse loads of gold and silver removed
from Fort Duquesne before its fall in 1758,
was thought to have been buried near here by
ten French soldiers in charge of it. It has
been hunted since the early 1800s.

ERECTED BY THE MINERVA AREA HISTORICAL SOCIETY 1982

Jesse glanced around the parking lot. He was alone. He smiled to himself as he envisioned finding the treasure. He wondered why the French buried it here in Minerva, in the middle of nowhere, at least to him. They obviously meant to come back for it. He wondered how many buried it and how many stood guard. How many actually knew where to find it? Was it still there or was it just a hoax?

His thoughts carried him to the spot where the secret path intersected with *The Great Trail*. He stopped for a moment. He wanted to continue, but Collin's warning rang in his ears.

"I promised not to return. I promised to keep her secret...the princess...a secret...."

Collin had followed through with his promise, and he warned Jesse to do the same. So far, Jesse had listened, but his restless nature found him standing at the crossroads of this place. He could continue to follow *The Great Trail* and maybe pass a few other people now and again, or he could run up through 'Whispering Trees' to 'Dead Man's Lookout.' He didn't debate long. With a quick glance in all directions, he ran up the hill.

His heartbeat quickened as he neared the edge of Old Man Crafter's farm. He drew in a deep breath. His intentions were fully exposed as he burst through the thick mass of multi-floral roses. A shot of hot nerves ran through his body as he saw Collin sitting on top of the boulder where he had slipped a few weeks earlier and tumbled to the darkness below. He had a rope in his hands, and he was staring at Jesse.

Jesse tried to cover by yelling, "I knew you would be here!" Collin didn't buy his innocence.

Collin had been sitting on the boulder for nearly an hour wrestling with his thoughts. He wanted to see the princess again. He was sorry anyone had shared this experience with him. He wished Jesse didn't know. He wished he could keep her all to himself.

In his imagination he felt the spiral in his hand. He remembered how it felt, smooth and cool, with a sharp tip. He closed his eyes and held it again in his mind. He remembered how physically sick he felt when his pocket was empty and how his heart leapt when he found the spiral in a pool of vomit, Jesse's vomit. He had decided to let her go, again, when he heard rustling at the wood edge. His eyes burned with anger when he saw Jesse.

Jesse walked to the top of the hill and sat on the rock beside Collin. Collin's face was flushed.

Jesse repeated his comment with disdain. "I knew you would be here. Keep her a secret, huh?"

Collin didn't respond. He was too angry.

"What did you find down there anyway?"

Collin gritted his teeth at his pushy friend but didn't speak.

"What's the matter, princess have your tongue?"

The tone in Jesse's voice and his attitude pushed Collin into action. Collin lunged at Jesse and forced him from the rock. Jesse slid backwards and landed on his back with his feet in the air. His eyes flew open wide from the inability to breathe. He pulled at his neckline to release pressure and pounded his chest to encourage air intake. He started to panic.

Collin stood over him and watched his antics. He had seen Jesse fake seizures so many times, yet he was surprised how real he made this one look. He felt as if he was watching a movie. An odd feeling of bondage hindered his movements. He heard singing from beneath the ground. At first it sounded muffled, but then it broke free. It swirled around him. He watched Jesse with indifference.

Jesse jumped to his feet and pounded his chest. He made motions for Collin to pound his back. He leaned over slightly and braced himself for the blow, but none came. Collin just stood there staring at him.

Finally, the panic in Jesse's eyes made Collin realize his friend was in serious trouble. He forced his friend to bend over and pounded on his back. With the third hit, the wad of bubble gum flew out of Jesse's mouth. He fell to the ground as he gasped for air.

Within a minute Jesse was screaming at Collin, "You asshole! I couldn't breathe."

Collin felt confused and numb from his lack of action. He couldn't explain why he had done nothing. Even worse, he couldn't admit that he didn't want to do anything.

He stuttered with his response, "I thought you were faking!"

Jesse glared at him, but said nothing. They left the hill without a word to each other. The rope lay coiled on the rock.

Collin stared at the ceiling. Sleep eluded him. He couldn't rid himself of the guilt he felt. His friend nearly choked to death today as he stood and watched. He didn't understand what had come over him. The thoughts that passed through his mind were not his own. He tried to shake his head free. He decided to not return to that place again. He didn't like who he became when he neared the chute. Something took over his mind and it scared him.

# 14

Jesse's sleep was restless. Every sound from inside the house seemed to underline his agitation. He heard his parents arguing in the kitchen. Each word fell thick on his ears. He heard the loud slap against bare skin blended with his mother's cruel laughter. He heard the scuffling across the floor magnified by the slamming of the screen door.

For a moment, the sounds subsided until the revving of a motorcycle engine stabbed through his heart. Jesse knew who drove it, and he knew what his mother did for a fix. He remembered that day well. His mind saw the man's tattoos, the spitting gravel, and his flapping t-shirt as the motorcycle screamed its exit.

He heard a bottle crash in the kitchen. Shards of glass waltzed down the wall and met the floor with the sound of twinkling bells. The kitchen wall bore the impressions of many similar dances. He knew his father's backhand well. Jesse covered his head with his pillow.

He heard his father walk up the stairs. The sound of his footsteps paused outside Jesse's door. He walked to the bed, gently uncovered Jesse's head and placed his pillow beside him. Jesse pretended to be asleep. Bill stroked his son's hair, and then quietly closed the door. Jesse held back the tears.

In the morning he woke angry. He stomped down the stairs to find himself alone. He glanced at the clock. It was 7:30 a.m. He pounded his feet on the stairs and down the hall as he approached his parents' bedroom. The bed was empty. He shook his head with disgust. She had not come home. He tied his tennis shoes and trudged out the door.

He walked with purpose to the hill where the princess lay below. The rope was still attached to the tree. He held it in his hands and winced at the memory of the pain. He wrapped both hands around it and tested it for security. He walked to the other end, uncoiled it from the face of the rock, and tied it around his waist. Without a thought, he walked to the edge of the opening and slipped down through the hole.

His hand ached, but his desire was stronger than the pain. Collin was hiding something from him, and he wanted to see this place for himself. Adrenaline ran hot through his veins.

The narrowness of the chute made him uneasy, yet there was security wrapped throughout this tight space. He touched the walls with his hands and felt the stone ledges Collin had described. He wasn't prepared for what happened next.

After ten feet the chute opened up to a large room. He wrapped the rope around his feet for extra protection. Jesse fumbled for his flashlight as his body swayed in suspension near the top. His fingers found the switch and the beam of light settled on the wall with the writings.

"Wow!" Jesse whispered as he looked at all the symbols and pictures. They were drawn in perfect lines all leading to the opening he had just climbed down through. Arrows were the last symbol. They bent around the ceiling and disappeared in the carved earth of the chute.

"Wow. This is cool," he exclaimed. His voice echoed around the chamber.

He moved the light down the wall to the floor. He gasped when it settled on the skeleton. Collin only mentioned a princess. He hadn't said she was a pile of bones. Slowly, he lowered himself toward her resting place. When his feet touched the ground, he found himself holding his breath.

Gently he brushed aside the dirt and pebbles which partially covered her body. He glanced toward the opening. He remembered how Collin said he thought he would be buried alive.

Much of the dirt had fallen down within the bones themselves and Jesse felt intimidated to reach through the rib cage to pull anything out until his light caught the edge of something shiny. He leaned in closer and saw a piece of metal hidden under a few stones. He took a deep breath, held it, and moved his hands through the bones as if he was playing the game Operation. His fingers found the smooth cold metal and pulled it from her chest cavity. He blew the dust from its surface. It gleamed in the light and appeared to be gold. He spat on it to clean the rest of the dirt from the surface and immediately it burned hot in his hand.

"Ow!" he yelled as it fell to the ground. He spit on his hand again and checked for blisters. "Damn. That was hot!"

The echo of "...hot...hot," bounced around the room. Jesse shook off the rising feeling of fear. He scanned the area for the gold piece. He moved his position of his feet. He looked close to the bones and farther away. He slowly backed up until…his feet fell from under him. The flashlight hit the floor and blew out with a flash. His hands groped in the darkness and his right hand rested on a pile of soft fur. He let out a loud yell of surprise. He searched the floor riotously with his hands until he found the flashlight. He shook it for resurgence. The domed room burst with light. He silently thanked his father for buying this special flashlight.

He moved the light around to reveal the lump of fur lying on the ground was a decaying ground hog. Once again, he glanced to the ceiling. He figured it fell from the ground through the opening and crawled a few feet and died. Collin hadn't told him that either. He sighed from relief. He thought it odd that there was no odor from the decaying flesh, no bloating from maggots, just a lump of fur slowly receding and curling away from its frame exposing tiny fragments of white bone.

When he stood, his feet skirted something metal across the floor. He followed the sound with his light and it lit the gold piece. He gathered it in his hands and sat on the floor to inspect it closely.

It formed the shape of a bird. Its wings were widespread as if ready to take flight. One foot was drawn to its belly; the other was pointed straight down. It was mounted on a long flat platform, which reminded Jesse of some of the stones that had been placed in the circle directly above. Tiny holes had been drilled through the piece, one on the top, and the other in perfect alignment on the bottom. He held the piece to his eye and brought it to the light. A narrow beam of light revealed its purpose. He thought it was some sort of bead strung to make a necklace. Curious, he crawled to the skeleton and held the light to search for others.

His breath felt hot as his level of excitement rose after finding another bead. This one was made from copper, he guessed. It was round and had several spikes sticking out from the center. They varied in length and thickness. Most of them remained very sharp. He tried to break one of the spikes from the sphere, but his malicious attempt was sabotaged as it glowed and burned the palm of his hand.

"Son of a bitch!" he said as he hopped up and down and shook his hand from the intense strength of the heat.

"...tch...tch..." echoed around the room.

He didn't understand it, but he decided to not try that again. He touched the bead lightly with his finger. It was cool. He picked it up and placed it on the floor next to the bird.

He returned to the princess again. He searched for other pieces. He found a clear cylinder wrapped with gold threads. He held it to the light. It seemed to gather and magnify the light. His thoughts drifted to the wall where the symbols and pictures had been etched. The gathered light seemed to obey its command. Within a second a flash of light came from within the cylinder and lit the entire wall in flash.

"Cool!"

Jesse was thrilled with his discovery. He hovered over the skeleton and began to rummage through the bones. He gave no thought to the destruction, nor did he think of reverence. He tore through the fragments until he found all of the pieces that he could.

The last piece he found was the spiral. The sheer size of the piece versus the others he had found left no doubt in his mind that this piece was the centerpiece of the necklace. He rolled the spiral around his hand and placed it over his finger. He held it up in the light.

Whether by accident or subconscious thought, his finger pointed directly to the chute as he lifted it into the air. His mind didn't make the connection. He was too excited about his loot. He couldn't wait to show Collin. He wondered how he had missed these pieces.

He kicked the rummaged pile of bones as he walked to the rope. His hands were filled with the unique pieces. He shoved them into his pockets and spit on his hands. After rubbing them together, he started his climb.

He didn't give much thought to the difficulty he would have using his weakened hand. Sharp pain shot through it and continued up his arm. He stopped just a few feet from the floor. The pain in his hand was severe.

"You're so stupid," he shouted at himself.

"...Stupid...stu...," came the echo.

The resonance was choked and the chamber fell eerily silent. Jesse hung from the rope. An oppressive feeling came over him. Fear gripped his thoughts. He heard the sound of movement below him. It sounded like something heavy being dragged across the floor. He couldn't move.

The beam of the flashlight swung around the room. It spun slowly at first, and then began to gain speed. Jesse felt dizzy as he watched the spinning light. He closed his eyes and held his face to the rope. He couldn't control his breathing and his arms felt numb from inactivity. For a moment, he thought he would faint.

Without warning the light went out. Jesse choked on the air. He heard the sound of laughter, cruel laughter, ringing in his ears. He wanted to cover his ears, the sound was deafening, but he wouldn't let go of the rope. When the laughter stopped, there was no echo, only the sound of crawling things slithering beneath him.

He tried to cry out, but his words stuck in his throat. In the darkness, he fumbled for the feel of a knot. He forced his injured hand to hold his weight. Something seemed to pull at his legs. His body felt twice his normal weight. Panic struck him. He had to get out of there. He was too petrified to notice the pain.

When he felt the blades of grass touch his face, he began to breathe. The warm air burned in his lungs. He scrambled from the chute and ran down the hill. He dared not look back. He struggled through the thicket of briars, imagining someone chasing him. He couldn't shake the strange sensation.

He didn't take the normal path home. Instead he ran the long way around, hoping to see some people. He would feel safer if he knew he wasn't alone. He whispered, "Please...please...someone..." constantly as he ran down the trail toward the railroad tracks. He never saw the woman he pushed with his arms as he rushed past her. She yelled to him, but he disappeared down the trail without a word. His legs carried him through the downtown area. When he ran past the barbershop, he nearly pushed an elderly man to the ground.

"Slow down, sonny," he shouted, but Jesse never did.

When the screen door slammed behind him, he locked it. His mother, wrapped in her bathrobe, was sitting at the table smoking a cigarette. She had a coffee cup sitting in front of her. Jesse glanced at the clock. It was 3:12 p.m.

"You look like hell," his mother said. "What's wrong? Did you see a ghost?" She mocked as she eyed her son from head to toe. Her hands were dangling in the air with her palms wide and outstretched. She dropped her arms as if they were just attached to a heavy weight. "My God Jesse,

104

your pants are in shreds." She tried to stand. "Where have you been?" Her tone was agitated.

Jesse looked down at his jeans. They were torn to his knees and some of the strips were missing. His shoes were covered with mud and his t-shirt was torn. He wiped the sweat from his brow and felt the clumps of mud stuck in his hair.

His mother shooed him away with her hands. "Go clean yourself up. Little Miss Perfect, who can't pay her bills, just cleaned." She took a long sip from her coffee cup.

Anger flashed in his eyes. He wanted to slap her, hard. His hand was clenched in a fist. He wanted to return all the unnecessary, unprovoked abuse, but instead, he walked away from her without speaking.

"I'm talkin' to you, boy," she sneered. "Don't you walk away from your momma!" Her words were slurred.

She wasn't drinking coffee, Jesse thought to himself as he walked up the steps. He started to unzip his pants, but his fingers were swollen and his index finger looked oddly contorted. It was then he noticed the pain. He held his hand under cold running water. If he broke his finger again, his father would kill him. He grabbed his finger and yanked it hard to straighten it. His mother never acknowledged his screams.

# 15

Liza held her hands out to the wind as she sat on the back of the motorcycle. She felt her entire body itch with fire from nerves. She needed a fix and she needed it bad. The half bottle of whiskey she had hidden in the front closet inside an old cowboy boot called to her until she finished it. It wasn't enough. She needed more.

It didn't take long for Dale to come for her. He knew she would call. She always did. Even if she swore this was the last time, he waited for the phone to ring. He was always ready for some good sex, even if it cost him a bit. He had plenty of drugs around, so it didn't bother him. Personally, he did not touch the stuff, but it made for a good living. He smiled every time his Harley engine purred.

Bill had chased her out of the house. The drill was always the same. Dale rode around a bit, letting Liza enjoy the wind in her face. He usually drove with one hand. She always wore a skirt. It's one of his requirements. Dale knew he could set the rules. She did whatever he asked for a fix.

Tonight was no exception. After the fifteen-minute ride, he took her to his home.

He lived on the outskirts of town. His house was a nice brick ranch built in the sixties. It was secluded, had several out buildings, and a finished basement. The driveway was over a mile long and crossed two streams. He had both bridges wired with explosives, just in case. He installed a state-of-the-art security system so he could monitor the property. He owned sixty-seven acres without a mortgage.

He never married. He had plenty of women around, most of them like Liza. All of them had been good girls at some point in their life, but once they found drugs, life forgot about them. They only existed.

Dale and Liza pulled into his driveway. Gravel spun. From behind a clump of bushes, a hidden gate closed behind them. Dale drove over the grass to a metal pole sticking out of the ground just a few feet from the gate. He lifted the metal lid and pushed a red button. He closed the lid and drove up to the house.

By the time they walked into the house, Liza was extremely agitated. Her nails clawed her skin. Her internal temperature fluctuated from cold to hot, and back again. She shifted her weight from left to right. Dale walked past her without a word. He knew she was no good to him unless she was flying. He returned with a vial and a needle.

It seemed curious to him after all the years she had been using that she never stuck herself. When he entered the room, she held out her arm. Dale examined all the possible spots and shook his head. She extended her other arm. Again, he motioned no. She jumped on the table and spread her legs and lifted her skirt. She squeezed her upper thigh. He drove the needle into her leg. She never winced, nor did she change her position.

After he used her body to his complete satisfaction, he poured two drinks of vodka, one with ice, one without. He sipped his chilled drink. Liza chugged hers. She always did.

The following afternoon, Dale took Liza home. He dropped her off at the end of the road. It was another rule. She slid from the back of the motorcycle enjoying the resonance of her latest fix and began to walk home. They said no goodbyes. She had already stated this was her last time. Dale smiled as he drove away.

She walked into a quiet house. She yelled up the stairs for Jesse. She assumed with no answer that he wasn't there. She never checked to be sure. She walked past his room without looking in. Her clothes slithered down her body and lay in a pile on the floor. She grabbed her robe and walked back to the kitchen. She poured herself a coffee cup full of vodka and sat at the table. She slid the bottle between her bare legs. She had finished her third cup of vodka when Jesse rushed through the back door.

She watched his actions with disengaged curiosity. She opened her mouth to speak, but her thick tongue strangled her words. When she tried to speak again, she spit her words with venom. She didn't mean to insult her son—it just spewed out of her mouth.

With the pouring of another cup, the bottle was empty. She held it upside down until the final drop rippled the liquid in her half-empty cup. She placed the bottle on the table. She stared through the watery glass until it became clear. She tipped the bottle and stuck her tongue into it as far as it would reach. Through the glass, she caught a glimpse of Jesse standing there. The look of distain on his face spoke silent volumes. Jesse ran out of the door.

She wanted to call after him. She wanted to tell him she loved him. She wanted to tell him how handsome he was and how proud of him she had become, but she wasn't even sure if it was true. She wasn't sure of anything. She felt like she had been involved with drugs all of her life, but it had been less than six years.

It started at a chance meeting with an old high school friend, Candice. Liza and Bill had a huge fight over something minute as always. Their fights always escalated out of control. It was a way of showing their unhappiness with each other.

She was walking down the street to cool off and Candice spotted her while driving. She pulled to the curb. They talked for a brief moment and Candice invited her to come to a party with her to forget her troubles. And forget them she did. She should've said no, but she was weak. Everyone was encouraging her to try Crystal Meth. She heard a little about it, but not enough. As she watched the rising of the curled smoke, she whispered, "Just this once." She couldn't have been more wrong.

Her body was etched in stone on that broken kitchen chair, riddled by needle tracks and collapsed veins. The constant search for a better high left her with fifteen years of facial lines that appeared in less than six. Her skin was an odd shade of grey and she had lost all muscle tone. Her ribs and hipbones seemed abnormally advanced from the lack of food. Her hair and life hung in strings. She took the last swallow of the vodka.

She tried to stand. Her body moved forward, but her feet didn't. She slammed to the floor without any reactions to brace herself. Her mouth was bleeding and started to throb. She stumbled to the mirror to look. She had broken her two front teeth. One dangled in a sliver; the other cracked at the gum line. With her body still numb from the alcohol and

109

heroin, she fumbled on the floor to search for her teeth. Her hand found a tiny carved idol.

It was about an inch and a half long and looked similar to what you would see on a totem pole. It was some sort of a brown stone with white and taffy colored veins running through it. The head was larger than the body and the eyes were overly exaggerated. There were several tiny holes in the top of its head, but only one in the bottom.

For whatever reason, Liza stuck it in her mouth. She ran her tongue over the carving. It felt good to bite down on it where she was missing her tooth. She felt it begin to heat. Before she could pull it from her mouth, it burned her. She spit it on the floor.

She looked in the mirror again. It had seared her gum and stopped the bleeding. She leaned over the sink and rinsed the blood from her mouth.

She held this curious object in the palm of her hand. It was covered with her own bloody saliva. She held it to her lips again, but thought better of it. Instead, she rinsed it in the sink. She stared at the idol as she walked to her bedroom.

With her mouth pounding and beginning to swell, she pulled on her jeans and a t-shirt. Her only thought was to take this thing to a pawnshop. She figured it was stolen by the way Jesse was acting earlier, so she better act fast before the police were notified. If that were the case, she wouldn't get a dime, just a rest inside the town jail. She had been there before and it was not fun. She slipped on her sandals and walked out of the door.

She found it difficult to take her eyes off of the thing. She held it close to her face in her left hand. It was skillfully carved, but severely out of proportion. By the time she came to the end of the road, she figured it was part of a necklace.

She made a mental note to search the house for more pieces if the pawnshop gave her a good price on this one. By its appearance, she knew it was old. How old, she couldn't guess.

Her walk downtown to the pawnshop seemed to take an eternity. She knew this feeling well and didn't like it. Her fix was wearing off and the amount of booze didn't camouflage the rising feeling of agitation. She began to scratch at her skin and pull at her clothing. Everything bothered her.

She began to swat the air. She saw flies, thousands of them, swirling around her, landing on her rubbing their filthy little legs. She ran to get away from them, stumbling many times. She tripped up and down the sidewalk curb as she waved her hands in the air. She cupped her hands over her ears trying to drown out the noise of their buzzing. The sound grew louder. She shook her head until she was disoriented.

In the distance she saw the word PAWN lit in red neon. She stepped off of the sidewalk. She wanted money to get another fix. She never saw the semi-tractor trailer until a second before it struck her. The only thing she saw was the bead flying out of her hand, bouncing on the pavement as she reached for it. Her body slid from the grill when the semi screeched to a halt.

The jack-knifed truck blocked traffic for several hours in downtown Minerva. A small crowd gathered as an EMT collected the pieces of her dismembered body. Her left arm and hand were separated from each other and rested twenty feet from her body. A large pool of blood stained the asphalt. The black tire tread traced the erratic pattern of the truck as the driver struggled to stop.

"She came out of nowhere. I...I...didn't see her...," he muttered again and again as the ambulance took him to the hospital.

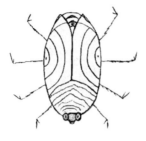

# 16

Jack was raised by his grandmother, a wonderful lady according to the town's people. A downright saint they claimed. She was perfect in every way, but she had one vice, bingo. She paraded on the front steps of the town hall against the evils of the game. It disgusted her that gambling would be allowed within the four walls of a church. Food of the devil, she would claim. The only problem with her visual confrontation was how she had to disguise herself to play.

She spent hours in preparation for the sinful evening. She had a special case with all of the trinkets and wands. She prided herself on the number of cards she could handle at once. She would wait anxiously for her sister, Mary, to arrive. When she saw her sister's car, she would yell a few last minute orders to her grandson and disappear out of the door. If she was lucky enough to shout 'Bingo!' first, she split the winnings with Mary as payment for the ride.

She was very strict with Jack and allowed him no room for mistakes. Living with the constant double standards and the old adage of 'Do as I say, not as I do' strangely contorted Jack's view of many things. He struggled with his deep hatred for his grandmother. Though she never raised a hand to him, the verbal abuse was oppressive. He hated only one woman worse than his grandmother and that was his Aunt Mary. He moved out of the house at sixteen and never visited them since.

Jack Hilbert was known as an odd fellow. He would stand about six foot five if he were able. He had scoliosis that left him with misaligned hips and a hump on his back. The children in town referred to him as the hunchback. The adults called him the barber.

He owned a tiny building downtown that was always packed with patrons, standing room only on most days. The old men came for their 'daily' shave, which he performed every other day, young boys came for their first haircut, but women, they weren't welcome. Even if a youngster came for his first haircut, mommy had to wait outside.

"This ain't no place for a lady," Jack mumbled under his breath as he escorted women to the bench outside. "You wait here 'til he's done." He slipped back inside the safety of the shop.

Truth be told, he hated women. When his grandmother grew old and frail, he had her admitted to a psychiatric hospital and he never once visited her. She blamed him for everything that was wrong in the world. He told everyone she was insane.

He opened the barbershop when he was about thirty. It took him two years to learn how to properly use the scissors, but he was skilled with knives. Many people said

114

he had a strange shine in his eyes when he held a knife in his hands, but that he gave the closest shave with a straight edge not a man in town could deny. He had a full head of hair, but as a true testimony to the steadiness of his hand, he shaved his head every day. Never once did he cut himself, nor anyone else for that matter.

Town gossip filled his shop. Most people think it's the women who spread rumors, but one afternoon spent in Jack's shop would change their minds. They never cared who was present. Nothing was sacred. They discussed every subject except religion and politics.

On wedding days, men placed their wagers on how long the marriage would last. Kit Miller boasted of the biggest pay out for the Saunder-Brown union, which only lasted three days. He made five hundred fifteen dollars on that divorce. The closest one to him was Jack himself who made seventy-five dollars on the Henry-Donaldson annulment.

In the spring of 1999, Jack had severe wind damage to his shop. The antique barber pole blew away and was never found. He replaced it with a new spinning one encased within a clear cylinder. The men complained for weeks how it made them dizzy. Jack finally gave up and pulled the plug out of the wall. The bare wires still hung from the ceiling.

He collected pigs with wings. Most days he wished people didn't know this fact because he was flooded with samples of all sizes. Some hung from suspended string, other sat on his shelves. They were so crammed they were literally thrown on top of each other. Most of them were covered with chunks of hair and all with many layers of dust. But, the best swung around on a motorized wire above the shaving chair. He did this on purpose to offset the comments about the spinning barbershop pole. No one had said a word about the flying pig, yet.

115

It was Jack who called the ambulance the day Jesse was hurt. He knew Bill Williams well. He had married his cousin. Jack was the one who gave Liza away that day at the courthouse. He had a standing wager on that marriage. He had one more year to go.

He didn't come to family reunions. He didn't go to church. He didn't play bingo. And he didn't like Collin.

Jack and Sharon Sims did not share values. She was the only woman who refused his rules. They had a little problem a few years back, one Jack remembered well.

She brought Collin in for his first haircut when he was two. His hair was long, curly and blonde and in Jack's opinion, too long for a boy. Sharon specifically asked for only two inches be cut from his hair. She also asked for the first lock to be given to her.

She knew the rules. She knew women sat outside, but she wouldn't budge. She stood with her feet planted on the floor as if they grew there. The room erupted with laughter. One look from Jack's face hushed the unruly crowd. Not a single man offered his seat to Sharon, so she stood with her hand extended waiting for the first tuft of hair to be placed in her palm.

Jack sneered defiantly but spoke not a word. He had a lot of admiration for Mark Sims and didn't want to disrespect him. With the first snip of the scissors, Jack held out the curl to Sharon. It filled the palm of his hand. He cut much more than asked. She never wavered. She kept her palm facing upwards, waiting for Jack to place it in her hand. He tipped his palm and the lock floated to the floor. Only the left side of his mouth curled from pleasure. Their eyes locked. Sharon never moved.

With her hand still extended and her palm empty, she said, "This time only two inches, please."

116

Jack obeyed like a defiant child. He never took his eyes off of her as he placed the two-inch curl in her hand. She smiled and thanked him but made no attempt to move. She stood just a few feet away as he worked his way around Collin's head being careful to only cut two inches off his curls. The only sound in the shop was the occasional ring of the bell that hung above the door. Every man that walked through it, as well as the ones seated, sat frozen with amazement that a woman graced this space and the floor did not consume her.

Jack closed the door of the shop with the thoughts of that day nine years ago burning what was left of his soul. It was 7:30 p.m. He had been there for twelve hours. He decided to walk to the beer distributor for a six-pack. He ordered a twelve of talls and carried the cardboard box out of the side door. He drank two before he walked three blocks.

He lived above the shop. Beside the large picture window was a narrow wooden door. He stuck his key in the lock and opened the door as he had done a thousand times before, but this time it only opened halfway. His mind did not register the change and he walked into the edge of the door, nearly dropping his precious cargo.

"Son of a bitch!" he yelled as he rubbed the lump that had already begun to form.

He yanked on the door again, but it was stuck. He set the box of nine beers on the sidewalk, along with his half empty bottle, and knelt to inspect the problem. It seemed stuck on a tiny rock. He pushed and pulled at the door until it worked its way free of the obstruction. He was about to kick the stone into the street in frustration when he noticed it was shaped like a bug. He picked it up and shoved it into his pocket. With his beer in his hand, he climbed the twenty-

117

two steps to his apartment, subconsciously counting each one.

He tossed his body on the couch and picked up the telephone. He dialed the local Chinese restaurant and asked for a number seventeen, extra spicy, for delivery. He hung up without any additional information required. They knew who he was. His order was always the same.

After lobbing back three more beers, he walked out of his door. He placed a brick fragment in the door to hold it open as he walked to the bottom of the stairs. When his feet touched the bottom step, there was a rap at the door. A young woman held a brown paper bag in her hands.

"Six dollars, please."

He pulled his money from his pocket and began to count his singles. The tiny beetle fell as he fumbled for an extra dollar for the tip. Had the delivery person been the young man who usually came, he would be walking away with two dollars, but this girl only deserved one. She picked up the carved insect and handed it to him with a smile. He stuck it into his pocket and closed the door in her face.

He lunged into his Chinese food with the skill of an accomplished chopstick guru. He prided himself in the ability though no one viewed his art. He had enough uneaten to scoop into the small take-out container that the restaurant knew to include. The last floweret of broccoli would not fit, so he ate it with his fingers. A pang of guilt ran through him, but he quickly dismissed it as necessity.

He returned to the couch with his remote. After flicking through one hundred channels, he turned the television off. Even the XXX channels didn't satisfy him tonight. He walked to his bedroom and emptied his pockets.

The bug made a strange sound when it settled on the chest of drawers. He picked it up and examined it closely

118

for the first time. It was carved from bone or ivory, which he couldn't tell for sure. The markings on its back simulated wings and a segmented body. He thought it looked like an Egyptian scarab with one distinct difference — it had legs, eight of them equally distended from its body. It was carved from one piece and its measurement from head to butt was an inch long and 3/4" wide. He noticed a small pinhole in the top and looked at the bottom to find a second hole. He pushed a piece of thread through it and was not surprised to see it peek out the opposite side.

He decided to take it to the jeweler in the morning for authenticity and toyed with himself as his imagination played with its worth as thousands, maybe tens of thousands of dollars. It appeared old to him. He was surprised at the narrowness of each leg, and that none broke when his door drove it into the brick sidewalk. He carefully placed it beside his pile of pocket coins. He showered and settled into bed.

Jack woke with a start. He tried to bring to his memory what sound woke him. He thought he remembered hearing buzzing, a loud buzzing noise. He rolled over onto his side placing his bad ear against the pillow. He took a deep breath and exhaled it slowly.

He heard it again. He lay there still as he could. He held every other breath trying not to miss it again. He squeezed his eyes closed and bent his entire thought on the sound.

By the second time he was wide-awake. It sounded like a blowfly stuck on its back, unable to free itself. Jack woke easily and was instantly agitated when his sleep was interrupted. He threw the sheets from his feet in one motion and stomped across the floor. He didn't want to turn on a light because he knew that was the end of his sleep regardless of the time.

119

He thought the sound came from his chest of drawers. He fumbled in the semi-darkened room with his hands until he found his wristwatch. He held the face toward the filtered street lit window. It was 1:23 a.m. He sighed heavily.

He scanned the top of his dresser once his eyes adjusted to the level of light coming through his window blinds. A city street lamp beamed just beyond his window, so his bedroom roller blinds were always closed even when the sun shone bright. Bright lights were not his favorite. Cloudy days were the best in his mind. His grandmother hated cloudy days.

The buzzing sound came again. He focused on the shine of the wood to find it. He nearly had his nose touching the surface when he saw the spinning bug. He pounded it with his fist.

"Ow! What the hell..." He brought his hand to his mouth and licked the burning sensation.

"Damn!" he yelled. He flicked on the bedroom light and winced from the imaginary daggers that pricked his eyes from the brightness. The side of his hand was on fire. He looked at the top of the dresser expecting to see a dead hornet lying there, but he saw only the carved bug. He moved his fingers to pick it up, but the bead was so hot it blistered his fingers immediately.

"Good God!" he screamed as he dropped it on the chest of drawers.

He stared at the curious object. He wanted to touch it again, but three had never been his lucky number. He pulled his blistered fingertips from his mouth and with a thoughtless motion, flicked the bug with his other hand.

He would have enjoyed the satisfaction, but the stupid thing hit his brown fabric roller blind, burned a hole through it and went out of the window like it had real wings. He huffed, turned out the light and went back to bed. He tossed and turned trying to think of anything else but that stupid burning beetle, but he couldn't. It taunted him. The fact that it had some sort of a power increased the value in his mind. He dismissed the idea it was worth tens of thousands and escalated the price to hundreds of thousands. The thought of someone else finding it and profiting from it tormented him. It was his rare find and he would be the one to yield from it.

He pulled on a pair of sweat pants and walked barefoot down the stairs. He secretly opened the door and looked in all directions for an unknown thief. He thought he saw someone crouching in the dark alley, but after a minute of watching closely, he realized it was only a piece of fabric half pulled from a dumpster flapping in the night's breeze.

He opened the door and listened for the buzzing sound. When he wanted to hear the noise, it defied him. He crouched down on his hands and knees and rubbed his hands over the brick to search for it.

After nearly one half of an hour and two people questioning his actions, he spotted it. It was against the base of the lamppost perched as though it had flown there. He moved his hand toward it and quickly withdrew.

"What are you thinking?" he asked himself. "It will burn the shit out of you."

He sat cross-legged until he solved his dilemma. He ran up the stairs, taking three at a time. He turned on the bathroom light and rummaged through the drawer until he found a pair of tweezers. He scurried out of the door and slipped at the top of the steps. He caught himself before he fell.

He had seen the last of his sleep tonight. His heart was racing as he held onto the railing. When he calmed his nerves, he started down the steps.

Fifteen steps he had hurried down. On the sixteenth one, he slipped again, but this time he couldn't catch himself. He tumbled down the last seven steps. His crumpled body lay head first at the bottom. His head rested at a ninety-degree angle.

# 17

She loved nature. It made her feel closer to God. She admired many of the wonders around her and found herself repeatedly saying, "With all of this, how can someone not believe?"

The truth be told, Julie Garrett had many gods, many her own making. She held a high financial position with a previously local, now national bank. She had worked her way up the ladder, starting as a part-time teller to her current position as president of loan operations. She assumed much of her importance as higher than her superiors', yet her humble aura enveloped many with a sense of admiration or pure hatred. The line between the two was as thin as the silk threads woven into her suits.

Her sense of fashion came at an extremely high price. Ralph Lauren, Armani, and Dolce & Gabbana were only a few names that hung in her closet. She never wore her pumps for two consecutive seasons, and she had a matching Gucci or Kate Spade bag for eighty percent of them. On Fridays, which was 'dress down day,' she wore her Tahitian pearls with her Calvin Klein Couture jeans. Somehow, the colors of black and blue symbolized so much more than a bruise.

She drank martinis, very dirty. She twirled the double olives around the rim of her glass until she plopped them one by one into the volatile liquid. With the final sip of the Vox vodka, she swallowed the olives whole while her eyes read the thoughts of her table guests.

She was thirty-nine, brunette, thin and extremely attractive. Her face was flawless with or without Chanel, and most of the men in her office had night fantasies about her. She was married without children of her own, though her husband had three with his second wife, two boys and a girl. They didn't like her but tolerated her because she made their father extremely happy.

Her husband, Ralph, traveled extensively due to his executive position with the premier European-American automaker. If he slept in his own bed, covered with twelve-hundred thread count sheets, for more than three consecutive nights, it was a rarity. Their relationship was as solid as their faithfulness. When they spent time together, it felt like a continuous honeymoon.

On several occasions, dressed only in a trench coat, she picked him up at a private airport terminal. Occasionally she would surprise him with a lace bustier and stockings hidden under a sea of khaki. She would reveal herself to him in the parking lot of a five-star restaurant and make him suffer through dinner knowing what awaited him.

He was twelve years her senior, but neither of them minded. They had a large historic home, decorated in period furniture, two Jaguars in the garage, and seven maxed-out credit cards.

They never fought over money. They never fought over anything. They enjoyed the whispers of moments together their careers gave them and thanked God for the opportunity to share them wrapped in white Egyptian cotton until noon.

They met over a business deal, Julie at one end of the mahogany partner table and Ralph at the other. After several hours of negotiations with a myriad of attorneys and no consensus in sight, they excused themselves for a private cooperative plan. They had a few drinks at the hotel bar and discussed the deal. After the second martini, Julie had all the appropriate papers signed. She slid them into her Tumi briefcase. She gladly accepted his dinner invitation.

Ralph knew New York City well. Instead of taking Julie to one of the well-known restaurants, he took her to The Purple Pickle. The building was small, secluded, and packed with locals. They were known for their fresh seafood, homemade pasta, and of course, eggplant. They served only top shelf liquor, local micro-brewed beer, and Italian wine. The food was exquisite, but the company was better.

They ate, laughed, and drank, but not too much. They both wanted to remember this evening. They sat at their bistro table until the restaurant began to close. They ordered a caramel-laced tiramisu to go and walked out of the door.

Ralph hailed a cab from the corner, and they rode together back to the hotel. He followed Julie to her room and helped to gather her things and carried them to his suite. They had a nine-thirty meeting with both groups to finish the negotiations Ralph had already signed.

At the auto group's nine o'clock meeting, Ralph's absence was unsettling. By nine-fifteen the associates were agitated and moments before nine-thirty, silent panic filled the room. The embarrassment of Ralph's actions glowed from every face.

Precisely at nine-thirty, Julie's team arrived. They stood at attention like a well-trained unit. At 9:31 a.m. a knock on the door interrupted the cold stares. The auto group held their breath, silently praying that the unknown guest was Ralph.

A smile from a courier greeted them. He was dressed in a silk suit and tie. His teeth were as polished as his Ferragamo shoes. He handed the sealed envelope to the bankers without a word and left the room.

Julie's boss thumbed through the pages. Although he knew everything would be perfect, he double-checked Julie's handiwork. Once he found the signatures, he distributed the opposing group their copy, slid the original into his briefcase, and walked out of the room. With their silent mouths open, Ralph's associates watched as the sea of Armani suits ebbed from the room while he and Julie were feeding each other tiramisu in bed, sipping on fresh-roasted Sumatra.

The auto group was shocked at Ralph's actions. His absence at the meeting was frowned upon, but Julie's crew knew her well. This wasn't the first time she didn't come with the signed papers. Her reputation as a closer was well known though she always kept it professional. This was the first time she crossed the line. Julie and Ralph were married in Monaco two months later.

It was a week shy of their fifth anniversary. Julie spent the morning finishing her plans for their anniversary party. When she made the arrangements only one location would do – The Hart Mansion.

The stately Italianate structure was built in 1869 for George F. Yengling and after his death was sold to Hiram Hart through a public auction. After Hiram passed the home to Paul and Gertrude Hart, the couple spent many years restoring the home to its current beauty. For ninety-three years the Hart family enjoyed the view overlooking the quaint town of Minerva, Ohio.

The Hart Mansion was Julie's favorite restaurant. Many romantic conversations took place over the chef's special creations. Julie's favorite appetizer was the Mansion's shrimp cocktail with white sauce. Ralph enjoyed their crab cakes, so Julie was certain to pick both as the anniversary evening's starters. She added Hungarian peppers for a spicy touch and to round out the number of appetizers to three.

Happy hour was set to begin the moment the guests entered the front door. Trays of red, white and blush wines were to be placed in the center hall. They would be asked to join the group in the upstairs bar for a few more drinks and light conversation. Once precisely an hour had expired, the appetizers would be set in the front adjoining dining rooms. The guests would be encouraged to walk the four acres of ground while the main course was being prepared.

She chose the Mansion Salad to be served with a side of chicken or steak just prior to the main course. One main dish was fresh garden pasta prepared without the normal seafood addition for her Vegan guests. Pork tenderloin, seasoned with an apple cider peppercorn demi-glace and grilled to perfection, was an easy second choice.

Her only hesitation was the seafood selection. Fish was her personal dinner favorite, and the Mansion's Orange Roughy melted in her mouth. Whether it was finished with their spicy glaze or a lemon and herb sauce, it was luscious. However, after last week's tasty dinner of Horseradish Salmon, Julie was undecided. She thought for only a few minutes, and then decided on the Alaskan Salmon.

With the basic dinner plans decided, Julie was anxious for Ralph's return. He was expected to fly home on the company Lear Friday evening. She had arranged to pick him up in a limo and drive to the party after at least an hour of driving with the privacy window closed. She gave Ralph specific instructions to be well rested. He smiled as he thought of the trench coat.

She had her black silk dress delivered by the seamstress after the alterations were completed. It was the new 'little thing' from Valentino. She had to split the cost between two credit cards to buy it, but when she slipped it over her hips and had the seamstress button the thirty-two buttons up the back, it was worth it. The silk chiffon scarf that was wrapped in ribbons swirled around the dress and added to its mystery. She envisioned it with the garter belt, thong and back-seamed stockings as she looked in her three-way mirror built inside of her dressing room. She slid on her Jimmy Choo's and smiled at the image staring back at her. She could hardly contain her excitement. Friday was four days away.

The guest list was small, but powerful. Three of the auto executives would be attending as well as six from her bank. Julie had met most of their wives on a business/shopping trip last spring in Paris. She applied for a specific credit card for that excursion. The limit was thirty thousand. She didn't want to run short and be embarrassed.

For the final time she counted the number of her guests and called the Hart Mansion to confirm. She spent twenty minutes finalizing the menu. She made no changes. She never did, once she made her decision, she never looked back. She couldn't afford to waste time second-guessing herself. It made her who she was today: strong, confident and extremely successful.

She slipped into her cashmere yoga ensemble and walked out of the door. When her car stopped at the entrance to *The Great Trail*, she paused and read the sign. She loved this place. It's where she came to get in touch with herself. She glanced around the parking lot and saw she was alone. She smiled. She enjoyed her own company.

She walked leisurely as she checked off her party list in her mind. Satisfied she had covered every detail with exquisite design, her shoulders relaxed and she picked up the pace. She never ran. She didn't like the long-term effects it had on a woman's body.

The birds sang gloriously that afternoon. Her smile radiated contentment. She stopped to watch a kingfisher hop from branch to branch and descend on a minnow in the stream. It flew to a narrow branch as the fish wiggled in its beak. With a quick snap, the kingfisher threw the minnow down its throat. It chattered its song of pleasure while eyeing the water for his next meal.

Life sounds filled the woods as she walked deeper down the trail. She had just decided to turn around when she heard the sound of someone running toward her. She winced at the thought of running. The path was well traveled, but nature showed its dominion by spreading tree roots throughout. One misstep and a hard fall was certain. She moved to the side to allow the jogger to pass.

Jesse's sweat-soaked head popped over the knoll. Julie was surprised to see a young boy. His eyes were filled with fear and his stare empty. It was obvious he didn't see her. His swinging arms hit her body as he hurried past. She yelled, "Hey! Slow down," but as quickly as he appeared, he vanished. She could hear his fading footsteps pound the trail in panic. Fear slithered down her spine.

With a backwards glance she took her first step. A scream of pain echoed through the woods. She moved her twisted ankle and saw a spiral lying on the ground. As she bent to pick it up, a burst of glacial air settled around her. Without thought she shoved the spiral in her pocket and tried to hurry from the growing feeling of dread.

Frost stilled the air. It was difficult to breathe. She forced her quivering body to move, but her limp was fierce. She opened her mouth to shout, but her voice was stolen from her. She gave up and sat on a rock.

The leaves beside her began to stir. They swirled in a hurried fashion around her body. She covered her face from the chilled assailant. Finally, the tempest of debris moved from her and disappeared deeper into the trail. The feeling of oppression slid from her thoughts as the air returned to the normal temperature. She exhaled her held breath.

Her thoughts returned to her throbbing ankle. She tied her shoelaces tighter to prevent swelling. Her fear turned to disgust when she thought about her new pumps that she would be unable to wear to the party.

Julie placed her hands on both sides of her ankle and rolled it around in tight circles. She was thankful nothing was broken. She tried to stand, but winced from the pain. She settled back on the rock and shoved her hands in her pocket with irritation.

The tip of the spiral pricked her finger. She sucked the pinprick until the bleeding stopped. Slowly, she slid her hand into her pocket and wrapped her fingers around the sharp object.

She held the spiral with both hands to inspect it. It glowed a strange shade of green yet appeared opalescent. The ring at the end left no doubt in her mind that it was a pendant from a necklace though to her it appeared to be upside down. The pendant was wider at the bottom and continued to narrow until it settled to a loop at the tip.

She twirled it around in her fingers. She was unsure of the type of material. It appeared to be made of silver, yet it had the ability to change its appearance to simulate a rare stone. She was very familiar with jewelry but had never seen anything like this. She wondered where it came from, and then remembered the young boy who ran past her. Assuming he must have stolen it from his terrified reaction, she covered it in her hands and listened for any sound. Convinced she was alone, she opened her hands for closer inspection.

One side of the spiral was slightly flattened. She held it to her chest and thought what a beautiful pendant it would make for the anniversary party. She unzipped her cashmere jacket to lay it against her skin. She visualized the other women's jealous stares. She smiled at the thought of her rare treasure. She didn't care if it was stolen. She found it and her ankle paid dearly for it.

Once again, her thoughts moved to the party. She envisioned standing at the top of the hillside stairs to personally greet each guest. A private firm was hired to valet the cars to the parking lot, but they were given specific instructions to stop the vehicles at the bottom of the garden staircase. It was Julie's favorite approach to the Mansion — one she and Ralph took often.

The stroll was breathtaking as the house slowly came into view with each ascending sandstone stair. The garden walk, which passed clusters of golden day lilies and cherry knockout roses, was punctuated by variegated Weigela and Forsythia. At the top of the winding staircase the full beauty of the Mansion could be embraced. The arched windows were accented with decorative lintels centered by a large keystone. They were painted a rich green that stood out from the white brick.

Julie's plan was to greet each member of her party at the stone overlook patio on the 33rd stair. With Ralph at her side, the evening could not be more perfect, especially with her new spiral gracing her neck. For a moment, the pain in her ankle was forgotten.

She focused on the women's envious eyes, as she placed it against her skin. Immediately it glowed a deep red and seared her chest with a mark. The stench of burning flesh was sickening. She tried to pull it from her but it wouldn't release.

Her heart raced. Her fingers worked furiously to pull the spiral away from her skin. With a quick flick of her finger the piece flew through the air. Julie's eyes tried to follow it, but she lost sight of it. She looked down at the image of the spiral seared into her skin.

Her shoulders drew together from the tightness in her chest. Her hands covered her heart. Numbness crept into her left arm. Her mind was confused. She was young, healthy, and had no history of heart disease in her family.

She forced herself to move through the pain and hobbled back toward her car. With her third step the pain left her body as quickly as it came. She felt her limbs tingle from its release. A crooked smile covered her lips. She turned to look in the direction of the spiral's resting place and saw her own lifeless body lying slumped over a rock

.

# 18

The following morning, The Daily View boasted a reporter's dream headline:

**FAMILIES DEVASTATED IN TRIPLE, UNRELATED DEATHS.**

Sharon sat at the kitchen table and read the eyewitness account of Liza's accident. The look of horror on her face could not be mistaken. The reporter enjoyed sharing every gory detail and relished in the opportunity to smear the community. It was a cruel and senseless act.

Listed in a small section under obituaries were three names:

## LIZA GINGER WILLIAMS
## SPENCER (JACK) HILBERT
## JULIANNE NINA GARRETT

Bill and Jesse had a private, closed ceremony for Liza. Only Sharon and Collin stood by their side. The sorrow in Bill's eyes came mostly from what could have been rather than what was. Jesse stared at the floor. He never let go of Sharon's hand.

Jack's funeral was a bit different. The church was filled with most of the men from town. The drudgery and blasphemy of 'what a good man' was difficult to take after the tenth person uttered those words. The only woman who attended was Jack's aunt Mary. She never shed a tear. She was consumed with thoughts of winning last week's bingo jackpot and relished in the fact of spending it, all of it. She didn't hear a word of the ceremony and walked home unmoved and unaffected.

Ralph grieved through anger. He burned with the desire to kill the responsible party. He was furious that his lifeblood, his flower, his reason for living had been taken from him. When he entered the coroner's office to identify her body, he was shocked at the mark burned into her chest. Convinced it was a gang-related symbol, he charged into the police station.

After only a minute of descriptive details, the chief drove him back to the coroner. Several photos were taken as the investigating officers struggled to scribble pertinent information on yellow notepads. The coroner filled the room with words and phrases only he understood, but when he mentioned heart attack, Ralph was certain his thoughts were accurate. His next stop was The Daily View.

The following morning, a suspenseful story filled the cover page. Not a single detail was eliminated: the position of her body, her Jaguar untouched with the key still in the ignition, her unzipped jacket exposing the branding of the spiral. An eyewitness account from the couple that found her body added to the growing fear. A close up of Julie's burn mark with the plea for any information leading to the identification of the 'Corkscrew Gang' underlined the photo.

Telephone calls flooded the police. They investigated every lead. None, of course, were valid. Ralph insisted on an hourly update from the police with their investigation. The Daily View made no mention of Jack or Liza's death as related.

Sharon shook her head at the headline. She walked to her front and back door and locked them. She checked every window for security. She closed the last one and turned the lock mechanism when Collin stumbled sleepy-eyed into the kitchen. His eyes fell on the photo in the newspaper. His mother recognized his horror.

"Collin. We'll be fine. We have wonderful police. They will catch whoever is responsible."

Collin's head was reeling from the photograph. "Huh?"

"Don't worry. It will be fine."

Without a word, Collin slipped into his tennis shoes. Sharon had her back turned from him filling a glass of orange juice.

"I don't want to you go out...," the screen door slammed shut, "...today." She called to him, but he was running down the street and didn't hear her.

His face was flushed when he tried to open Jesse's door. It also was locked. He pounded on the door.

"Jesse! Get up!" He pounded more. "Jesse!"

Slowly the screen door opened. Collin burst through the door with the newspaper crumpled in his hands. His words came through gritted teeth.

"What did you do?" he screamed.

He threw the newspaper at Jesse. It hit his chest with a thud and landed on the floor open to the front page. The spiral taunted Jesse.

"I *said* what did you do?" His tone was angry and accusatory.

Jesse hung his head.

# 19

Everyone in town knew Rosemarie Phillips. If you didn't attend church with her, you waved to her as she went for her daily walk every day precisely at 7:30 a.m. - sun, rain or snow. She lived her last forty-seven years as a widow. Her husband died of a heart attack when he was thirty-eight years old. She had been blessed to live on this earth eighty years today.

She woke up with a smile, wider than normal. She spent an hour in prayer and devotions and spent the next thirty minutes uttering a prayer for each person who had sent her a birthday card. She picked up each card, held it in her hands and whispered a special thought just for them. Her faith was powerful, but her demeanor humble.

Arthritis twisted her hands, but she never complained. She took whatever ailment came her way and wore it with

138

honor. She often said, "If Jesus could die for me, then I certainly can handle this." They weren't empty words.

She kept a beautiful cottage garden in front of her small house. She worked in the yard as much as weather and her health permitted. She talked to her flowers as if they were dear friends. Many visitors stopped for a quick chat as they rushed past her home. They always left with a gathering of fresh flowers from her garden. She had one child, but he died as an infant. She groomed his gravesite weekly.

Her finances were humble though she said she was blessed. Much of the maintenance completed on her house came from the church members as a small payback for what she had done for them. She touched nearly every member in the congregation by her thoughtfulness and generosity.

She was the first one to greet a new visitor to her church. Her warm smile wrapped in a plump face made one feel at home. When she brought a baked good from her kitchen later that week as a follow up visit, she was always welcomed. She brought many people from 'out in the cold' into the church simply by her acts of kindness. If she noticed a member had been absent for a few weeks, she made it her mission to visit with another homemade goodie. Their returned presence was her payment.

Often, she accompanied the pastor to visit shut-ins and hospitalized members. Eyes would be filled with hope as Rosemarie placed her twisted hands into the oversized bag. She catered her baked goods to their needs. If they were diabetic, she made something sugar free. If one had difficulty swallowing, she would bring pudding or jello. If they were terminal, she brought whatever they wished. Her presence was the best gift of all. She sat with them until she saw their face light up with the presence of the Holy Spirit. She wrapped her arms around them and prayed with them before she walked out of the room. One of her spiritual gifts was the gift of compassion, and she shared it well.

Her walk this birthday morning was particularly Spirit filled. The weather was cool, but crisp. It felt invigorating to walk at a more rapid pace than normal. Her feet felt light on this day as she walked beyond her turn around spot. She walked around the town's shopping district, past the grocery store and barbershop. She greeted each person whom she met with a wide smile and a hearty, "Good morning."

Rosemarie listened to the songs of the birds and tried to match each call to the proper bird. She paused to witness a pair of cardinals as the male courted the female by feeding her. It brought a smile to Rosemarie's face and took her memory back to younger days when her husband would accompany her on these daily walks.

He loved watching the birds as much as she did. They challenged each other to identify their songs. If the truth would be told, Raymond taught her most of the birds' calls. She wiped a tear from her cheek as she thought of him. She missed him as much today as she did the day God called him home.

Her feet continued to carry her as her mind took her to long-lost places. When she finally became aware of her surroundings, she was standing in the middle of the old factory's abandoned parking lot. She chuckled out loud to herself and turned to head back toward her home.

The sunlight reflected off of something that lay deep in the weeds. She shielded her eyes from the glare as she walked closer. It almost seemed to shine brighter as she stood over it. She bent down and cradled a tiny vial in her hands.

"What is this?" she questioned herself.

She stared at this tiny glass container, which seemed to be energized by the rays of the sun. It was about two inches in length and about an inch round. It had tiny filaments of gold thread twisted around the outside to protect the glass from breaking. It swung gently from a tiny ring at the top but curiously had a second ring attached to the underside. When she turned it upside down, the light inside the vial vanished.

Rosemarie drew in her breath in surprise. Slowly, she turned the object upright and out from it came a ray of light that flooded her face. She closed her fist tightly around it and waited for her blinded vision to return to normal. Her heart rate quickened.

For a moment Rosemarie thought she had been blinded. She uttered a quick prayer of release and grew calm when her sight returned. She stood still in the parking lot for a minute longer before venturing another step forward. She slid the strange object into her pocket daring not to take her hand from it or to look at it again.

She couldn't recall the long walk home, but when her feet touched the green wood floor of her front porch, she felt herself take the first breath she could remember. She plopped down in a wicker rocker and untied her walking shoes. The ferns she hung from her macramé hangers swayed gently in the morning breeze though Rosemarie could not feel it on her face. She pulled in a deep breath of the fresh morning air, thrust her hand into her pocket, and withdrew the tiny curiosity.

She squinted expecting to see the bright light again, but the vial was empty, though it felt warm to touch. She held it closer to her face. The glass was shaped like a teardrop and was completely empty. It was feather light and made no sound as she gently shook it. The gold strands, which protected the vial, were finely braided. They looked extremely delicate but they could not be moved. Again, she shook the vial. No signs of any moisture could be seen, nor any opening in the seamless glass container.

Rosemarie stared at this strange object in the palm of her hand. She wondered where it came from, how long it had lain in the parking lot, who its owner was and how she could find out. She was startled by the sound of a man's voice. She closed her hand around her treasure and shoved it back into her pocket.

"Happy birthday, Rosie."

She had been so preoccupied she nearly forgot. "Thank you, Pastor Joe. What brings you here?"

"To give you this." He handed her a new Bible wrapped with a white ribbon.

Rosemarie smiled, "Oh, you shouldn't have. This money could have been spent on someone less fortunate. I already have a Bible."

Their eyes moved to the worn black leather book lying on the table beside her wicker rocking chair. Its edges were frayed from overuse as was the lettering. Many of its pages were pulled from the binding and carefully folded and tucked back into place.

"You mean that?" Pastor Joe laughed.

Rosemarie chuckled, "It has seen better days."

"After you left last Sunday, I found this on the floor." He handed her a few crumpled pages. The top page was half missing. "Your Bible wouldn't be complete without the book of James." He shook his finger at her. "That young preacher had much to teach all of us about living a Christ-filled life."

Rosemarie took the pathetically worn papers from his extended hand and placed them inside her birthday gift.

"I'll put these in here for safe keeping." She picked up the tattered book and ran her hands gently over its binding. "I guess it's time to retire this one if it keeps losing important lessons." They both laughed.

After a short visit, Pastor Joe was on his way. Rosemarie stroked her new leather Bible and rocked herself on the front porch. She couldn't wipe the smile from her face. She opened her new gift and thumbed through the pages. She caught a glimpse of the color yellow. Slowly, she moved back through the pages until it was opened to the sixth chapter of Matthew. Her eyes settled on the twenty-first verse. 'For where your treasure is, there your heart will be also.' She placed her hand on her pocket.

She felt the vial began to warm and within a matter of seconds, it began to burn her leg. She pulled the bright light from her pocket and cast it to the corner of her front porch. Her hand bore a small burn mark mimicking its teardrop shape. Instinctively, she brought her palm to her mouth. She looked into the corner where the vial rested. The light was gone. She was apprehensive as she picked up the piece but as quickly as it had heated, it cooled. She placed it in her pocket again.

Rosemarie sat in her kitchen with a damp towel wrapped around her injured hand. She placed the tiny vial on the table in front of her. The clock on the wall ticked the hours away without any movement from her. She remembered checking the time once at three-fifteen but when she finally rose to dampen the dry cloth wrapped around her hand, it was dark outside. The clock on the wall read 9:56 p.m.

She stumbled from stiffness as she walked to the sink. When she unwrapped the cloth from her hand, the burn mark had vanished. Confused by what she saw, she picked up the vial and walked to her bedroom. She didn't bother to undress but settled herself on her bed. She fell asleep with her hand in her pocket.

She woke startled at two o'clock. Her room was filled with a bright light. Without looking, she knew her treasure had fallen from her pocket. Afraid of the power of this object, she began to pray. She fell asleep with the pillow over her head.

The morning was clear and bright and if she hadn't slept in her clothes she would have forgotten about the vial. She searched her sheets for the small object but it could not be found. She looked under her bed, under the pillows, on both sides of the bed and even under the rug, but the vial was gone. She panicked as she searched. Nearly an hour had passed and she sat exhausted in the pile of tossed bedding. Nervous laughter gurgled from her parched throat. She stood, kicked a pillow, and walked out of the room.

This day passed much like the one before. She sat in silence, thinking about the strange object that consumed her. Today was the first day in a long while that she did not read her Bible or bathe.

She woke again a two a.m. to a bright light. She rose from her bed and followed it down the hall. The unmistakable glow came from the spare bedroom. She entered the room with caution. Her thoughts were filled with anger as she reached for the vial. Just as she was about to touch it the light extinguished. She stumbled forward from surprise and lost her balance. Her head struck the corner of the dresser.

Rosemarie winced from the pain in her head. She covered the large bump with the palm of her hand. She stared at her bruised face in the mirror. The only light in the room was from the vial. She stumbled out of the room and down the hallway to her bedroom. Her head pounded from the pain. She managed to lay herself down on her bed. She remembered the pillow feeling soft. She remembered the sound of silence. She remembered feeling herself float. She remembered seeing a bright light. She remembered reaching for it. Then all went dark.

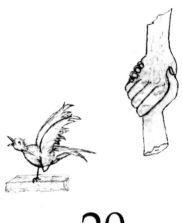

# 20

Jesse hung his head and stared at the floor. The sharp tone in Collin's voice was not one he had heard often. He felt ashamed.

"Answer me, Jesse! What did you do?"

"I...I...I...dunno," Jesse stammered.

Collin moved closer. His hot breath misted Jesse's face. "Damn it, Jesse. Why did you go back? What else did you steal? What were you thinking?" His voice squeaked from strain. He would've felt guilty for swearing, but he was consumed with anger.

Jesse stood in the kitchen dressed in his pajamas with his head down. He shrugged his shoulders to every question. He knew what he did was wrong, but he couldn't explain why he did it. His eyes stared at the shape of the spiral burned into a woman's skin on the front page of the newspaper.

Collin began to shake him for a response. He was screaming at his friend. "She's dead, Jesse! She's dead because of *you*!"

Suddenly, Jesse turned and ran up the stairs to his bedroom. He held his breath as he took the steps in pairs. He fell to the floor, grabbed the tattered pants he had hidden under his bed, and started rummaging through them. His lungs burned as he searched all the pockets looking for the pieces he stole from princess. Collin appeared breathless at the door just as Jesse was hovering over his cupped hands.

Collin was silent as he approached Jesse. He was rocking back and forth cradling his hands. Collin grabbed his wrists and forced his hands open. Lying on his palm were two objects–a gold bird and a pair of hands clasped together carved out of some sort of black stone.

"I knew it!" Collin screamed at his friend. "I told you not to go back. I told you I made a promise...to the princess...you...you...make me sick!"

Collin collapsed on the floor. He sat cross-legged staring at Jesse. Neither spoke.

Finally, Jesse lifted his head and saw anger mixed with bewilderment in Collin's eyes. He stammered as he spoke, "I...I...don't...know why I...did it." Collin didn't respond. Anger and resentment burned deep in Jesse. The tone of his voice changed. He stiffened his back and spat, "Maybe if you hadn't kept that stupid bag of bones so secret, I wouldn't have gone back!"

Collin wanted to strangle his friend. Somehow hearing the princess being referred to a 'bag of bones' infuriated him. He spoke to Jesse through clenched teeth.

"She's not a bag of bones!"

"How do you know she's a she?"

"I just know."

"How?" The questionable tone in Jesse's voice sounded like mockery.

"I just know, Jesse," Collin spewed back.

Jesse stood over Collin, placed his hands on his hips and bobbed his head back and forth as he spoke in a sing-song voice, "Oh Collin is so smart...Collin is the smart one...Collin is the nice one...blah, blah, blah."

Collin lunged at his friend. He tackled him at his knees and pulled Jesse to the floor. The beads flew through the air and danced themselves into the corner. Fists and feet rattled across the floor as they fought.

Jesse was the first to draw blood. He punched Collin's nose and blood rushed from it. Collin wiped the blood with the back of his hand and with as much strength as he could find punched Jesse in the mouth. It was a solid hit. Jesse fell to the floor and held his mouth moaning. Collin stood over him with clenched fists waiting for his friend to lunge again. Jesse never moved.

After a few minutes, Jesse stood. Blood and saliva oozed from the corners of his mouth. His lip was cut and began to swell. His eyes held a strange look. He spit a tooth into the palm of his hand.

Jesse was dumbfounded by Collin's response. Of all the times he tried to provoke him to a reaction, Collin always resisted. The left corner of Jesse's mouth curled in a triumphant smile.

Collin gasped at Jesse's missing front tooth. He jumped to his feet and showered him with apologies. The smile left Jesse's face.

Jesse twisted his lips to chastise his friend but as he opened his mouth to speak, the sound of a bird singing filled the room. They both looked in the direction of the

148

sound. It came from the corner of the room. Lying on its side next to the pair of hands was the golden bird.

Their eyes were wide, but they made no sound. Both boys held their breath as they walked closer to the objects. Together they knelt on the floor.

Collin reached for the bead. It was about an inch long and an inch and one half high. It was flat on the bottom and had two holes in it for a string to be pushed through it. The sunlight in the room bounced from its shiny surface. It was silent.

Again, the sound of the song continued. Both boys laughed when they saw the robin outside of the window perched on a tree branch. Their sigh of relief came simultaneously.

Collin whispered, "Are you okay?"

"Yep."

"I'm sorry…I…."

Jesse cut him off. "It's just a tooth. No big deal."

"Your dad's gonna be mad.'

Jesse sat in silence thinking of the conversation that would have to take place. He would have to explain that they were fighting because Jesse stole the pieces of the necklace from a bony princess in a hole in the ground that Collin fell through and that's how he hurt his finger and how he ran and how scared he was and how he lied and how a woman died…. His mind raced through all of the 'ands'.

"I'll tell him I fell off my bike. He won't be mad at that."

"But…."

Jesse's voice was desperate, "It's the only way, Collin. It's the only way."

Collin stared at his friend. It was hard to imagine a moment ago he wanted to strangle him and now he felt sorry for him. He forced a smile.

"Whatever you say." They sat in silence.

Collin picked up the other piece from the princess. It was two hands clasped together. He ran his fingers over the smooth black stone. He moved the piece around in his hand until the holes were on the top and the bottom. One hand appeared as if it was coming down to grasp the other as it was reaching up. The hand reaching down had a firmer grip on the other. His face was filled with questions as he studied the carving closely.

Jesse's voice broke his thoughts, "I think it's onyx."

Collin shook his head. "I think you're right." He squinted again and looked at Jesse. "This was resting on one of her rib bones."

Jesse's eyes flew open, "You saw it and left it there?"

"I didn't think it was mine to take."

Jesse hung his head. He knew Collin was right. He usually was.

"How many did you take?"

"All of them."

"All of them?"

"Yep."

"How many, Jesse."

"Seven."

"Including the spiral?"

The magnitude of what Jesse had done struck him as a piercing sword. He covered his heart from certain death. A woman died because of him. He was unaware of how he had also caused Liza and Jack's death, and how his selfishness and disregard for others had left Rosemarie in peril.

150

The words stuck thick in his mouth as he shook his head to signal yes, "Including the spiral."

# 21

When Rosemarie opened her eyes she expected to be standing before Jesus, but instead the familiarity of her own home greeted her. Her eyes fell on the print of her Savior that hung on the opposite wall. Tucked in its oak frame was a blade from a palm branch formed into a cross from last Easter. The color had faded from green to beige, but the meaning remained the same. She smiled.

The morning sun shone into her east bedroom window. She moaned just slightly as she climbed out of her bed. She walked over to the mirror and sighed at the sight of her bruised face. She still wore the same outfit from two days prior. She stripped off her clothes and slipped into a warm bath.

She was amazed at how she had lost hours and days. She tried to force the thought of the glass vial from her mind. It obviously held strong powers, ones she did not consider pleasant, but she thought about it constantly. She thought about its value and how the money could offer her late years a bit more comfort. She felt the pang of guilt for lusting after more than she had.

After her bath she dressed, but before she walked out of her bedroom, she slipped the vial once again into her pocket. She had to have it with her. She settled herself on her front porch and picked up her new Bible. Her thoughts wandered to the vial many times as she tried to read. She was startled by the sound of the church bell ringing.

She jumped off of her chair and ran into the house. She fumbled for her dress shoes, but decided her walking shoes would be better. In her best recollection today was Saturday, but with the chimes ringing its Sunday song, she realized she had missed a day. How that happened perplexed her, and by the time she reached the front door of the church, she had worked herself into a sheer panic. She slipped into one of the back pews just as they began to sing the first hymn.

She tried to calm herself by concentrating on the words of the familiar song. "Then sings my soul, my Savior God to Thee, How great Thou art, how great Thou art..." she heard herself singing. After the end of the third verse she felt the rush of nerves, which colored her neck red, begin to fade to pink. She lifted her voice in praise and sang the last stanza with zeal. For a moment she forgot about the vial.

Pastor Joe took his position behind the pulpit. He began his sermon with a story. He told of a man and his addiction to gambling. His words spun a sordid tale of self-destruction as this man continued to feed his addiction. In

153

the end, of course, the man lost his life's savings, his house, and worst of all, his family. He spent his final days homeless and in despair.

Rosemarie found herself correlating the story to the vial. She held her hand in her pocket tightly over the smooth shape. She pushed her fingernails into her skin until it bled. She never relaxed her grip.

Pastor Joe finished his sermon by quoting the very verse he had highlighted in her new Bible. She felt the movement of hot nerves as they traveled down her body and back up the opposite side. She felt he was speaking directly to her. He was showing her the evils of holding onto treasures here on earth instead of laying them up in heaven as instructed. Without thinking she pulled the vial from her pocket and tossed it into the offering plate. Her body relaxed from its release.

Sharon and Collin also had arrived late. They slipped into the back pew just as the last stanza of 'How great Thou art' was sung. Collin plopped himself down on the pew with a thud. Sharon gave him a stern stare. He mouthed the word sorry.

Collin had a hard time focusing on the sermon. He was still angry with Jesse and felt guilty about the punch although he continued to justify it in his mind. Jesse and Collin traced each of Jesse's steps from the mound to home and no treasures could be found. Collin found himself badgering his friend. Jesse never looked up from the ground.

Collin stared at the back of the church pew. He felt his mother's elbow nudge his side. She held out the offering plate for him to pass. He took the plate and as he started to pass it, he saw the vial. His eyes opened with surprise. Again his mother nudged him and whispered for him to pass it. He quickly glanced around. He was the last one. The usher began to walk toward him. Collin's heart raced and his mouth went dry. He had to get this vial, but he didn't want to reach in the offering plate and take it.

As the usher neared Collin, he became desperate. He quickly stood and in an act that looked like an accident, he tripped and spilled the contents of the brass plate. The look of disgust on the head usher's face was unmistakable. Collin hurried to gather all of the envelopes and loose change that were scattered on the red carpet. With the ushers help, everything made it back into the plate except the vial. Collin had slipped it into his pocket.

When church was over, Rosemarie had a crowd of people surrounding her. The level of questions was overwhelming. She felt relieved to have rid herself of the oppressive object of desire, but she dared to mention it to a church member.

She shook Pastor Joe's hand in the vestibule, "Thank you for a wonderful message, pastor." Her smile was genuine but contorted with her swollen, bruised face.

"What in the world happened to you, Rosie?"

She brought her hands to her face remembering her ordeal, "Oh, I fell in the middle of the night and hit my head on my dresser."

"Should we call the doctor?" His face was filled with concern.

Rosemarie fanned her hand in the air, "No, I'll be fine. I just look a mess."

"Are you certain?"

"Most certain," she replied with another puffed smile.

"Wait for me and I'll walk you home."

"That won't be necessary. I look worse than I feel. Truth be told, pastor, I couldn't feel better." She smiled and turned from him.

She smiled the entire walk home. She was thankful for the strength to be rid of the vial though she worried about the person who would find it in the offering plate. She paused for a short moment and uttered a prayer for them and continued to walk home.

Collin couldn't wait to burst through Jesse's door. He had to show him what he found. He wondered who had put it in the plate. He tried to remember who sat in front of them at church, but the only one he could think of was Rosemarie Phillips and he was certain it wasn't her. He pounded on Jesse's back door.

Jesse rubbed the sleep from his eyes as he yawned at the back door. Collin spoke not a word but held out his hand, palm up and fist closed. Again, Jesse yawned. When he opened his eyes, he was face to face with the mysterious vial.

"Whaaat?" His eyes flew open. "Where did you find that?"

Suddenly overcome with secrecy Collin snapped, "What does it matter? I found it." His voice was filled disgust.

"Where did you find it?" Jesse spoke through tight teeth.

"Jesse, get dressed. We've got to find the rest of them."

"But we have looked everywhere!"

"Not good enough." Collin held out the vial again. Quickly, he closed his fist over it and shoved it deep into his pocket. He padded the outside to feel if it was secure. "C'mon we gotta keep looking."

Jesse pulled on a pair of denim shorts and a t-shirt. He hollered to his dad who was working on the car in the garage. "Hey dad? Collin and I are going. Catch up with ya later." His feet never stopped moving. He heard his father mumble something from under the car, but he didn't stop to listen.

Bill Williams slid from under the car on his homemade dolly. He continued to talk to Jesse as if he was standing there. "It's just not safe. You boys aren't careful enough...I don't want you leaving the house. What about the Corkscrew Gang? Jesse?" He raised his voice, "Jesse!" The boys were out of sight.

Their lungs burned long before they reached 'Indian Hill'. They stood at the edge of the woods staring at the burial mound. They were silent. Collin thought he heard singing. Jesse thought he heard that same cruel laughter; the one he heard when he stole the pieces from the princess.

Jesse was breathless. He whispered, "Did you hear that?"

Collin didn't answer. He stared at the mound. He couldn't shake the feeling that she was calling to him. He felt the tiny hairs rise on the back of his neck.

Jesse spoke a bit louder, "Collin, did you hear that?"

Irritated from being disturbed he snapped, "What?"

"That...that...laughing."

Collin looked at him puzzled. The singing had stopped. He cupped his hands behind his ears to hear more clearly. All he heard was his own rapid heartbeat. The sound was so loud it drowned out all else.

He lowered his hands to his side in defeat. "I don't hear nothin'."

They turned to walk down the trail. Collin urged Jesse to try to remember everything. His multiple questions made Jesse feel increasingly agitated.

He snapped at Collin. "Shut up and just let me think."

"Chill out. I'm just trying to help the princess."

With the mention of that word, Jesse felt as if he was being watched. He turned around several times to check but no one was there. He felt a hand lie on his shoulder and pull at his shirt.

"What?" he snapped at Collin again assuming it was he.

"What? I didn't say a thing."

For a moment Jesse felt the oppression leave him. "Let's go farther down here." He pointed to a direction that he had not run that day.

As soon as the words left his mouth, a rush of cold wind blew through them. Without a word Jesse ran. With every footstep he relived that day. He remembered feeling heavy as he tried to climb up the rope, the relief of the feel of grass on his face as he reached the top. He remembered the feeling of being chased. He ran faster down the trail. Collin yelled to his friend to slow down, but Jesse ran faster. He had no idea what his friend was going through but watching him from a distance was a strange experience.

He watched Jesse as he seemed to struggle with an unseen foe. He watched him stumble and push at the air. He nearly tripped but at the last second, regained his balance and continued to run. Collin followed him the long way around. He again watched him trip and nearly fall in the middle of the abandoned parking lot. When Collin reached the same spot, he noticed a hunk of concrete that must have caused him to trip.

They ran through the downtown area. Collin's legs were weak from overuse, but he pushed himself to follow his friend. Jesse's arms flung wildly as he passed the barbershop. He struggled to stay on his feet and managed to stay upright. He ran past the ice cream shop, the bank, and the grocery store. His final struggle came near the rose fence at Mrs. Henderson's place. Collin thought it was odd that he ran home the long way.

Jesse struggled to jump the fence. He batted at the air and shook his leg free as he tried to pull his exhausted body over the fence. The thorns of the rose bush ripped through his flesh and tore his clothes, but with one final effort he toppled head first over the other side. His feet never stopped moving until he was inside Collin's barn.

When Collin finally entered the barn, Jesse was nowhere to be found. He yelled several times, but Jesse did not answer. Playing on his own experiences he decided Jesse must have been hiding in the haymow. He climbed the ladder and saw Jesse's t-shirt under a layer of straw. He plopped his tired body on the soft hay and tried to slow his breathing.

"What spooked you?" he asked after a long while.

Jesse did not answer. He was struggling to hold back the tears. That was the second time in his life he had felt that level of fear.

"Are you okay?" Jesse didn't answer. "Jesse, are you okay?" he asked with more assertion in his voice. Still there was no response.

Collin pushed the layer of straw off of Jesse. He was shocked when he found his friend crying. He didn't mean to appear insensitive, but he began to laugh.

"What's the matter Mr. Tough Guy? Did the wind at 'Dead Man's Lookout' scare you?" Collin taunted.

Jesse glared at him with hate-filled eyes. "Cut it out!" he shouted. "You have no idea."

"No idea about what?"

Jesse was silent. Collin continued to repeat the question until Jesse hollered, "Shut up! She was chasing me!"

Collin spoke not another word. He knew what his friend meant. He understood that feeling. He was patient until Jesse felt comfortable to continue.

"I...don't understand it...It was the weirdest feeling...I heard her laughing at me. Then, she pulled on my shirt. I got scared and ran. But, it was like I had done it before except this time I could see myself doin' it. Like I was watching a movie, but I was in it at the same time." His voice was strained. He wiped the wetness from his face. He had bits of hay stuck all over his face and his hair. He looked comical, but this was not the time for laughter. Collin was silent as he continued.

"I saw the woman that died, Collin! I almost knocked her down as I ran past her!" Fear gripped him as his eyes filled with tears. They raced down his cheeks as he continued. "I didn't remember until today." He began to sob. Collin sat motionless. He had never seen Jesse cry. He didn't know how to react.

Within a few minutes, Jesse wiped the tears from his face. He felt the pieces of hay stuck to him and tried to pick them off. He wiped his runny nose on his arm and sighed.

"It's my fault that she's dead. It's all my fault!" They sat in silence.

# 22

Mrs. Henderson placed her hands on her hips with disgust. Her roses looked terrible and her lawn hadn't been cut for two weeks. The fertilizer her lawn care company had sprinkled was too heavy and patches of her yard were brown and burned. She wished she hadn't switched landscapers.

"If it sounds too good to be true, it is," she spoke in repulsion to herself. She picked up her telephone and dialed Greg Chardt's Green Team.

The sound of the answering machine clicking on made her hang up with a scowl. She hadn't walked two steps when the phone rang.

"Hello?"

"Mrs. Henderson?"

"Yes."

"It's Greg Chardt. I see you called."

Caller ID she thought, "Yes, I did. My yard looks terrible. The fertilizer burned it and I have brown patches everywhere. And the places that are growing are almost to my knees," she exaggerated. "Not to mention my roses haven't been touched this season."

161

"I..." he tried to respond to her accusations, but she wouldn't let him speak.

"The promises you made are not being done. I have never been so disappointed or so embarrassed in my life!" She finished her words with a snap.

Now was his chance. "I was planning to come cut your yard and prune your roses this morning. Would that be convenient?"

She stammered just a bit. She wasn't used to being so assertive, but he had pushed her too far. "That...would...be fine." She quickly gathered her wits, "We need to discuss your plans for the brown spots." She hung up.

Greg smiled at the receiver. Old ladies cracked him up. He knew he could re-charm her. After all, it was his gift.

Greg was six-foot-two, weighed 195 pounds, had long wavy brown hair, blue eyes, his muscles had muscles, and he sported the most charming smile a woman could find. He was the most popular guy back in high school. He was the captain of the basketball team and the most aggressive point guard the area had seen in twenty years. He alone was the reason the team won many games.

After high school he attended Bowling Green State University for two years. His father had a massive heart attack at forty-three and passed away the summer before his junior year. He stayed home to help his mother manage their family's landscaping business. He was one of two boys, but his younger brother had special needs, so his help was limited. The business was lucrative, so it made sense to quit college and bring in the cash.

Greg was very aggressive. The first year of running the family business, their revenue doubled. The second year it doubled again. After ten years they had four locations and thirty-two full-time employees. Greg had free rein to do as he pleased. His mother remarried the prior year and moved to Marco Island, Florida. He found himself spending more time on the golf course than behind the desk; second only to the time he spent 'working out his deals' in his special way.

He was a natural charmer. He could sell any service to anyone and upgrades were never a problem. The men saw him as an aggressive businessman. Their wives saw him as an opportunity.

Greg flirted with all the ladies. He could talk his way out of any negative situation and turn it around to his good. Their age didn't matter; the result was always the same. His brother referred to him as a 'shit man' meaning he could fall into it and come out smelling like a flower. Greg didn't mind Pete's pet name for him because his speech was so deplorable no one could understand him except Greg and Pete's private nurse; and Greg already had snared her into his trap.

Along with his ability to charm came the skill of lying. He never worried about keeping his lies straight because he was so talented in twisting the truth or lies he could make one believe anything that spilled from his lips. The only woman who knew his game was his ex-wife, Dawn.

She tried to ruin him after the divorce, but no one believed her. Greg was an elder in the church, was always the first one to volunteer to help, had a wonderful positive attitude, and talked a good game. In the end Dawn just looked like the bitter ex-wife with an agenda. After eight months she moved to Idaho.

Somehow over the past year, he grew bored with his life. He decided to leave many of the basic operational decisions to his management staff. He spent more and more time on the golf course. He spent a lot of money gambling and threw his money around as if it were bottomless. He drove a loaded Hummer and bought a condo in Beaufort, South Carolina. He soon had a harem of Southern ladies flocking around him. He made most of his business deals between the tees or waves. He liked this life better.

He went into the office on Tuesday and Wednesday mornings only, if he was in town. He had excuses for the other days. He pretended to be at nursery auctions every Friday but only went once a month. He had a hot babe on the back of his Harley every Saturday and sat in the church pew every Sunday. Appearances were everything.

He watched the books closely and skimmed as much as he could. He made more cash deals than anyone around and they always lined his pocket. If the business had a bad month, his 'tighten our belts' speech inspired the entire staff, all but the accountant, who was also on the take.

Mrs. Henderson was one of those 'cash' deals. It was a small job, but he smelled an opportunity for improvement of his pocket lining one evening at a restaurant. Two men were having dinner and too many drinks laughing about the dollar amount they had raised their clients. They were having a contest and Mrs. Henderson was the one who lost. She was the highest raise without complaint.

The next day Greg showed up at her doorstep unannounced. When she hesitated to switch companies, he promised her the moon at a reduced rate. She signed the three-year contract on the spot.

On this particular Wednesday, for whatever odd reason, Greg decided to do Mrs. Henderson's work himself. He hooked up a trailer to his Hummer, loaded the equipment and drove off.

It was a typical late summer day in Ohio. The early morning haze hung like a thick blanket a few feet off of the ground. It swirled around the treetops covering their leaves from sight. The drive to Mrs. Henderson's through this mystified world seemed like a dream except for the sweat that beaded on Greg's face.

By the time he pulled into her gravel drive it was 7:05 a.m. The humidity from the day before lingered like an unwanted guest. He was dressed in long pants, a long-sleeve shirt, and gauntlet gloves to his elbows. He tackled the rose trimming first. His plan was to be finished pruning by 8:00 a.m. By order of the city's noise ordinance, no equipment could be operated until after that time.

He had the first section of the fence finished before Mrs. Henderson came outside. He could tell by her gait that she was not happy. He smiled to himself as she approached.

"Good morning, Esther. You're up early."

She was about to chide him a bit more when he pulled a cup of coffee from his trug. "Cream, no sugar, right?" He held out the coffee for her.

Taken by surprise she stammered, "Why...thank you...Greg. How did you know?"

He smiled at his success. This is what he did well. He made it a point to remember minute details about each of his customers. One never knows when they could come in handy.

"A little birdie told me," he smiled. He continued to keep control, "It's going to be another sweltering day again today." He took of his hat and wiped the sweat from his brow. "I hope you aren't planning any outside activities. I wouldn't want you to ruin your hair. It looks beautiful. Did you just have it done?"

In fact she had. All of the older ladies in town went to 'A Cut Above'. Grace Deemas was the best hairdresser in town. Most of her clients were the older women. They kept their weekly standing appointments. Her schedule was well

165

organized and set in stone. The only time a client changed was if she died.

Grace's only day off was Sunday. Her schedule was packed Monday through Saturday, eight in the morning until four in the afternoon. She ate her lunch between perms and sets. Tuesday, 11:30 a.m. was Esther Henderson's concrete time.

The gossip at the beauty parlor did not differ much from the barbershop save the people speaking. The women were much more discreet as they tore their topics apart. It usually began with 'I wasn't to say anything, but...' or 'Bless her heart'. The really juicy ones mostly began with 'Keep this in your prayers'. It always ended with an eruption of surprise and a headshake by all in attendance. Yesterday, the topic of conversation was the now notorious 'Corkscrew Gang'.

Mrs. Henderson sipped on her cup of coffee as she watched Greg trim. Her rambling rose was precious to her. It was a cutting from her wedding bouquet. Her mother had been careful to snip each stem with care. 'Cut five, bury three' she sang to herself as she clipped the morning of Esther's wedding. After the celebration, she helped Esther plant the stems and cover them with cloches. The following spring they found three had lived through the winter and within a few years, those three cuttings grew to cover the arbor and surrounding fence. It was one of Esther's greatest achievements.

She knelt to gather a few appropriate stems. Lost to the task at hand she spoke out loud, "These will be perfect for Sarah. She said she wanted at least ten." She sifted through the cuttings for enough pieces with at least five leaf nodules showing after the bud. She glanced at Greg.

"Oh, not too much now," she chastened. "We mustn't cut off all the blooms." Greg smiled under the shadow of his brim.

Holding the bouquet of greenery in her hands, she said, "I'll be back out in a minute. I must place these in water."

"I'll be here," Greg responded.

"You're doing an excellent job. And I do appreciate it." She walked across the back yard and disappeared inside the north porch. Greg wiped the smile and sweat from his face.

He was about to take another cut when he saw something glimmer deep from within the thicket. He pushed his gauntlet-covered hand through the taunting thorns and pulled out a piece of copper. He rolled it around in his palm. It was nearly an inch in size, flat on the back, and had multiple spikes protruding from the sphere. The spikes varied in length and thickness. It resembled a sun, he thought. There was no doubt the piece was handmade and it was old.

He wondered about its value. He allowed his mind to wonder about hundreds, maybe thousands of dollars. He was lost in thoughts of grandeur when he heard Esther Henderson's soft swish in the dewy grass. He quickly stuffed the sphere into his pocket. He didn't care if it were hers. He found it.

"What's wrong, Greg?" she questioned his idleness.

"Huh?" He hesitated for a moment and quickly recovered. "I found some cane borers," he lied. "I think I removed the diseased area, but," he envisioned his pockets bulging, "I'll have to come back weekly for the next several weeks to be certain." He tried to conceal his smugness with an aura of concern.

Esther gasped, "Greg, I can't lose these roses. They are too precious to me."

Greg gently patted her shoulder, "You're in great hands, Esther. I'll be sure to rid you of the borer." His eyes and words were reassuring. She smiled at his concern.

He turned from her to finish trimming the roses. He worked at a feverish pace creating more of a sweat from the effort than the oppressive air. Esther watched with grave concern as the snips of buds and stem were tossed to the ground. He finished in record time.

He pulled the sweat-soaked shirt from his body. Esther blushed with thoughts of his damp naked chest. The years of the well-used gym membership showed by his sculpted six pack. He tossed the wet shirt into his Hummer and slipped on a muscle shirt.

Greg loved his tractor time. It gave him the opportunity of uninterrupted thoughts as well as cell phone calls. This morning, instead of the usual process, he was consumed by thoughts of the patina sun. He wondered whom he would call for an appraisal. None of the local antique dealers would do. It could be traced back to Esther and he couldn't have that scandal in this small town. He had decided a trip to New York would be the perfect idea. He patted his pocket again.

Immediately, the piece felt hot. It burned through his pocket lining and seared itself to his leg. Without a thought he jumped from the tractor and unzipped his pants. He tried to pull the piece from his skin, but it would not yield. He screamed from the pain. He couldn't be heard. He flicked the spikes with his fingers trying to free it from attachment. The smell of burning flesh was nauseating.

He covered it with a patch of fresh grass and tried to pry it from his leg. He splashed water on it from his water bottle. He flicked it repeatedly with his fingers. Tears and panic flooded his face. No matter what he tried, he couldn't get it off.

He couldn't breathe. He felt tightness in chest. He grabbed his heart and leg. His scream, though deafening to his ears, was muffled by the sound of his running motor. His leg burned with the branding fire.

With one last effort, he flicked the sphere from his skin. It flew towards the rose arbor. Greg's life flashed before him as it moved through the sky.

He watched in slow motion as he witnessed his life's deeds. He saw each time he punched his brother. He saw the first time he stole money from his father's wallet. He witnessed each lie he told and how it hurt the people involved. He saw the multiple times his mother cried and he was too busy to comfort her. He heard his thoughts of deception to his clients. He felt the back of his hand burn from hitting his ex-wife. He saw the pain in her eyes. He witnessed the many hateful words he screamed at her.

The vision began to move faster and the pain in his chest began to lessen. He saw his accountant plot against him. He watched as he fixed the books and padded his pocket. He watched his most valuable employees steal money from the 'cash customers' as well as supplies from the office. He watched as they filled their automobiles with gas from the company's commercial tank. He watched the local oil company prepare two receipts. He wondered how he could have done things differently and led a better life.

He felt his legs buckle. The pain in his chest stopped. The numbness in his arm resonated to prickling needles. His vision narrowed and instead of being faced with the bright light he expected, he was surrounded by total darkness. No light could be seen. His ears were flooded with screaming. His body was being pulled and pinched by things unseen. Laughter, cruel, evil laughter drowned out all other sound. His empty body hit the ground with a thud.

Esther hummed to herself as she folded her laundry. The drumming of her dryer bounced contentment in her ears as it covered all outside noise. She felt comfortable with the care of her roses in Greg's hands. He would take care of those cane borers, she reassured herself.

The steam from her iron fogged her bifocals. She wiped the mist on her apron. She admired her white blouse perfectly pressed on its hanger. The buzz from her dryer alerted her that the load was finished. The alarm stopped when she opened the door. The smell of fresh clothes brought a wide smile to her face. From outside she heard the sound of the lawn tractor's consistent hum.

# 23

The town was churning from the headlines the following morning:

**MAN FOUND DEAD, BRANDED BY GANG.**

Tim Lorie, the aspiring reporter from The Daily View, struggled to find an appropriate headline. He was so proud of his original name inspired by the burn mark on Julie Garrett's body, but with this new branding mark he was reluctant to use it. He had spent the past week flooding the paper with hysteria surrounding the 'Corkscrew Gang', yet he felt his fear grip slipping from his readers until today.

He was the first reporter on the scene. He placed numbered tent cards all around the scene and snapped five rolls of film. He wanted to make a name for himself in this small town to be recognized by 'the big guys' so he could further his career in reporting. He was single, nice looking with dark hair and brown eyes, quick-witted, and filled with ambition.

He spoke on camera to all of the local stations. Everyone was eager to interview him. He reported any lead he could uncover himself or anything his 'sources' leaked to him. The police had been tight lipped about the investigation because of Ralph's involvement, but information always found its way to Tim. He never hesitated to put it in print.

He was extremely careful with his wording to not reveal his manner of gathering the information. He never mentioned a name even if he had permission. He felt it added to the mystery he worked hard to create. His language was direct, intelligent, and polished. He never dropped a sentence, misspelled a word, or used wrong tenses in his pieces. The truth was he belonged with the big guys. He was that good.

In high school and through college, he annoyed most of the people he came in contact with. He was always the kid with questions. He challenged everyone's language and beliefs, and it was difficult to carry on a conversation with him because he mostly put the other person on the defense. Instead of finishing a story, they would end up in an argument over an unrelated subject. Tim smiled if his opponent raised the tone of his voice.

In his professional career he was quite admired. His attention to detail never went unnoticed. His bosses loved him. And he always got the big stories. This one was the opportunity of a lifetime.

He stayed at the scene most of the day. He typed enthusiastically on his laptop. When another vehicle arrived, his face was the first they saw. His spilled all of the details permitted and a few he shouldn't, the biggest one being the photo of the burn mark. The second was the fact Greg's pants were off his body.

Esther Henderson stayed inside her house. Tim was the only interview she permitted. Tim's grandmother had been a good friend of Esther. She told him in great detail when she found Greg's body, the position he lay, the description of the burn mark, how the lawn mower was still running, where his pants had been thrown, what he was doing there in the first place, how remorseful she felt for chastising him, how kind he had been to bring her a cup of coffee just the way she enjoyed it, how he trimmed her roses and found the cane borers....

She talked and wept for thirty minutes. Tim recorded every detail in writing and with his mini recorder. She finished with a sigh, "Who will rid me of these cane borers now?" Tim decided to use that very statement to begin his broadcast.

"Did you see anyone else in your back yard?" he asked with anticipation.

"That's the strangest thing. I didn't see a thing." She shook her head. Her eyes flooded with tears once again. "What am I going to do, Tim? That could have been me."

Another good quote Tim noted to himself. "Just be sure to lock yourself in tight. Don't open the door for anyone."

She looked at Tim through watery eyes, "Would you double check my windows and doors for me?"

He hugged her tightly and said, "Of course, I will."

After he had checked all of the home's openings, he timidly asked, "May I broadcast from the north porch? The big boys will be coming in soon."

She hesitated for only a moment. She knew how important this was to him. Her house had been plastered all over the news, and she had shooed people off of her porch all day. Her fear melted for a moment as she thought of Tim growing up and how he pretended to have a microphone with him constantly.

She smiled, "If this will help you move one step closer toward your dream, the answer is yes."

Tim hugged her for the second time. He smiled as he looked out of her window. They were coming.

When the cameras from Cleveland and Pittsburgh arrived, he was the face on the television. He finished his live report without a mistake much to the dismay of the police and jealousy of the other reporters. He was focused and extremely proud of himself. New York would arrive in a few more hours. He was almost giddy.

A large crowd gathered behind the yellow crime scene tape. Tim scanned the crowd for possible gang suspects. He knew often times they gathered to watch their handiwork unfold. His eyes skimmed over Collin and Jesse. They were in the front row.

Collin's eyes filled with fear as he stared at the picture of Greg's leg. Tim held it steady for the cameraman to capture a close-up. Jesse's mouth hung open like a panting dog. They both felt the fear in their throats.

Collin tugged on Jesse's shirt. Without a word the two of them slipped from the crowd and ran home. Sharon wasn't there. She was cleaning Bill's house. Collin prayed she didn't have the television on so they could be left alone for a while. Once inside, Collin locked the back door.

"Jesse!" he spoke with a strained voice, "What are we gonna do?" Jesse stared at the floor. Collin paced the kitchen. He had his hands on his head. His thoughts raced. His head throbbed. He knew he had to do something. The princess was angry and he could feel it.

He turned to Jesse, "Okay, let's try to think. We know the spiral is on the trail." He held up his pointer finger. "We know the sun is in Mrs. Henderson's yard unless someone found it." The lump in his throat chocked him at the thought. He held up two fingers. He clasped three fingers together with his other hand, "We know you have the bird and the hands." He slipped the fourth finger to join the others. "I have the glass thing." He held up all five fingers. He turned to Jesse, "And how many did you say you stole?"

The accusatory tone in Collin's voice broke Jesse. He never moved his down- turned head. Tears fell to the floor. Collin did not feel sorry for him. He told him not to go see the Princess. He had warned him. It wasn't his fault Jesse didn't listen. Anger burned inside him.

"Jesse!" He yelled, "You gotta think! Get a grip. We have to put this necklace together and give it back to the Princess. We have to find the pieces. She wants them and she's mad!" He drew in a deep breath trying to calm his nerves. He walked over to Jesse and spoke in a softer voice. He held his hand on his friend's shoulder. "How many Jesse? Please. How many pieces?"

After a long silence, "Seven," was the only word Jesse spoke.

# 24

Jesse couldn't sleep. His sweat soaked the sheets. Why did he lie to Collin? He slid from his bed and quietly walked to his sock drawer. He unrolled his favorite pair of super hero socks. Lying in the palm of his hand was the eighth piece of the necklace.

It was an arrow made from some kind of pink stone, possibly quartz. It was larger than most of the beads except for the spiral. It was nearly two inches long and flawlessly smooth except the point. It had two holes drilled into it, one at the top and the other at the bottom, although which way was the top was hard to tell.

Jesse remembered the carved arrows in the tomb. They were near the top of the ceiling and pointed toward the opening. He turned the arrow to point upward. It cast a soft glow in the darkened room. Like the vial, it seemed to gather light, but it did not disburse it on command. Jesse closed his hand tightly around his tiny treasure and crawled back into bed. He smiled at his find.

His thoughts drifted to his mother. He squeezed his eyes trying to remember her before the drugs. He couldn't. His father had done the best he knew how, but Jesse was starving for guidance. He needed the love of a mother and leadership from his father. The closest thing he found was Sharon, and he was jealous of Collin for having her all to himself.

His head hit the pillow but his eyes stared at the ceiling. He tried to remember the last time he was happy. He thought about his younger years. All he could recall were angry words and arguing. He had no memory of his grandparents or any other family. Any happy times he remembered included Collin or Sharon. Even during his recent accident, it was the smell of the chocolate chip cookies that resonated. His chest ached from anger toward everything and everybody. He squeezed the arrow tightly.

He finally drifted into a restless sleep around two o'clock. His eyes fluttered with rapid eye movement. His breathing became labored. He felt as if he were being choked. He sat up in his bed with his eyes opened wide.

Sitting on the edge of his bed was an image of a young girl. She had a frown on her face and her arms were folded in front of her. By the way she was dressed there was no doubt Collin was right. She was a princess.

Her clothes were adorned with tiny shiny beads made of silver and gold. She had a bracelet around the top of her arm. Jesse recognized it from the tomb. She had many scarves wrapped around her head. The tails swirled beyond her dark hair. Pain filled the dark circles under her eyes.

She was about the same size as Jesse. Her stare was empty and accusatory. Frightened, Jesse tried to speak. No sound came. She held out her empty palm to him waiting.

177

In defiance Jesse shook his head no. Her eyes flashed with anger. She rushed her body toward his.

Her tiny fingers gathered around his throat. Jesse couldn't pry her hands from his neck. He felt her grip tighten; yet he couldn't feel the weight of her body. He tried to push her from him, but his hands moved through her. The vision was solid but he couldn't touch her.

He began to panic. He knew she wanted the arrow. Thoughts of surrender never entered his mind. He found it. He wanted to keep it. Her grip closed tighter.

Jesse's arms began to flail. He felt weak from the lack of oxygen. The room grew darker and her body seemed to grow more powerful. Jesse was no match for this fight.

His feet kicked at the air and his bed. In a thud his stuffed animals tumbled to the floor. He felt his energy slide. His arms hung limp at his sides. He lost the battle. She pried his hand open and snatched the arrow.

Bill Williams burst through the door. He awoke out of a dead sleep when he heard the muffled crash. His first thought had been that Jesse fell out of bed.

He found Jesse wheezing for air. He picked up his limp body and carried him down the stairs. He shook Jesse gently and assured him everything would be all right. As he ran out of the back door, Jesse began to cough uncontrollably.

He jerked his truck door open and laid Jesse on the seat. The pickup roared without its muffler. Bill spun gravel from his drive as he hurried toward the hospital. His white knuckles clung to the steering wheel. Jesse held his hands on his neck, clawing for air. His eyes were wide with panic.

As they made the second turn, Jesse's body flew against the door. Out of his mouth flew the pink arrow. His airways were opened.

He pounded on his father's arm. Through a weak voice, "I can breathe."

Bill slammed on the brakes. Tears flooded his eyes. He grabbed Jesse and hugged him. "Oh my God, Jesse, I thought I was going to lose you. You really scared me!" He stared at his son, "What happened?"

"I don't know. I felt like something was choking me." He remembered the princess. A flash of hot nerves ran through his body.

"I...I...guess I was having a nightmare."

Bill pulled his son close beside him and placed his arm around his shoulder. "Are you sure you are okay?"

"I think so," he answered timidly.

"We're just a few minutes from the hospital. We should have you checked out."

Jesse sat up in the seat. He fidgeted as he pondered the question. He kicked his father's boot over on the floor in front of him. Lying on the floor was the arrow. He brought his hands to his throat and covered his mouth. Nerves choked his voice.

Through the tears he whispered, "Let's go home."

"Are you sure?"

He shook his head 'yes.' He couldn't speak. He had a brush with death and lived to tell about it. He stared at the arrow on the floor. Collin was right. The princess wanted it back. She wanted all of the pieces, not just seven. He dreaded the thought of telling Collin he had lied. He hung his head and sobbed. Bill never moved his arm.

# 25

Collin was speechless as Jesse told his tale. Jesse braced himself for the chiding he expected from his friend, but it never came. Collin stared at his friend with his mouth swinging open.

"Are...you...okay?" he stammered.

"Yeah," Jesse answered sheepishly.

"You almost died?"

Jesse stared at the floor. He was ashamed of all he had done. He was sorry for stealing the pieces. He was sorry for kicking her bones. He was sorry for the way he acted with disregard toward everyone but himself. He was sorry he lied to his friend. He was sorry that people had died because of him. He was sorry for everything but not sorry enough to tell Collin about the arrow.

Collin held out his hand to Jesse. He placed the bird and the pair of hands in Collin's palm. He never mentioned the arrow.

"You're right, Collin. She wants these back. She held out her hand to me and when I shook my head no that's when she started to choke me." His eyes welled with moisture, "I can't go back there, Collin. She hates me! I can't go back."

Collin felt sorry for his friend. He had been through a terrible ordeal.

"C'mon. I have an idea." Collin jumped to his feet.

"What?" Jesse asked reluctantly.

"Just wait. I need to see if you think the same way."

"What the hell are you talking about, Collin?"

"I have a theory." Jesse opened his mouth to speak, but Collin cut him off. "I'll explain when we get there. I want to show you something first." The irritation in his voice couldn't be missed.

Jesse followed him into Collin's house. Sharon was cooking dinner.

"Hello boys. Are you ready to eat? There's plenty for all of us if you're hungry."

"We'll be down in a minute, Mom." They disappeared up the stairs.

Once inside Collin's bedroom, he closed and locked the door. He knelt on the floor and pulled the newspaper articles from under his bed. They were full of post it notes and scribbles in all the margins. He laid them out across the floor.

He took a deep breath. "Now," he whispered, "she was the first one to die, right?" He pointed to photo of Julie branded on *The Great Trail* on the front page of the paper.

Jesse's stomach flipped. A lump formed in his throat. "Yeah," was all he could manage. Jesse didn't understand where he was going with this. He wanted to forget about the dead woman. After all, it was his fault.

"Look, Jesse." Collin pointed to the burn mark of the spiral. "She obviously found it." His fingers tapped the newspaper. "We've looked everywhere for it and can't find it."

"So?"

"So..." Collin mocked, "What if *he* found it?"

Collin's finger pointed to the name Jack Hilbert.

Jesse felt sick. His face was contorted from confusion. "I don't get it."

Collin sighed with disgust, "Okay, listen to me." He lowered his voice to a whisper, "What if Jack found it? What if his death wasn't an accident? What if the princess tripped him and he broke his neck that way?"

Jesse's eyes were filled with fear. He held his breath as Collin spoke.

"What if we've been looking for it in the wrong place? Maybe it's not on the path at all, but somewhere around his house." His fingers tapped the name in print again. "I think the spiral is here."

Jesse's head felt light from denial of air. He gasped and covered his mouth, "But...how did it get there?"

"You don't remember anything, do you?" Again, Jesse was confused. Collin rolled his eyes in disgust. "Didn't you say you almost knocked her down?" He pointed to Julie's picture.

"Yeah." Jesse hung his head.

Collin's voice grew louder and more agitated, "And didn't you say you ran into an old man outside of the barber shop?"

"Yeah," Jesse looked at Collin. He was beginning to follow.

"And Jack Hilbert was the barber, right?"

"Right." Jesse tried to follow what Collin was saying, but it didn't make sense. He rolled the thoughts around in his mind, and he couldn't figure out how the spiral could have burned the woman and then ended up at the barbershop. Collin was so convincing in his speech, though, Jesse quickly dismissed his own thoughts as wrong.

"And when you got home, you only had two things in your pocket, right?"

"No, three," Jesse was caught up in his own thoughts as well as Collin's detective skills and forgot to lie.

Collin sat up straight, "Three?"

Jesse's face flushed from exposure. He wanted to keep the arrow. Now he had done it. Now he was gonna have to tell him. He was so stupid. Too much information. Why couldn't he keep his mouth shut?

Collin interrupted his thoughts, "I thought you only had two? The bird and the hands."

Hands that was it. That was Jesse's out. He relaxed his shoulders, "Yeah, three. The pair of hands and the bird."

Collin rolled his eyes again, "You can't count the two hands as two things. It's only one bead, one part of the necklace," his tone was curt.

"Sorry," Jesse shrugged. He smiled to himself. The arrow was his.

The boys jumped as a knock came to the door. Sharon tried the doorknob, but it was locked. "What are you boys doing in there?"

Collin's face flushed. "Detective stuff," he said as he swished the evidence back under his bed. He motioned for Jesse to unlock the door.

Sharon walked into the room. Her smile degraded to a frown when she saw the newspaper of Julie Garrett sticking out from under Collin's bed.

183

With her voice full of concern, "I don't want you boys trying to play detectives with this gang stuff. Let the police handle it." Her voice became strained. Both faces stared smugly at her. "This is serious business. People have died. No one has any suspects." Her voice rose, "I don't want you two messing with this." She placed her hands on her hips, "Bill and I would not know what to do without you two!" The tone in her voice left no doubt. Jesse got it. Collin didn't.

Collin hung his head from being scolded. Jesse smiled at the thought of Sharon being his mother.

"We'll have no more talk of this." She shook her finger at them. "Do you hear me? No more excursions. No sneaking around. All of these terrible things happened in broad daylight. I want you boys to pay careful attention and I want no excuses!"

"Yes, ma'am," they said in unison.

"Now throw that stuff away and wash up for dinner." She turned to Jesse, "Your father is downstairs."

In Jesse's mind that was confirmation. They had become more than just friends. Sharon walked out of the room.

Collin glared at his friend. "What are you smiling about?"

"Nothin'." Jesse followed Sharon down the stairs.

Dinner that evening was filled with pleasant conversation. Collin couldn't help but notice that change in Jesse's attitude. As much as he tried, Collin couldn't keep his mind on the table talk. He convinced himself he was right about the spiral. Jack must have found it, though he had no idea how it could have been transported. Maybe it had special powers of which he was not aware. His skin tingled. Maybe Jack found another bead, he thought. Maybe it wasn't the spiral he had after all. He closed his

184

eyes and tried to recall the missing pieces. He had no fear of the 'Corkscrew Gang' because it didn't exist. He decided he would slip out later that evening to investigate. The thought brought a smile to his face.

"What are you smiling about?" Sharon asked Collin.

With a red face he glanced at Jesse. He was smiling too but for a different reason. "Nothing."

"Now, Collin Robert Sims, I know that grin. What are you up to?" Her smile radiated warmth and adoration.

"I'm...just happy, Mom. Just happy." He knew how to make his mother stop asking questions, but he did mean it. Sharon stared at her son curiously. He bent his eyes toward his plate and shoveled the food into his mouth.

Jesse sat with a stupid smirk plastered onto his face. He was happy. Thoughts of a real family filled his mind. He watched his father's eyes follow Sharon around the kitchen. He watched the tender way he touched her shoulder. He smiled throughout dinner. Yeah, his dad was also happy. Jesse finally had a moment he could cling to, a memory of love and happiness, and he was a part of it. It was too long in coming. It felt good.

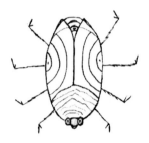

# 26

Collin closed the screen door quietly. He was sure to walk on the edge of the first step to avoid the creaky spot. He glanced at his watch. It was one-thirty a.m. He took three steps on the sidewalk and turned to run through the soft grass. It was too early for the morning dew if in fact it didn't rain first.

He ran as fast as he could. He dodged open spaces to avoid discovery. The night air was a bit cooler and it was easier to take deeper breaths. He stopped just around the corner from the barbershop. He leaned his body against the old brick building and tried to catch his breath. He was about to move when he heard some voices.

Collin pressed his face against the west wall. He held his breath as the voices moved closer to him. His arms clung to his side as he pinned himself motionless. His final move was to turn his head toward the sound of the voices. The brick was cool against his cheek. A rumble of thunder rolled in the distance.

"...had bruises all over her face. It looked like she had been in a hell of a fight."

"Who would want to fight her?"

"I don't know, but she was pretty beat up."

"Poor Mrs. Phillips."

Collin watched the two men walk past the alley. He pressed his body harder against the building hoping not to be seen. He held his breath.

"She kept repeating that she had a strange experience. She was pretty vague about it, but she kept mumbling the word light...."

Collin gasped and coughed at the sound of the word. The two men stopped and stared in his direction. For a moment he stood frozen. They turned their bodies and took one step toward the sound.

"Who's there?" one of them questioned.

Collin's feet moved first. He ran back down the alley into the darkness. His foot caught the barbershop's garbage can and spilled its contents into the alley. The sound of bottles rolling around on the pavement drowned out the men's voices.

"Stop! Who goes there?" The men never moved beyond one step. The skillful printed words of Tim Lorie kept their feet from moving toward the noise.

Collin's heart pounded louder than his footsteps as he ran through the naked streets. The shouts grew fainter as he ran. He didn't stop until all was quiet. He held his breath to be sure he wasn't followed. When he was certain, he doubled over and placed his hands on his knees. He tried to slow his breathing by taking deep deliberate breaths. The word 'light' kept rolling around in his mind.

By the time his breathing was normal, he had convinced himself his suspicions were right. He slowly walked back toward the barbershop's alley. He strained his ears to listen for any sounds. Certain he was alone, he peered around the corner. Sure enough, the men were gone.

He took one step into the alley and froze from the sound of a bottle rattling against the ground. He strained his eyes to focus through the darkness. He jumped at the sound of a raccoon's scream. He relaxed his shoulders and tiptoed past the animal as it rummaged through the scattered garbage.

He inched his way along the wall until a lamppost lit his face. He ducked back into the shadows. He listened for voices. He placed his hand over his heart trying to slow its rapid beat. He drew in a deep breath and walked into the lit sidewalk. He was alone.

The neon beer sign from the bar down the street flickered. The open sign faded to darkness. Two people stepped out of the closed bar. The sound of the key turning in the lock echoed through the street. Collin slid back into the shadows. Their footsteps moved farther from his. A muffled female voice spoke. A car door slammed. The sound of a car engine sprang to life and moved in the opposite direction. Within three minutes, all was silent.

Collin moved to the door at the bottom of Jack Hilbert's apartment stairs. His palm was sticky as he tried the locked door. He pulled his movie rental card from his pocket and a butter knife from the other. To his surprise the card released the lock. The door creaked open and rested against the bottom wall of the staircase. He moved into the dim hallway and closed the door behind him. He twisted the doorknob to ensure its release from the inside.

He moved timidly up the steps. The sound of the moaning stairs reverberated through the narrow passageway. Collin felt his throat close tighter as he moved up each stair. The air covered him like a heavy blanket. He tried to take in deep breaths but the thick dampness choked him. He covered his mouth and pinched his nose trying to suppress his cough.

When his hand finally touched the doorknob to Jack's apartment, the door swung open. The doorknob was locked, but the door had not been closed. He stood with his mouth open and eyes wide as the door slowed with a loud creak. It rested nearly three quarters ajar. Collin stood motionless as he listened for other intruders. It was silent.

He took one step into the doorway. His sneakers chirped across the wood floor. Through the torn blinds the streetlight created an eerie effect across the aged furniture. Collin forced himself to move through the rooms.

The musty smell of old dirt blended with stale cigarette smoke stole Collin's breath. He slipped past the dark brown sofa and plaid rocking chair without tripping over the humps in the old rust shag carpet. Everywhere he looked he saw cigarette butts. He lost count after nine full ashtrays. He rounded the corner into the bedroom.

His eyes scanned the room before entering. Every picture on the walls hung at a strange angle. Bits of frayed wire could be seen behind a photograph of a nude woman. Each lamp in the room was without a shade, and in the corner taller than Collin were stacks of old pizza boxes. Collin shuddered at the thought of their contents. He stepped through the doorway into the bedroom.

The bed was left just as it had been, unmade. The sheets and blanket were rolled into one from a sleepless night. He searched the dressers for the spiral or anything else that looked remotely familiar. All he found were ashtrays heaped with spent butts. The smell was sickening. He tried not to gag.

He fumbled through the rest of the apartment. He stubbed his toe on the kitchen table. He scanned the kitchen counter but found nothing. His eyes sifted through the dirty dishes in the sink. The smell of moldering food was difficult to take. He placed his hand over his mouth to suppress the nauseating feeling. Disgusted he turned to leave.

His eyes examined the living room furniture once again for a piece of the necklace. His nose led him to the neatly packaged take-out box. He carefully lifted the container by its wire hanger. The oil-soaked bottom burst open and spewed its rotten contents onto the coffee table.

"Ugh!" Collin pulled back his hand. A look of distain covered his face. "That's gross!" he exclaimed out loud. He shook the slimy cabbage remnant from his fingers and wiped it on his pants.

He paused for only a second as he slipped out of the open door. Convinced he was still alone, he walked through the faded yellow doorframe. His throat closed as he heard the sound of something heavy tumbling down the stairs. His feet blended with the approaching attacker as the racket echoed throughout the tight stairway.

He burst through the door at the bottom and stumbled onto the sidewalk. The skin of his right cheek was no match for the rough concrete sidewalk. It ripped at his flesh until his head slammed into the iron lamppost stopping his body. His unseen assailant crashed into his skull. A piece of brick rested an inch from his nose.

Collin groaned from the searing pain. Slowly he moved each limb until he was satisfied nothing was broken. He was careful not to touch his face, but the sting told him his cheek resembled hamburger.

He started to sit upright when he heard the sound of buzzing only inches from his face. He tried to focus on the sound, but it was too close. He moved himself to rest on his elbow. He couldn't believe what he saw. Concealed on the base of the streetlight was a tiny carved bug. It was still, yet the sound of its flutter mesmerized him.

A smile lit his mangled face. There was no doubt. He was right. Although it was not the spiral he had expected to find, it was one of the missing pieces. He smiled and shoved the fluttering bug into his pocket.

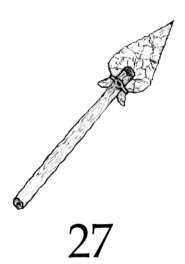

# 27

Collin lay awake on his bed. His cheek throbbed, but all he could think about was the necklace. His fist closed tightly around the tiny bead. He could feel the coolness of the stone. He forced himself to go over his theory one more time.

Slowly the light of morning crept through the window. Within a few minutes he could distinguish the objects in his room. He wanted to avoid a confrontation with his mother, so he slipped out of bed. He hadn't changed last night's clothes.

He scribbled a note to his mother:

*I'm in the barn.*

The barn door groaned under its weight. The smell of security surrounded Collin. He slid his father's metal tackle box over to the edge of the workbench. The hinges were

192

covered with rusty neglect. Collin had to force them open. He smiled at what he saw.

His father had this particular box filled with bits of unfinished pieces. He sifted through feathers, hooks, yarn, string, and fishing line. He clamped the magnifying glass to the edge of the bench as he had watched his father do many times before. He removed three plastic film containers from the bottom of the box and popped the tops. He tumbled the pieces into his hand.

He carefully placed the vial he had pulled from the offering plate beside the pair of hands and bird that Jesse surrendered to him. He pulled the newspaper photos from his back pocket and smoothed the image on the surface. He rummaged through the metal box until he found an exacto knife. Carefully he traced the edges of the images with the sharp blade.

"Okay, let's see," he said. "The spiral is the biggest, so I'd say it goes here." He placed the wispy paper cut out on the workbench closest to him. He scanned the vial and the other pieces. He wiggled his fingers above them secretly hoping they would fall into place. "Next...would be...." he stopped. The corners of his mouth turned down. He slumped his shoulders. "Hmm...I don't know what's next." He stood with his hands on his hips.

He heard the door move. He scrambled to stuff the pieces back into the film cases and the crumpled cut out image of the spiral in his hand. He shoved the container into the bottom of the box and tossed the bits of string and feathers to cover it.

"Collin, what are you doing?" Sharon asked timidly. She noticed he stood before the workbench with one of his father's tackle boxes open. She knew how important those snippets were to her husband and how precious they had become to her son.

Collin never turned around. He scanned the table top for any signs of his true intentions. Satisfied, he answered, "Just lookin', Mom."

Sharon stood beside her son with her arms around his shoulder. "Just looking at what?"

"All this stuff," he waved his hands over the box and looked at his mother.

Sharon's knees buckled at the sight of her son's face. She gasped and grabbed for the bench to steady herself. "Collin! What happened?"

Collin's hand instinctively moved to his face. He had forgotten for a moment and he hadn't planned what to say. "Oh...this?"

Sharon placed her hands on his shoulders and turned his face toward the light. "Oh my God, Collin! What happened to your face?"

"I...fell...slid...on the...side...wa...wall. Yea...on the sidewall of the haymow. I fell and slid across the wood floor."

Sharon carefully inspected the wound for splinters, "We've got to get this cleaned up, honey. I don't want it to become infected."

Collin's thoughts slid back to the film container and its contents. "Okay, in a minute, Mom. I wanna finish."

Sharon twisted her face and her voice grew stern. "You will finish whatever you were doing later." She nudged his body toward the door. "You're coming with me to the house, young man."

"But...."

"Right now!" The tone in her voice left no room for argument. Collin listened as she chided him the entire walk from the barn to the back door. She had warned him about going out. Note or no note, he was homebound.

Bill Williams rooted through the kitchen cupboards for a vase. He had picked some wildflowers for Sharon and wanted to have them on the kitchen table when she came over to clean today. He knew today was going to be a rough day for her. She had another appointment with the bank at nine o'clock. He knew her time in that house was limited. He pounded his fist on the counter for not being able to help her out. His eyes fell on the card he bought.

He tried to remember the last time he had been in a card store. He shook the memories of Liza from his mind. He sighed and picked up the card.

A serene winter landscape was painted on the front. The calming blues of a frozen creek blended with the bare beauty of leafless trees. The starkness of the snow-covered ground was broken by clusters of field grasses defying the call to yield to the bitterness of the winter temperature. A small cluster of pine trees stood in the distance dusted by a fresh powder of snow. He could almost taste the chill in the air. His hands shook as he opened the card.

*When you are feeling down*
*for no apparent reason*
*When a smile seems to take too much effort...*

*Think of the warmth of the sun on your face*

195

*Laughter of your friends*
*A warm fire on a snowy day*

*The taste of salt on your lips ~*
*with the waves touching the beach*

*And soon the energy you've lost – returns,*
*and each step forward becomes a little lighter.*

He closed the card and looked at the back. It was written and painted by a local artist. The title of the watercolor painting was "Frozen Stream." He rubbed his head with his hands and opened the card again.

There was something erotic about the message to Sharon. His eyes rested on the word *smile*. He pictured her sweet face. He scanned down to the word *laughter* and heard Sharon's giggle in his mind. It brought a smile to his face. He blushed at the thought of the word *lips*; hers tasted of longing. Then reality set in as he stopped at the word *lost*.

Who was he kidding? She was only lonely, he told himself. He stretched his hand over the card and began to crumble it, but the memory of her soft touch on his arm made him stop. He closed his eyes remembering the look in her eyes. He snatched a pen before he lost his nerve. He scribbled the words *I'm thinking of you.*

He hesitated with how to sign it. He tried to swallow the lump in his throat at the thought of the word *love*. 'Too soon to say that,' he thought. But what should he say? How should he sign it? He had never been a man of many words, and the thought of signing this card terrified him. He shook his head at his fear and laughed out loud. He held the pen to the card and simply scribbled his name. He slid it into the envelope and wrote 'Sharon' on the front. He placed it on the counter as he continued to look for a vase.

After a few more rummaged cupboards, he found a vase. In it he arranged the daisies, chicory, goldenrod and Queen Anne's lace. The vase was much larger than what he had picked and he had plenty of room to add more color. He checked his watch. He still had twenty minutes before he needed to be at the shop. He darted out of the door for a specific flower he had in his mind. He didn't know what it was called, but the only place he saw it growing was by the downtown sidewalk. He hoped the city hadn't mowed.

Jesse had waited long enough. In the dim morning light he worked his way toward his closet. He picked up his pair of good church shoes and dumped the pink arrow into the palm of his hand. He heard his father moving around the kitchen, but then all fell silent.

He opened up his door and yelled down the steps, "Anyone home?"

No response came.

He ran down the stairs and slid across the kitchen floor. He quickly rummaged through the junk drawer until he found a spool of fishing line. He pulled about two feet from the spool and sat down at the kitchen table. He strung the monofilament through the tiny hole in the end of the arrow. He held it up in the air and watched the downward pointing arrow swing from the unseen thread.

The light seemed to pass through the object without affecting its appearance. He was filled with pride. He could feel the silhouette warm his chest. He glanced down at his bare chest filled by the shadow. He thought it odd that the silhouette felt warm. His eyes moved back toward the arrow itself. It seemed to glow.

He noticed a loop on the backside of the arrow point. He hadn't noticed it before. He moved closer to it to investigate and as soon as he touched it his fingers blistered from the heat.

"Damn it!" he yelled as he stuck his fingers in his mouth. He shook his hand in the air. He looked at the string. The arrow was gone.

In a panic he slid around the kitchen floor but saw nothing. His eyes and hands moved the dishes toward destruction as he wiped the countertop clean. Bill's card for Sharon landed in the sink.

Jesse started to panic. Fear widened his eyes. He never heard the sound of his father's pickup truck return.

When Bill walked into the kitchen, he was furious with the mess Jesse had made. He had toppled his orange juice glass onto the floor, and the bits of broken glass were mixed with Jesse's blood as he fumbled his hands over the floor once again.

"What's going on here?" Bill's voice was agitated. Jesse didn't answer. Bill picked his son up by the shoulders and looked at his bleeding palms. He ran his hands under the kitchen faucet to rinse the blood from his hands. "What are you doing? "Agitation colored his voice. Still no reply. Jesse's eyes were dazed.

Bill grabbed Jesse's shoulders and shook him slightly, "Jesse!"

Jesse's pupil's returned to normal. The world became clear. "I...I lost something."

"Look at your hands! You've got a thousand cuts all over them." Bill noticed a piece of glass sticking out of his flesh. "Hold on a minute. I've gotta get that out." With his thick fingers he grabbed the piece of glass and pulled it from Jesse's palm.

"What in the world were you looking for?"

For a moment Jesse wanted to tell him everything. He wanted to tell him about the princess, her necklace, how he stole the pieces and how so many people have gotten hurt, but the words would not leave his lips. He willed them to move, but his tongue would not yield. He collapsed on the floor and whimpered.

# 28

Samantha Aaron was an attractive woman. She was nearly six feet tall, had short blonde hair and green eyes. She was proud of her fit body and spent an hour a day at the gym trying to maintain it. She had two children, Tom and Terri. They were seventeen year-old twins.

She had a pleasant personality, a wide smile, and warm words of greeting to those she knew. Her laugh was robust and her voice distinct. She had a quality about her, which one could neither forget nor discern.

Sam married her high school sweetheart, Tony. They celebrated their nineteenth wedding anniversary in February. They always appeared to be happy, at least in public.

Tony owned the local grocery store and was a butcher by trade though he never touched any meat. His purpose was better served as he pushed his pencil when he wasn't sharpening it, and he spent much time 'tripping over the wastebasket' during inventory to lose unwanted count sheets.

They had several employees who were paid an honest wage according to Tony, but if they arrived for work ten minutes early they were forbidden to clock in until three minutes had passed. Government payroll standards allowed for those seven minutes to be forgiven by the owner at his discretion. Tony never paid those seven minutes, or the seven minutes after their shift ended if they clocked out late.

Both of the children worked at the market. Sam and Tony felt it important to teach a good work ethic. Terri had her sights set on college for something in the medical field while Tom was being groomed for the head butcher. It was Tony's dream that Tom would one day take over the business.

Tom had shown an interest in the business at a very early age. He was instrumental in encouraging his father to retain a liquor license to sell beer and wine. It had been the most profitable segment of the business thus far. That proved to Tony his son was a fine asset and an early retirement sounded good to him. He spent the next year talking him out of college.

"I'll give you the money I would spend on your college education to you in one lump sum," was the carrot most often dangled. Occasionally, "You'd just be wasting your time," would spew out in a heated argument. Usually the sugarcoated reaction was, "Your talents would be better spent running the family business. You can buy me out and do with the market what you wish." That was the winning argument.

Tom had visions of grandeur when it came to the store. He wanted to upgrade the outside, give it an old train station façade. He wanted to showcase a grand entrance with local farmers selling their 'natural' produce. He wanted to hire a wine steward and hold wine tasting classes. He thought of flying the 'fresh catch' from the shore daily and hiring a cheese maker with a see-through window for the interested customer to view. Several additional cash stations would be installed with many of them offering the convenience of self-service. In Tom's dream what would make the market the finished product was to offer a babysitting service complete with a secure playground at the parents' disposal while they shopped.

The market already had a baker fresh from the coveted New York City, but he only worked part-time. Tom wanted to change Joseph to full-time mostly because he had his eyes on Joseph's hot daughter, Lizzie, who was a year younger than Tom. If Tom had his way, it would all stay in the family, though Lizzie was in no way attracted to him. She thought he was arrogant and extremely rude. Unfortunately, she was right.

Terri, however, was content to play cashier. She loved playing a game with herself to see how fast she could move the items across the scanner and how quickly she could bag them. There were few cashiers as quick as she or as often out of balance. After all, she had learned a few things from her daddy.

Samantha kept the books for the business. She produced all of the payroll reports, 1099's, W2's, W9's, 941's, 1090's, 1040's, as well as the monthly on account statements. She had her own system of pocket padding.

The entire family had a self-serving attitude while masking it with the plastic façade. It fooled most people, but not Sharon and Collin. Tony and Mark were half-brothers.

Sam did her best to pretend to like Sharon, but she talked about her constantly even if Sharon wasn't completely out of hearing distance. The words hurt, but Sharon never spoke of them. If she didn't hear what Samantha said directly, she would hear of it through her daughter, Terri. Sharon was unsure which woman was more cruel or self-centered. She tolerated both of them because of the family ties, but after Mark died, her contact with them became less frequent. Sharon was crushed by the fact that they never offered any assistance, financial or emotional. It was a tough realization to see that they didn't offer because they were incapable.

If Sam could admit the real truth, she would say she was extremely jealous of Sharon. Sam and her family had the respect of the town's people, a position in the local church, a reputation for helping out those in need, and all of the worldly possessions one could acquire. Why she saw green each time she looked at Sharon was difficult to understand. Sharon had confidence in herself, she was a true giver – no strings attached, a great mother, and an honest person. Sam only pretended to be those things.

After a few minutes of listening to Sam, her true personality and agenda revealed itself. "The mouth is a window into the soul," Sharon's grandfather's words came as a whisper." How is it with yours?" Sharon took her sister-in-law as her personal cross to bear. She did it the best she knew how.

Sam and Tony woke at precisely six o'clock a.m. They dressed in their walking clothes and headed for the downtown area. They usually walked the same pattern each morning, except for Saturday. That was the day Joseph opened the market.

The sky threatened a downpour, so they walked at a quickened pace. Sam's new shoes rubbed her heels, but she dared not to mention it. It didn't take much to change the mood of her husband.

Tony walked slightly ahead of Sam. He always did. He had an agenda this morning. Joseph was to open the market. He needed to arrive by four thirty to make the cake for a retirement party this afternoon. Tony needed to be sure he remembered to unlock the door.

Joseph was a great baker. He came from the 'Big Apple' with glowing references. His past was littered with financial trouble after his divorce, so he decided to move to a rural town. Anywhere in the country would have been fine. For some reason a friend emailed him The Minerva Market's telephone number. He made the call to Tony and was hired over the telephone.

Tony had a strict set of standards for the store as well as for its employees. He had quite a round of discussions with Joseph about the length of his hair, but in the end Joseph won. His concession was a ponytail. Tony didn't miss an opportunity to chide Joseph about the length as it grew, but Joseph decided to take the Sampson approach. He vowed to never cut it as long as his boss mentioned it. This was only one of the tests of their wills.

Tony arrived at the front door. It was locked. He glanced at his watch; it was 6:31 a.m. With the look of disapproval on his face he peered through the glass doors. He fumbled in his pocket for the key and was startled by the sound of the thumb turn being unlocked from the inside.

"Good morning, Mr. Aaron," Joseph said cheerfully as he swung open the door.

"It is past time," Tony said as he tapped the crystal face of his Timex.

Tony brushed by Joseph without another word. He moved as if he was carrying a heavy load on his back as he walked toward the bakery. He could smell the cake before he saw it.

The stainless steel counter was littered with bowls of different color icing. Pastry knives of all sizes were haphazardly placed around the work area. Five bags were filled with sweet confection all with different tips. A row of pink roses was drying on a cake stand. Tony was pleased he had been busy, but irritated with the disarray. He mumbled something under his breath and walked out of the room. Joseph continued assembling his masterpiece.

Sam knew this drill well. She walked in circles around the parking lot of the market as Tony tended to his business inside. He would flag her down from the doorway and tell her to continue without him or, if all seemed in order, he would rejoin her. This morning he was satisfied.

After a few minutes of ranting about how late Joseph had unlocked the door, added with the usual "It's hard to find good help," they continued their brisk walk in peace. The clouds hung heavy above them. Within a few minutes it began to sprinkle.

They were only a few blocks from home when they passed by the clockmaker's shop. Chester Tote was bent over from the weight of a bucket of bleach water. He was about to step off the curb when Tony offered his assistance. Without a word Tony carried the bucket out into the street and poured it on the darkened asphalt.

Chester managed a smile and nodded his head as Tony returned the empty bucket to him. He turned and walked back into his shop. He followed this ritual every day since Liza was killed. He felt relieved somehow by washing the bloodstained road with a bucket of bleach each morning. He had been a witness to the tragic accident and this helped to erase it from his mind.

A loud clap of thunder startled Sam. She jumped from the curb and landed sideways on her ankle. She heard a loud crack. The pain shot through her leg like a hot spear. She screamed out in pain. Tony looked at her broken ankle with disgust. He didn't have time for this today.

"What did you do?" he spoke in an accusatory tone. Sam couldn't manage her plastic smile. Her ankle was too painful and the tone in his voice made her feel worse. She hung her head and cried.

Tony let out a disapproving sigh. "I'll go get the car." He ran a few feet and yelled back to her, "Be ready when I get back."

Sam's tears turned to sobs in the absence of her husband. She cried for her current situation. She cried for her life of pretending. She cried for love. She cried for acceptance, but most of all she cried out of self-pity.

She thought Tony would soon be coming down the street and decided to try to stand. She had been barked an order, so she pulled all of her gym strength together and tried to stand. She couldn't. She noticed a light pole a few feet from her and thought she could use it to get on her feet. She pulled herself to it.

She watched her limp ankle drag behind her. The distorted position made her sick. She moved her head to the side and vomited. She carefully moved her foot in a better position. She screamed from the pain. She started to slide again when her hand skirted something brown. It made a strange sound as it moved across the pavement.

Sam forgot about the pain for a moment as she picked up a tiny carved bead. It looked like stone yet held the weight of metal. It was an inch and a half long, brown and white, and was carved to resemble an idol. The eyes of the god were over-exaggerated and its hands were folded together over its chest. It felt cool to touch. She was so captured by the raw beauty and form she didn't hear Tony pull close to her until he blew the horn.

Startled, Sam stood and waited for Tony to help her to the car. He never moved. He motioned over the steering wheel. She could hear his voice rambling over the car's engine, but she consciously tuned out the words. She managed to hop to the open door and sat gingerly in the passenger side. She barely had the car door closed as Tony raced for the hospital. They drove in silence. He never asked how she felt.

After four hours in the emergency room, Tony gathered Sam's personal effects that had been placed in a hospital ID bag. He threw away the unused tissue, put her lip balm in his own pocket, held the house key in one hand, and looked curiously at the idol cradled in the center of his left palm.

"What's this?" he spoke out loud but mostly to himself.

Sam was trying to balance herself on the new pair of crutches while she fumbled with her air cast. Her appointment with the surgeon was in three days after the swelling had reduced.

She'd lost patience with Tony's tone, so she snapped, "What?"

Tony never changed his voice. He held the idol between his fingers and pushed it close to her face. "This!" he mocked.

Sam immediately felt possessive of her new found treasure. Somehow seeing it in the hands of another made her furious and strangely jealous. Her face flushed as she lunged at Tony's hand like a small child. Her response startled him. She spoke not a word, but her facial expression told the tale.

"Geez, what's up with you?"

She pretended not to hear him. She closed her hand tightly around the idol. It was hers. She was the one who found it.

The only sound in the rest of the ride home was Tony's chiding. "You know we're told in the Bible to not worship graven images."

The conversation Sam screamed in her mind never passed over her tongue. Secretly she knew she got to him. She knew it bothered him and it made her want it keep it all the more. Her heart was filled with hatred for this miserable, angry, selfish man she had married. He was so hateful, yet in the midst of it all, he managed to preach to her. Religion was a convenience to him, something to dangle in front of others for show, not faith. Through her total disgust, Sam smiled an evil smile and enjoyed the moment. Her hand squeezed the desired image.

# 29

Collin helped Sharon prepare stuffed shells for her sister-in-law. Despite the division between them, she felt sorry for her. She knew Tony wouldn't cook and neither would the twins. She pictured the strained smile and sad eyes of her sister-in-law as she tried to convince them that everything was wonderful. If Sharon hadn't been repeatedly spit on by Sam's gossip, she would do more.

She gathered a few herbs from her garden to dress up the salad. She rinsed some garlic chives, salad burnet, French sorrel and gathered nasturtium and borage flowers for the finishing touches. Collin helped by chopping cucumbers, carrots and squash. The smell of the Italian dinner filled their car.

When they arrived at the Aaron home, the door was unlocked, and the alarm did not announce their arrival. Both were abnormal. Sharon's voice echoed in the silent house.

Sam came home from the hospital and crawled into bed. Tony placed a glass of ice water on the bedside table and left for the market without a word. Sam's eyes burned from sadness and anger.

Her emotions competed with her mind. She tried to remember a time when she was truly happy. Even when Tony and Sam dated in high school, he displayed anger toward her and life in general. He spent much of his time trying to outdo anyone who stood in his way. He acted as if he had much to prove, not only to himself but also to his family. He spent most of his life comparing himself to his half-brother trying to shade his true feelings of jealousy.

Mark seemed to have it all going for him. He was well liked yet not extremely popular. Football was the only sport they played together. The coach played them fairly equal, but he chided Tony constantly about keeping his emotions in check. Mark didn't particularly care for his half-brother, but he held it together for his mother's sake. They were barely two years apart and had enough peer pressure spawned by different last names. Mark learned to let the comments roll off his back unaffected. Tony harbored deep resentment, and as he grew older it spewed from his mouth laced with his sharp attitude.

Sam replayed many heated arguments that happened within her own family, especially with Tony. She squeezed her fists so tightly she had nail prints in her palms. She tried to change her thoughts to something more pleasant, but anger consumed her. She sat up in bed and threw the water glass across the room. Slivers of glass shimmered as they danced across the floor. The ice cubes slipped over the cherry floor leaving tiny threads of water as evidence from where they had been. She watched them melt into a small puddle and slowly disappear. She rested her head back on her pillow and tried to relax.

Her thoughts returned to herself. She relaxed her tight grip and ran her fingers over the tiny object she held in her palm. She closed her eyes and tried to imagine where this little idol came from. She turned her thoughts to the age of the original owner and before she realized, she was holding the piece only inches from her face.

It was skillfully carved. Each detail had been meticulously engraved to perfect detail. The clothing looked to be ceremonial with wavy stripes in varied widths. She pondered their meaning, but her eyes were drawn to its own. Their sheer size was curious. She assumed the person who carved it meant it as a symbol. After a minute she whispered "Eyes to see you." Her smile was confirmation.

She turned the bead over and looked again at the bottom. She noticed a tiny hole, which ran through the entire piece. The hole at the top was the same size. There were several tiny pinholes placed around the top of its head. They encircled the center, larger hole. Her eyes squinted. She pulled it closer to investigate.

The medication blurred her vision. She fought the urge to sleep. She blinked repeatedly. Her eyes found the idol each time they opened. Its hands were folded over its chest, folded, folded, folded, left hand outstretched, folded, folded....

Fear threw her eyes open. She stared at the tiny bead. Its hands were folded across its chest. She blinked her eyes

211

again, still folded. Again, they remained folded. She repeated this process over and over again with the results being the same. She smiled to herself. The meds were playing tricks on her. She laughed out loud and opened her eyes one last time. The figure had both of its arms extended.

She drew in her breath. She fought the urge to close her eyes fearing it would change again. She held its tiny hands within the tips of her own. They felt strangely warm.

She closed her eyes and laughed at her luck to find such a curious object. She was careful not to close her palm tightly. She wondered what she would do with it.

She imagined herself standing in front of the press explaining how she came upon the idol. She heard the multitude shouting their questions. "One at a time," she heard herself say. The questions came in droves. First, she envisioned herself standing in her own living room holding the press conference, then the background changed to an outside marble staircase, then it stopped inside a museum. She stood next to a glass case protecting the tiny bead from prodding hands.

Her desire to feel it once again became unbearable. She saw the idol extend its hands, calling out to her. She wanted to feel the coolness of the stone against her skin. She wanted to hold its tiny hands within her fingers. It wanted her. She wanted it more.

She smashed the glass case with her fist. Glass slivers shimmered in the camera lights as it moved through the air. Sam's blood speckled the front row of spectators. Her face burned from the light of the cameras. The crowd gasped in horror as she grabbed the bead from the broken case. Their hands covered their ears from the noise of the alarm.

She felt her feet move as she fled down the flight of stairs. Her voice shouted, "It's mine! You can't have it! I found it!

It's mine!" She pushed several assailants from her path until at last she was alone, alone with her treasure.

She opened her hand. Her heart jumped at the sight of this tiny thing once again held within her grasp. Her smile was wide.

She pulled a hair from her head and slid it into the top of the idol. The tiny circle of holes held each hair securely. When she had finished, she danced with excitement. "I did it!" she squealed. "I figured it out. I made it my own. My very own!"

Sam opened her palm to look at the idol. It looked strange with her short blonde strands protruding from its head. She sensed disapproval. It seared its image into her palm. The strands of her hair shriveled from the heat. She heard screaming from a distance. She had no idea it was her own. She looked to the sky for redemption and delivery. Her vision went dark.

Sharon placed the hot dish of stuffed shells on top of the stove. Collin placed the salad bowl on the granite countertop. They shrugged their shoulders to the silence of the house.

"Samantha, are you here?" Sharon yelled from the bottom of the stairs. She turned to Collin. "She must be sleeping. I'm gonna go check on her."

Collin was busy checking out the house when his mother's scream drew him up the circular staircase. His sneakers squeaked to a halt on the marble floor. His aunt was lying on her bed with a pillow over her face. Sharon was screaming her name, but Sam didn't respond.

Collin made a motion to remove the pillow from her face, but Sharon held him back. Her hand trembled as she pointed to the burn mark in her palm. Collin's stomach flipped at the image of the idol. He knew what his mother was thinking. She was thinking *'gang.'* He was thinking *'princess.'* They stared in silence at the motionless body.

"Is she…" Collin couldn't finish his sentence. Sharon just shook her head.

"I need to call the police." Sharon whispered, "And, oh my God, I've got to call Tony!" She clasped her hands over her mouth, "How can I tell Tony?" she mumbled through her hands. Tears dampened her cheeks. "I'm going to call. Don't touch anything."

Sharon picked up the telephone from the mahogany partner's desk. Her back was to Collin. He inched a few steps closer to the bed. His heart pounded as he looked at Sam's palm. He knew it was here somewhere.

His eyes scanned the Egyptian cotton sheets. Her hand was on top of the covers, but it wasn't there. He inspected the bedside floor. It wasn't there. He knew it didn't walk off by itself. He knew it had to be there somewhere. He heard his mother's telephone conversation in the background. She called the police first. He heard the mention of a brand mark. Her voice was strained.

He stepped closer and knelt on the floor. His hand felt the hand-knotted Indian rug. His heart pounded trying to free itself from his chest. He peered over the bed to see his mother. She held her head in her hands, but she was still

214

talking. He knew he was almost out of time. He brushed his hand over the fringe of the rug one last time and he felt the stone bead. Without looking at it, he shoved it in his pocket.

Quickly he stood. His eyes were wide. He relaxed his shoulders and walked to his sobbing mother's side. He slipped his arm around her waist. Her body shook as she hung up the phone.

"Everyone is on their way." She never lifted her head. "Let's go downstairs." She glanced over to the body of her sister-in-law. "We shouldn't be in here."

Collin didn't respond. He patted his pocket and relaxed his shoulders a bit more. They walked down the staircase in silence.

The hands on the English tall-case clock seemed glued in place. Several minutes passed between the timed ticks of the swinging pendulum. Collin and Sharon stared through each other without words. Collin thought about the pieces of the necklace he had gathered; Sharon dreaded the imminent conversation with the police and Tony. She felt her throat close. She started to cry.

Collin counted the pieces in his mind. His right hand was in his pocket wrapped tightly around the newest addition to his quest. He thought of the sun and wondered how he would find it in the grass and how he could get away to begin to search. Paranoia etched his face as he thought of the questions the police were going to ask. How could his true intentions remain hidden? He watched his mother collapse on the floor. He opened his mouth to speak, but his words stuck as the officers walked through the front door.

With the mahogany double doors opened wide to the front lawn, Collin watched as two police cruisers joined the other pair on the circular cement drive. All but one extinguished their lights. He stood mesmerized by the alternation of red to blue. He nodded his head at the officer's questions. Sharon tried to speak through her sobs.

"Why were you here?" the captain asked again.

"To bring...dinner...," Sharon tried to speak clearly, "for the family." Officer Warren put his arm around her shoulder.

"How did you find her?" He waited for her reply with his pen touching his notepad.

"She...was lying on her back with a pillow...." Sharon covered her mouth with her hands and sobbed uncontrollably.

"I know this is hard, Mrs. Sims, but we need your help. Please." His eyes were kind but his voice was stern.

After a long pause Sharon continued, "The pillow covered her face."

"Did you move anything in the room?"

"No."

"Nothing at all?"

"No."

"You must be certain. Are you sure?" Collin's face blushed red.

"We didn't touch a thing." Sharon's response came as a scolded child. He glanced at Collin. His eyes told a different story. She squinted at his reaction. The officer turned to respond, but another policeman rushed into the room.

"Captain Warren, Mr. Aaron has arrived, sir."

Tony ran through the open front door. Red blotches covered his face and horror filled his eyes. He grabbed the double front doors and slammed them shut.

"Where is she?" was all he said. One of the officers at the top of the staircase motioned for him to follow. He ran up the stairs two at a time. When his screams filled the air Sharon covered her face.

216

The word, "NO!" echoed through the house. The volume seemed deafening. He fought the two officers who blocked the door from his passage.

"Let me go!" he screamed, but the officers held him at the threshold. His legs collapsed under him. His fists echoed against the marble floor. His sorrow couldn't be muffled.

All who stood at the base of the stairs watched the drama unfold. Slowly he stood and turned from the master bedroom. His footsteps were deliberate and heavy. Each one grew more intense. By the time he stood in front of Captain Warren, his teeth were clenched and his fists were drawn.

He spit his words, "You...you find whoever did this. You find who killed my wife! You do it quickly. You *will* keep me updated and you WILL NOT leak this to the press!" He stormed out of the door. His tires spun a cloud of dust that covered his vehicle. It hung in the air in defiance. The famous Tim Lorie from The Daily View scribbled wildly as he kicked a spent pen across the floor.

"All as it was," spoke the officer spoke through tight lips. His finger pointed to the pen. Tim never lifted his head. When the officer shoved the pen into his chest, Tim forced a smile. His hand never stopped moving.

Sharon and Collin drove home in silence. The smell of the stuffed shells still lingered in their small kitchen. Without a word Sharon placed three shells on a plate in front of Collin. She sat down with a glass of water before her. Her eyes were rimmed in red. They both jumped at the knock on the door. Bill rushed to her without a word and put his arms around her. Jesse stared at the floor.

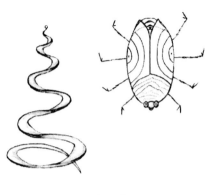

# 30

Collin lay on his back. His arms were folded behind his head. He looked at the clock for the fifth time. It read 2:49 a.m. He could hear muffled voices coming from the floor below. He knew Bill and his mother were still talking. His deep sigh was filled with disgust.

"What's wrong?" Jesse whispered through the darkness.

Collin curled his lip at the question and sighed again. He mocked his response, "What's wrong? You know what's wrong!"

"Shhh. They'll hear you."

Collin sat up in his bed. Jesse was lying on the trundle. "What are we gonna do, Jesse? This is getting out of control!" Jesse didn't respond. "We have to find all of the pieces. We have to give them back to the princess." Collin tried to calm his strained voice. "How many people have died, Jesse?" His tone was accusatory and close to Jesse's face. Jesse hung his head. "How many?"

"Three..." The lump in Jesse's throat cut off the rest of his words.

"Three, huh? Try four." Collin's voice moved to a harsh whisper, "Four, Jesse, four...because of *you*." He threw his head back onto his pillow.

Collin wrestled with his angry words. Sometime in the middle of the night, he whispered, "I'm sorry" to his whimpering friend. He couldn't be sure if it was true or a dream, but he thought he heard a reply.

Collin's body floated through the opening of the chute. Once again he stared at the strange markings on the wall. He saw the bones of the princess lying in ruins on the floor of the tomb. He heard his voice echo through the chamber. He heard her laughter and her cries. He felt himself being lifted from the dirt floor. An unseen source pulled his body.

As he moved through the chute it seemed to elongate. He heard the voice of an elderly man. The words spoken in a hushed tone rose and fell with the rhythm of written song.

"When the chute is opened, a helper will come. He will give you the light and show you the way. You will sing like a bird to announce your arrival. I will lift you toward the light and bring you to the gods."

Collin saw the princess smile. It seemed to take much effort. Her eyes were drawn and shallow. Her skin was the color of stone. She lowered her head to receive a necklace that the old man placed around her neck. The spiral was on the bottom.

"Wake up, Collin." Jesse stood over him and shook his arm.

Collin sat up with a gasp, "What?"

"You were having a bad dream."

Collin tried to remember but couldn't. He had a puzzled look on his face. "How do you know?"

"You were breathing funny and you kept mumbling."

"I...I can't remember." Collin scratched his head, "What did I say?"

"I dunno. I couldn't understand you. All I knew was I had to wake you up."

Collin managed a smile, "Thanks."

Jesse sat at the edge of Collin's bed. "You can't remember, huh?"

"Nope."

"Not a thing?"

"Nope."

"Really?"

Collin's voice was heavy with irritation, "You can really be annoying. You know that?" Collin put his head in his hands. He didn't understand what was happening to him. His patience for his friend was gone and the sight of him changed Collin's mood drastically. Overcome with guilt he whispered, "I'm sorry Jesse. I don't remember. And your questioning me doesn't help."

Jesse played into his friend's emotion. With his head hung he answered, "I just wanted to help. You seemed scared. I...I thought if I woke you...you wouldn't be scared anymore."

Collin managed a thin smile. "Thanks," was all he could say.

Bill cradled Sharon in his arms. He counted each step until he was certain he had climbed the last. He swung her bedroom door open with his foot and placed her on the bed. He covered her with a quilt that was folded at the bottom. He moved her hair from her eyes and kissed her cheek. He waited until the rhythm of her breathing was consistent. He kissed her once again and closed the door. It was four a.m.

He listened to her tale long into the morning hours being careful not to interrupt. He tried not to show horror at the description of Sam's body. He guided her through her complaints and reassured her feelings of Tony's misguided attention. He absorbed all the details of their relationship though much of it he already knew. It was a small town. He held her when she cried and calmed her when she panicked. She fell asleep on the couch.

Bill Williams sat on Sharon's couch and pinched himself. He never believed people could change and here he sat as proof. His body was tired but his mind was moving in overdrive.

He remembered Sharon in high school. She was voted 'Most Sincere' her senior year although the secret vote among the boys was 'Most Sexy'. She was the queen of her Homecoming court and the captain of the debate team. The boys picked the opposing side just to watch her move.

She was sweet, always smiling, and built like a shapely doll. She had plenty of male friends but never a date. The boys kept their distance out of respect for Mark, all but Keith Tynes.

Keith had been Sharon's grade school boyfriend. He lived on her street. They rode the bus together through every grade. Their mothers were good friends. As young children, they talked about getting married after their first kiss at age four.

The town nicknamed them 'the kids'. They barely had separate names. Even through junior high, they were always together, always laughing, and shared everything; everything but sex.

Sharon had held Keith at bay. She made him promise to wait until they were married. He was told not to ask, but his eyes told his tale. He was desperate.

Keith's parents divorced when they were in sixth grade. His mother refused to move out of the town because of Keith's relationship with Sharon. Everyone understood their destiny.

Keith's personality changed midway through their eighth grade year. Sharon was too close to him to see it. He needed more attention and looked anywhere to receive it. He became the class flirt and got into quite a bit of trouble from his 'wandering' hands with other girls. He spent a lot of time in the principal's office.

By the time they entered high school, their relationship was not much more than friends. Keith was still desperate for Sharon's approval, but he started spending more time with his buddies. By tenth grade they hardly spoke.

Sharon met Mark the summer before her first year of high school. He was the shortstop on the practice field that day although he also pitched. He was a senior, built and handsome. She couldn't take her eyes off of him.

"Hey, Sims!" Bill called to his friend, "Got someone here for you to meet." Sharon's face flushed. "This is Sharon Wells. Sharon, meet Mark Sims."

They both smiled as they shook hands. "Are you new in town?"

"No," Sharon blushed, "just new to this school."

"Did you transfer?" Mark questioned. She's a lot older than a freshman, he reassured himself.

"No, I'm a freshman," she spoke with pride.

Mark's face fell at the word *freshman*. He finished the conversation as quickly as he could and chided Bill for the introduction.

"She's fifteen."

"So? Look at her -- she's beautiful!" Bill turned to look at Sharon. She was watching them. He nudged his friend. "She's watching you."

Mark reacted with disgust, "She's fifteen."

Bill quickly became one of Sharon's friends. He wanted to be close to her. He guarded her against many wolf whistles and groping hands. He gave a few of his classmates a black eye for their comments.

In February of his senior year, he decided to ask her out. He waited in the hall around her locker before homeroom. He knew she was approaching from Keith Tynes' reaction.

"Leave her alone, Keith," Bill said with a shove.

Keith placed both hands on Bill's chest and tried to push back. Bill never moved. He had a good thirty pounds over Keith. Keith smiled a nervous smile.

"She likes when I do this," he said with an attitude as he twirled her hair in his hands.

Sharon ignored the rift and closed her locker door. "Go to class, boys," was all she said. They turned from her in obedience.

Bill took two steps and turned to face her, "Sharon?" He had to do this while he had the nerve.

"Yes?" Her china complexion stole his words. "What's up?"

Bill stammered for a few seconds and whispered, "Would you go to the prom with me?"

Her face lit from the gesture. "Oh Bill, that's so sweet but I'm already going."

Reacting as if he had just been slapped, he blurted out, "With who?"

Sharon smiled, "Mark Sims."

Those words cut through his chest. He couldn't respond. He walked away from her.

"Bill? Bill!" she yelled after him. He never turned around.

The night of the prom commemorated four months of dating for Sharon and Mark. He had admired Sharon from a distance since that day in August. He drifted slightly back when he heard she had just celebrated her fifteenth birthday in December. She was the third youngest in her class. She would graduate a seventeen-year-old.

After Christmas break he couldn't resist any longer. He asked her to the prom and was thrilled when she said *yes*. He knew she would be the prettiest girl there even if she were a freshman.

Mark was crowned king that night. Sharon was very happy for him although he was embarrassed. His half-brother sneered in the corner while Bill whistled loudly announcing his approval. Liza was the first one to kiss him in congratulations. It was a long wet kiss. Bill finally pulled her from him.

"Sorry, buddy. She's a bit tipsy." His ring clanged on the hidden flask in his pocket. Mark wiped the kiss from his lips. Sharon tried to suppress the jealousy.

The band played great music that night. Sharon and Mark only left the dance floor once, to steal a few kisses. They stayed for the 'after-prom' and made plans to meet a few couples at a local restaurant for breakfast.

Sharon stood in line for the ladies' room to change into street clothes while Mark and a few friends changed in the halls. When Mark approached her to leave, the line hadn't budged.

"Come on. Let's go."

"But...I'm still in my gown."

"You haven't moved." He yelled into the open doorway, "What are you girls doing in there?"

"Changing..." came the unison reply followed by a multitude of giggles.

Mark turned to Sharon and pulled her out of line, "Come on. You can change in the car." Sharon's mouth and eyes opened wide in opposition. "I won't look. I promise." Mark stood with his left hand over his heart and his right in the air. Sharon laughed and followed him out to his car.

It had rained that evening. Without a word, Mark scooped Sharon into his arms and carried her over the muddy parking lot to his car. She opened the door and he gently placed her on the front seat. When he sat behind the wheel, she was next to him.

The parking lot was jammed with junior and seniors trying to leave at one time. Mark stopped twice moments before he was hit. He blew his horn and yelled out of the window.

"Watch it!" Bill and Liza whizzed by with their car barely touching the pavement. Bill stuck his hand out of the window and threw the empty bottle from his car. "What an idiot!" Mark said with disapproval.

225

They waited in the parking lot until most of the students had gone. Mark's car purred as they talked about the evening. Mark took Sharon's face in both of his hands and kissed her.

"You make me proud," he said. "You were the prettiest girl there."

She thanked him quietly and kissed him. Her thoughts whispered the promise she had made to herself. A car pulled up beside them and blew its horn. Mark rolled down the steamed window.

Mrs. Donaldson sat in her Buick. "You kids best be getting on home now." She smiled and drove away. Their car was the last.

Sharon gathered her clothes and slid over the seat to change. Her gown caught on the seat belt. They both laughed as they tried to pull it free without tearing it. Through all the movement one of her shoulders straps tore and floated across her bare neck.

Her gown had an empire waist and the bust line was gathered with tiny ribbons and pearl buttons. It was slightly off the shoulder and had two straps tied at the shoulder. It was pink and paled to the color of her cheeks. Mark fumbled with the torn ribbon awkwardly.

"I'll just tuck it down here." She made a motion to hide it in her bodice. She pulled her dress open to tuck the strap inside and revealed her bare skin. Sharon's motion was innocent, but Mark was overwhelmed. From the look on his face, Sharon knew what she had done.

He moved his hands toward her tiny pearl buttons. The word 'Stop!' was screaming inside her head, but it never left her lips. She wanted the same.

She watched as he opened each button. He paused for a moment to caress the skin he had just revealed. He stopped to kiss her at each progression waiting for her to halt him. She only smiled.

He kissed her bare shoulders. The soft light cast a wanting shadow across her. He moved his hands across her in a gentle sweeping motion, caressing her bare skin with his fingertips. They pledged themselves to each other that evening and never regretted it. They were married a month after Sharon graduated.

Bill and Liza were one of the couples who had arranged to meet at the diner for breakfast. Between the two of them they finished an entire bottle of whiskey. His driving was erratic and neither of them felt any pain until the back window was filled with alternating red and blue lights. Bill was charged with driving while intoxicated and Liza was cited for underage drinking. They never made it to breakfast either.

Bill slipped quietly down the stairs. He waited at the bottom for any sound from Sharon's room. It was quiet. He rested his head on the couch's soft pillow. The last thing he saw was Mark's deer mount.

# 31

For the diminished Aaron family, hurried preparation filled their day. They visited the funeral home, picked out the casket, and talked about the service. The pastor helped with many of the tactical questions. They left the funeral home and drove to the florist. This was the only place Terri spoke. Tom never took his eyes off the clerk.

"No, Dad. Mom would not want any carnations. She hated them. She called them cheap filler."

Tony tried to hide his frustration. He thought funerals were ridiculously overpriced and everyone took advantage of the grieving. He picked the carnations *because* they were inexpensive. He didn't *care* what Sam thought. He was the one who was paying for it. Subconsciously he placed his hand over his wallet.

He smiled at his daughter the best he knew how. "Honey," he whispered, "Everything is so expensive...I just thought we could save a little bit on flowers."

Terri wasn't convinced. Her father couldn't manipulate her as he did her mother. She clenched her fists in defiance. "No carnations....not one!" She turned to the clerk to ensure the message was received. Tony turned from her in disgust.

"Write this down," she waved her finger in the air at the clerk. "We want a large spray to put on the top of the casket with fresh lemon and magnolia leaves. Clusters of larkspur, delphiniums, and white roses will be entwined with full stems of Stargazer lilies. Be sure to use the buds as well as the open flowers." Agitation colored her voice. She wanted her cheap father to have a lofty bill for all the times he denied her mother. She turned to walk away and added, "Be sure to pull the stamens from the open flowers and don't forget the Beloved Wife banner." She smiled as she turned.

"Oh, I forgot. Mimic the lemon and magnolia leaves surround, but use only white dendrobiums with English ivy trailers to be placed at Mom..." her words were stuck in her dry throat as she spoke the word *Mom*. Tears flooded her eyes and moistened her cheeks. She wiped them with her fingers. Her commanding voice softened, "Do you have a banner that says *Mom*?"

"Yes, we do. Is that what you would like?"

Terri couldn't speak any more. She shook her head and motioned for Tom to follow. They walked out of the door paying no attention to the cheerful sound of the ringing doorbell. Tony was sulking in the car.

They drove to the cemetery in silence. Tom and Terri sat in the car while Tony walked through the stone arch doorway. The door moaned as it closed behind him.

"She was hot!" Tom burst with excitement.

229

Terri looked at him with disdain, "What?"

"That girl, Kara, at the florist shop...she was hot."

Terri opened her mouth to speak, but couldn't think of an accurate word to describe how disgusted she was at her brother's complacency. She couldn't stop the tears.

Tony's hands shook as he paid for a family plot. He only bought that because it was cheaper than if he bought one at a time. He never thought about burial plots until yesterday. He shook his head at the price. The gentleman behind the counter misunderstood his silence as grief.

"I'm sorry for your loss, Mr. Aaron." Tony never responded.

He mumbled under his breath at the price and the expense of the day. He knew the final blow was yet to come as he jerked his car into the monument drive. He pounded the steering wheel at the thought of its cost.

"I'll be right back." He slammed the car door.

"Geez!" Tom mimicked. "What's with him?"

Terri never took her eyes from the view out of the side window, "He's a jerk. A cheap jerk! Serves him right."

Tom stared at his sister's comment. He had never heard this side of his sister before. He nudged her arm.

"What's up with you?"

Terri turned to her brother with hatred in her eyes. "You just lost your mother, you asshole! Don't you care? Doesn't it matter to you? All you think about is getting laid! You're worse than him!" Her eyes pointed to her father who was only a few feet from the car. He opened the door before Tom had a chance for rebuttal.

"Everything okay in here?"

Their eyes burned at each other, but not a word was spoken. No one wanted to suffer the wrath of Tony Aaron. His words always cut the deepest.

"Fabulous. Just fabulous," Terri's words were laced with sarcasm. Tom glared at his sister. She stared out of the side window.

As they turned into the drive, Tom tried to make small talk. "That didn't take long, Dad. What did you pick out?"

"Something simple. I told the man that Sam was a pretty plain person."

Terri looked at her brother. He sat with his mouth open. His mother was as far from 'simple' as he could imagine. He knew what his father did. Terri mouthed the word 'asshole'.

Tony sat in silence on the edge of his bed. How could he sleep in the bed where his wife was murdered? He looked at the pillow void of its case. The sheets had been taken by the police as evidence. The only piece of bedding, which wasn't confiscated, was the duvet cover and it lay in a puddle on the floor.

His thoughts moved from self-pity to rage. His mind could not comprehend what had happened. He stroked his beard stubble and placed his head in his hands. He heard shuffling at the door. It was Terri.

"Dad, are you okay?"

Tony sat in silence. *Okay,* he thought. *What is okay?* He stuttered his response. "Yeah...I'm...okay...I guess."

Terri's eyes were flooded with tears. More than anything she needed reassurance from her father, reassurance that everything would be okay, but Tony was incapable. He spoke no other words to his daughter, nor did he comfort her. After ten minutes Terri went to her own bedroom and cried herself to sleep.

Tony was immersed in self-pity. He moved through the events of the day. He thought of how Sam broke her ankle. How he sacrificed his time to take care of her. How he

231

helped her into their bed. How he brought her ice water and left her to rest undisturbed.

He thought about the staff in the hospital. He knew most of them well. He remembered one nurse, Janey Hemple, owed him money from last month and still hadn't paid. He remembered how her eyes drifted to the floor in shame when she saw him. He couldn't understand how people could simply not pay their bills. *How could they live with themselves?*

His thoughts moved in and out of deranged self-righteousness. He remembered how he helped Chester Tote with his bucket of bleach water. He smiled at the thought of how he knocked fifteen dollars off of Chester's bill three months ago because he was having a tough time. He failed to recall how he had overcharged him ten dollars the past two months to make up for his generosity.

He replayed most of the events of the day somehow building himself up as the hero as well as the victim simultaneously. His face moved through many emotions of joy and satisfaction, but ultimately ending in self-pity. It was in that moment he remembered the idol.

His back stiffened at the thought of holding that evil thing in the palm of his hand. He remembered the strange reaction from his wife. He forgot his snide religious comment.

He wondered how long Sam had the thing. He wondered where she found it. He couldn't shake the dark look in her eyes as she lunged for it at the hospital. Tony stared at the stripped bed in horror and shivered at the wickedness Sam had invited into the household by harboring that idol.

"Graven images...," he shook his head in disbelief.

Suddenly, he choked on the thought of how her last minutes on earth had been. He imagined how a group of

232

gang members entered his house to come back for their stolen piece. He wondered how long they had waited for her. He imagined them lurking in the shadows as they walked that morning. He wondered if they witnessed Sam breaking her ankle and if they waited outside of the hospital. He walked to the window to visualize where they hid until he left for the market. He wondered if he knew any of them, if they had open accounts at the market, or if any of them owed him money. He cursed Sam for falling prey to temptation.

He had the cordless phone in his hand ready to dial the police with his thoughts. He looked back toward their bed again. Filled with rage of Sam's irresponsibility toward her family and her faith, he cursed her name for the last time.

He threw the telephone across the room. It burst at the seams on impact. The sound of the dancing batteries on the hardwood floor echoed his hatred.

Tony walked calmly down the hallway into the guest suite and slid between the crisp sheets. He would be better off without her. She held him back from the man he knew he could be. Sleep came easy.

# 32

Collin and Jesse were awake for over an hour and dared not move. The digital alarm clock read 4:21 a.m. It seemed like hours since they heard Bill carry Sharon to bed. He slipped down the stairs so quietly it was difficult to hear him. Collin heard him settle into the couch. The squeak in the springs helped.

"Jesse? You awake?"

"Yep."

"Are you ready?"

"Yep."

"Got the flashlight?"

"Yep."

Collin whispered his last order from the edge of his bed, "Remember, quiet, quiet, quiet. If we get caught, we're dead."

"Got it," Jesse answered sarcastically.

"I mean it, Jesse. This is serious business."

"Got it." His tone was better.

They slipped from the covers and remade their bed like they had seen done in the movies. Collin pulled on Jesse's shirtsleeve, pointed to his wrist and then to the door.

Jesse obeyed and followed Collin.

Once they slipped through the door, they stood in the dimly lit hallway listening for any sound. His mother's bedroom door was closed, and neither could ignore the sound of the snores coming from the living room couch. Jesse pointed to his nose and crossed his eyes.

They moved down the staircase one step at a time. They both held their breath and concentrated on the rhythm of Bill's snore. They stopped when their feet touched the bottom stair. Colin held his index finger to his lips and after a few seconds motioned for Jesse to follow.

They walked gingerly past Bill as he slept. Not a single change was detected in his breathing. They tiptoed through the kitchen.

Collin moved slowly as he unlocked the latch on the door. The sound of its release seemed to resonate through the room. Fear settled on their faces as they bent their ears to listen for any sound. None came. Collin lifted the hook latch on the screened door, and they slipped outside.

The early morning air was crisp. The grass crunched under their weight. The rustling sound strained Collin's nerves. Collin became nervous from all of the rustling sound so they slowed their pace. Only their hearts raced.

When they finally arrived at Mrs. Henderson's rose arbor, the enormity of their task turned to a heavy weight. How were they going to find the sun? It could be anywhere. Jesse extinguished the flashlight.

The street lamplight cast a strange glow across the back yard. Mrs. Henderson's porch light still burned brightly. She had never tuned it off since the day Greg Chardt was killed in her backyard. Her doctor had prescribed nerve medication to help her cope with anxiety from the stress.

She lived her life between the balance of sleepiness and hysteria. It was not a pleasant place to be.

The boys stared into her lit kitchen. Satisfied she was not watching, Collin motioned for Jesse to search the yard while he took the task of rooting through the thorny branches. Jesse immediately dropped to the ground and started to search by crawling on all fours. He held his face just inches from the grass.

Collin walked to the far end of the fence. It took several minutes for his eyes to adjust to the dim light, but once he got his night sight he could see the fence and roses clearly. He worked in a slow sideways sweeping pattern. When he searched a three-foot area, he went back over it in the opposite direction. He had to feel absolutely certain that he hadn't missed it. With all the ridiculous press exposure surrounding this case, he was sure the sphere had not been discovered. He felt the police were looking for the gang members and when they found them, the searing objects would be in their possession. Only he and Jesse knew there wasn't a gang. He tried to swallow the growing lump in his throat.

They searched for nearly an hour, and the sky began to show the first sign of morning light. Collin watched Jesse as he combed the grass with his hands. He had been over Mrs. Henderson's back yard twice and was beginning his third search. The slump in the middle of his back magnified his growing discouragement.

Collin focused on the middle of the arbor growth. The foliage was dense and his fingers bled from multiple pricks. He sighed unconsciously.

"Any luck?" Jesse whispered.

"Nothing," Collin answered with disgust. He glanced up at the morning sky. "We don't have much more time."

"I know," Jesse's voice fell.

Collin was about to call off the search when he caught a glimpse of something foreign in the leaves. He thrust his injured hand into the middle of the thicket and wrapped his sore fingers around a cool metal object. He closed his fist around it and pulled his hand back through the thorns. He was amazed when he opened his hand, and lying in his palm was the sphere.

"Thank you. I promise to return them all. I promise," he whispered triumphantly.

He ran over to Jesse and pulled on his shirt. "I got it. Let's go!"

They leapt over the rose fence and ran through the field toward the barn. Collin's heart pounded through his chest. The morning was getting brighter and they had to sneak back into the house. It would be a miracle if Bill were still sleeping.

As they rounded the corner of the house, Collin's fears were realized. Bill was awake and making coffee in the kitchen. He pulled Jesse's shirt and fell into the holly bushes. Jesse couldn't speak. He knew they were caught. The morning newspaper hit the porch floor with a loud thud. The boys jumped at the sound.

Their breathing slowed to normal just as the door opened. Bill walked out onto the porch, bent over, and picked up the morning paper. The screen door closed behind him.

Collin watched Bill through the prickly holly leaves. He scribbled something on a piece of paper, scanned the news for the headline, and snatched up a cup of coffee. He tossed his work shirt over his shoulder. He whistled as he checked the door to be sure it was locked. Collin's face froze with his mouth hung open.

Neither boy moved or made a sound as they watched Bill slide into his truck. He took another long gulp of coffee and pulled out of the drive. No one moved until the roaring muffler could no longer be heard.

"Thank God!" Jesse announced. The tone in his voice sounded relieved. "Let's get back inside before your mom sees us." He started to crawl out of their hiding spot, but Collin grabbed his arm.

"What?" he asked agitated.

"I don't have a key." Collin hung his head.

The sound of defeat never entered Jesse's mind. "Isn't your window open?"

"Yeah?" Collin wasn't following his thought.

"We'll just climb the tree and sneak into your window."

The color returned to Collin's face as he smiled. "Great idea!"

Jesse climbed the tree with ease. Collin was quick to follow. He was surprised at himself that the thought of sneaking back into his house through his bedroom window had never entered his mind.

Jesse closed the window quietly. "How many times have you done that?"

"Lots." His eyes exposed his lie.

"You still have it?"

"Yep."

"Let me see it."

A feeling of selfishness overwhelmed Collin. He didn't want to show Jesse. He had already seen it. He was the reason they were in this mess in the first place. His body stood frozen while his mind wrestled his dilemma. Finally he withdrew his hand from his pocket and revealed the sun in the center of his palm.

"Wow!" was all Jesse could manage. His voice came in a distant singsong tone. He wanted to take it from Collin's hand, but somehow he knew he shouldn't. It was then he noticed the blood. "Holy cow, Collin, you're all ripped up. Look at your hands and arms!"

Collin looked at his hands and wondered how he was going to explain this one. "I gotta wash them off." He started to open his door.

"Wait!" Jesse whispered loudly. He pulled several leaves from his hair. After he inspected the rest of Collin's body, he said, "Okay. You can go now."

Collin tiptoed down the hallway to the bathroom. The water stung his open cuts. He scrubbed the dried blood from his hands, arms, and face. The torn skin started to bleed again. He whispered a silent prayer. After a few minutes the bleeding stopped, but the red welts remained. He closed the door and crawled back into his bed.

Jesse was lying on his back with his hands folded under his head. He stared at the ceiling. He thought about the trouble he had caused his friend and how each person had died. He thought about Jack Hilbert and wondered what his last thought was before he broke his neck in the fall down the stairs. He guessed that Julie and Greg had quite a bit of time to think before their hearts gave out in fear. He felt a cold shiver rush through his body when his thoughts turned to Samantha Aaron. Being smothered would have to be the worst one yet. He tried to shake the thoughts from his mind.

His mother, Liza, was another who met a tragic death, but he felt thankful it wasn't related to the princess. Somehow that soothed his mind. If he had known that he caused his mother's death, he wouldn't be able to live with himself. That burden would be too heavy for an eleven-year-old. He wiped the tears from his face.

The room was silent. The light through the window revealed the tree limbs as they swayed in the morning breeze. Their movement became frenzied and erratic. The roof was alive with the rhythm of the rain. Within minutes it came in torrents.

"We got in just in time." Collin didn't reply. He was sleeping.

Sharon woke with a start. She had overslept. She threw off the covers and ran out of her bedroom door. She was still dressed in the same clothes as yesterday. A shiver passed through her body as she thought about her sister-in-law. With as much distaste as she had for that family, she couldn't help feeling sorry for them. They had never been nice to her or treated her family with respect. They lived their selfish lives in a transparent bubble and it had just burst.

She read the note Bill had left for her on the kitchen table. His handwriting was fluid but a bit shaken.

*Sharon,*

*I wish there was something I could do or say that would make it all go away. In some ways it would make me feel more worthy of all of your kindness. You have been a great friend to me in my time of need. How can I return the favor?*

*Call me when they leave,*
*Bill*

240

She knew this man. She knew he had much more he wanted to say but afraid to say it. She wondered what Mark would think of her involvement with him. She could only see his tender side when they were together. She shook her head at her thoughts. A tear raced down her cheek as she answered the door.

Sharon held her head in her hands as she sat at the kitchen table. She had barely had time to comb her hair before the representative from the bank arrived. It was nine o'clock.

"Well, Mrs. Sims, I believe we have all in order." His voice was void of emotion.

"The bank will assume your property and all belongings if full payment is not received within thirty days. You are not permitted to remove anything from the property beside your personal items. All else is now, or will be, the property of the bank." He tried to sound professional, but he loathed this part of his job.

Sharon sat motionless. Her lips quivered as she tried to speak. Hearing those words was difficult. She suppressed her tears.

"And I have until, when?" she asked quietly.

"Thirty days."

They stared at each other for several minutes in silence. Quiet tears slid down Sharon's tired face.

"Would there be anything else?" she asked with what was left of her dignity.

"Only the list of inventory and equipment," he said sheepishly.

Sharon slid a single piece of paper with a few items scribbled on it. He frowned when he looked at it. He opened his mouth to question the content but thought better of it.

241

He slid the list into his briefcase. His chair chirped across the linoleum floor as he pushed away from the table.

"I'll show myself out," he spoke over his shoulder. "Have a good day."

Sharon scoffed at the comment. *Good day,* she thought, *Yeah, right!*

Collin and Jesse bounced down the stairs at ten o'clock. Sharon had her back to them as they entered the kitchen. Collin knew she was crying as she hung up the receiver.

Her eyes were red and swollen when she turned around. Jesse froze. Collin threw his arms around his mother. She gasped at the scratches on his arms and hands.

Through her tears she asked him what had happened.

Without thinking he said, "I had a bad dream." He wasn't really lying, he promised himself. Jesse woke him from his bad dream. He had dreamed about the princess, but he couldn't remember what happened. It seemed like an age ago.

Sharon threw her arms around him and sobbed. Without looking in Jesse's direction, her hand invited him into the circle. The trio stood on the cool linoleum floor and cried for different reasons.

# 33

Collin stood alone in the barn. Jesse had gone home to shower and change. He would return soon. Sharon was cleaning Mrs. Henderson's house. He was alone with his thoughts.

He pulled the newest piece of the necklace from his pocket and set it on the workbench. His hands shook as he pulled the other pieces from the bottom of his father's tackle box. A piece of abalone bounced as it hit the floor. He smiled when he picked it up and realized it was unharmed. The way it reflected the light and revealed its colors reminded him of the spiral. *"The spiral,"* he thought. He wished he could find it.

He pulled the sun, bird, bug, vial, idol, hands, and the paper cutout of the spiral out of the box and placed them beside each other. He slid them together on the workbench. He placed the paper cut out in the center. He scratched his head as he scanned the other pieces.

243

"Which ones go beside the spiral, I wonder." He cupped his hands over his mouth. He moved his hand toward the bird and thought about the day Jesse and he thought they heard it sing. He laughed out loud.

His gaiety was cut short when this tiny object that he held between his fingers moved and opened its mouth to sing. It tilted its head slightly skyward and sang its song through twice. Fear paralyzed Collin. He stared at the bead until it was finished. Its resting position was the same as before with its wings widespread, one foot drawn to its body and the other on a flat platform. Its beak was closed tight.

Collin squeezed it slightly with his fingers. He thought maybe it had a trigger somewhere within itself that when touched made it sing. He turned it around in his fingers and squeezed every possible spot. It was silent. Sweat covered his hands. Carefully he placed it beside the image of the spiral.

Next he picked up the vial. The gold threads which wrapped loosely around the object looked so fine yet they were hard as iron. He tried to move them but they remained steadfast to their position. It seemed as if they protected the vial from breakage. He remembered the day he found it in the offering plate. His thoughts drifted to the bruises all over Rosemarie Phillips' face. He knew that poor old woman had been through quite an ordeal. He wished he could ask her if she was the one who placed the vial in the plate. His gut told him he was right, but he knew he could not approach her about it. If in fact she was the one who placed it in there, she was the only one who lived to tell about it. His body grew cold from the thought.

His eyes moved over each bead and he thought about their strange ability to burn the skin. He wondered what made them do that. Intimidated by his thoughts, he hesitantly picked up the bird again. It was cool to touch. He stared at it closely, held his breath, and waited for it to sing. It was silent. He placed it again beside the paper spiral.

He placed the bug on the opposite side and the vial beside it. Beside the bird, he placed the sun and followed it with the idol. He picked up the pair of hands and laid them beside the vial. All was even, three pieces on both sides of the spiral.

He sighed deeply. He knew the order wasn't right, but how would he know? He closed his eyes and tried to picture the princess. He tried to remember how the beads were placed on her remains. He shivered at the thought and picked up the pair of hands.

He twisted and turned them around, staring at the alignment of the holes. Realizing the string had to be placed through each piece from top to bottom, it would make each bead lie on their side. He turned each bead sideways.

He shook his head in disgust, "That's not right. They look like they're lyin' crossways." He scratched his head in thought.

He shuffled and shifted each piece until every bead had been moved several times. It didn't seem right. He sighed again with disgust.

When he stopped shifting, he held the sun in his palm. He rolled the bead around in his hand, mesmerized by its movement. When he stopped rolling it, it rested on its flattened side. He noticed two of the spikes were particularly longer than the others. They were the ones directly behind the holes.

Quickly he rummaged through his father's tackle box and found a spool of microfilament fishing line. The box boasted of being rounder, smoother, and thinner than other

30-pound test line. Collin pulled the spool from the box and unwound a few feet of the moss green string. He snipped the end with his dad's clippers and carefully placed them back inside the tackle box.

His tongue wiggled back and forth over his tightly drawn lips as he pushed the line through the holes in the sphere. It slid easily on the line and slipped right off the untied end. It bounced on the barn floor without a sound. Collin stared at the object as it glowed at his feet. The bright red hues faded to orange then to a soft pink before returning to its original copper patina. He waited a few more seconds and knelt to pick it up. He expected it to be hot, but his fingertips told a different story. He picked up the cool bead and placed it on the workbench in front of him.

After tying one end of the fishing line, he restrung the bead. It slid to the bottom and rested on the oversized knot. He picked up the bug and threaded it onto the string. It rested awkwardly onto the sun. Collin slid the bug off the line and tried the vial. The result was the same.

He picked up each bead and checked the bottom and the top for an extra hole for the longer spikes to slip into but found none. He picked up the idol and slid it over the string. It settled beautifully onto the sphere.

Collin shouted with triumph. "One down, six to go!"

He tried to fit each bead on top of the idol and none worked. "Must be the top," he said as he slid the last one from the string. He pulled the sun and the idol from the line and laid them in place, the idol farthest from him, with the sun neatly tucked in place. He continued to try to fit each bead to the bottom long spike. Finally, the hands settled in skillfully.

"Hot dog!" His voice echoed in the empty barn. "I got another one!"

246

With renewed excitement, he moved each piece around until he found the perfect placement for each one. The spiral he figured fit on the bottom. Next, came the bug, followed by the vial. He was amazed how they fit into place so perfectly. The bird fit perfectly under the pair of clasped hands, but no matter what he did, he couldn't get the vial and the bird to fit. He was surprised at the vertical formation the necklace seemed to be taking, but it still didn't all fit together. Disgusted, he took the strung necklace apart and tried every other possible combination, but the end result was always the same. It seemed as if he was missing at least one piece, if not more.

A hot flash of nerves traveled down his spine. He wondered if a piece was still with the princess. He dreaded the thought of going back there. The princess didn't like being disturbed. He was instantly agitated. His thoughts were bent on Jesse.

Collin stood with his hands on his hips. "I don't get it. Jesse said he took seven pieces and there are seven here." Just to be sure he counted them for the tenth time. "One, two, three…" his voice trailed off as he counted, "seven," he finished with a snap. He held his head in his hands.

He glanced down at his watch. It was 12:32 p.m. Where was Jesse? He should have returned by now. He shook his head and drummed his fingers while he stared at the seven pieces before him.

247

Jesse enjoyed the walk home in the rain. He splashed through every mud puddle he could find because he could. He smiled at his freedom.

He really didn't mind being alone. Somehow knowing he would never have to return to the house and find his mother with another man calmed him. It was a strange feeling. Did he miss his mother or did he miss what he never had? After careful consideration he realized it was the latter.

He whistled as he neared his house. The shabby clapboard structure seemed to look a bit better to him these days. It was a terrific thing to be so jaded at eleven. Jesse had learned to build a sizable wall in front of him. He was very skilled at his craft.

He pulled his wet clothes off and threw them in the corner of the kitchen. He knew Sharon would pick them up, wash them, and place the fresh, clean clothes at the foot of his bed. All he had to do was put them away. He smiled at the thought.

He walked naked up the stairs to the only bathroom in the house. By the looks of the room, it was time for Sharon's visit again. Jesse pulled the last clean towel from under the sink. He drew it to his nose and enjoyed the smell of fabric softener, something he never knew until recently.

His heart fluttered as he washed his body and hair. When he finished, he quickly dried off and wrapped the damp towel around his waist. He took five steps down the hall toward his bedroom and swung the door open.

His bedroom was in shambles. His shoes had been tossed from his closet and strewn around the room. Some landed on his bed, some on the floor and one of his sneakers teetered on his windowsill. Most of his clothes were pulled from the drawers and thrown in piles on the floor. Only one drawer remained nearly untouched, his sock drawer.

Driven by sheer panic, instead of leaving the ram-shackled room, he dashed to his sock drawer. The wet towel fell from his waist. His hands dug to the bottom of the drawer searching for his favorite pair of super hero socks. The feel of the plush cotton made them easy to find. His heart raced as his hands pulled each pair of socks from his drawer. His eyes burned as he searched the floor again. Tears flooded and fell from his eyes.

"My arrow...," he whimpered. "It's gone."

He wiped his eyes and began to throw each pair of socks around the room. He moved into his closet and threw his own clothes over his shoulder. He grabbed his favorite flannel, padded its pockets, and threw it on the growing pile.

His anger brought fierce strength. His mind raced until he thought of the only person who knew about the arrow...Collin. Clothes continued to fly around the room. He gritted his teeth. His eyes squinted. He had no idea how or when Collin did this, but it was obvious he did.

One by one he pulled each piece of clothing from his closet until he found what he was looking for--his khakis. He remembered having the arrow in his shorts pocket. He pulled at them but they were stuck. He jerked hard but they wouldn't budge. He tried to search in the pockets, but they were twisted into a tight ball around his favorite belt. He felt the sweat pour down his face. The salt burned his eyes.

With his final frustrated effort he pulled at them one last time. He rolled backwards from their sudden yield. The oversized belt buckle smacked him in the face. The belt tangled around his neck. In a heated rampage, he struggled to free himself.

"He is the only one who knew!" He screamed until his voice was spent. In a moment of calmed assurance he heard the sound of laughter, cruel laughter. He spun to face his assailant expecting to see Collin standing there. Instead, it was the princess.

She sat cross-legged hovering over his bed. In one hand was the pair of super hero socks; in her other was the arrow. Jesse lunged at her but was stopped short by the quick jolt around his neck. He struggled to pull the belt from around his neck, but the more he pulled, the tighter it became.

Her laughter was all he could hear. It pounded in his ears with every rapid heartbeat. His face became flushed. He lunged at her again. He felt his knees begin to give way. With one final jerk, his body crumpled into a heap.

Collin impatiently glanced at his watch again. It was 12:34 p.m. He heard a thud beside him. He looked over the workbench and saw nothing. A tingling sound came from the floor. Lying by his foot was a pink arrow. Instinctively, he glanced upwards, but saw nothing.

He bent over and picked up the arrow. It was cool to touch. He knew from a quick examination it was the bead he was missing. He glanced up to the ceiling again.

Chills trickled down his spine. He heard singing. He knew it was she. He spun around, but he was alone in the barn.

With a loud bang, the barn door flew open. It swung wildly. He heard footsteps running towards him. Cold air froze the room. Collin could see his breath as he struggled to cry out. He clutched the arrow tightly in his palm. The breeze swirled tightly around him whistling in his ears as it moved through and around his body. In a moment, all fell still and eerily quiet. Collin choked. His feet were nailed in place. He opened his mouth once again, but all was silent. He squeezed his eyes closed and tried to calm his racing heart. Slowly he began to take longer, deeper, more relaxed breaths.

When he finally gained enough courage, he opened his eyes. He was alone. The barn was silent as if it also was holding its breath. He opened his hand and stared at the arrow. He didn't want to imagine how it came to be in his hands. He turned his attention back to the necklace that he had laid out before him. The arrow slid into its proper place.

The corners of his mouth turned upward as he slid the last bead onto the fishing line. There he had it. It was complete. He watched it spin around just a few inches from his face. The paper spiral, at the bottom, spun wildly in a circle. He knew that wouldn't do, but for now it was all he had.

Collin counted all the pieces out loud, "One - the spiral, two - the bug, three - the vial, four - the arrow, five - the bird, six - the hands, seven - the sun and eight - the idol." His shoulders relaxed. "Eight pieces, Jesse. There were eight."

His eyes settled on the pink arrow. He tilted his head in curiosity as he stared at it, wondering how it got to him just in the nick of time. The vision of Mrs. Phillips came to his mind. Her face was so battered and bruised. His eyes fell on the vial...Poor Rosemar..." His eyes flew open wide. He stared at the pink arrow. "Oh my God....Jesse!"

251

Collin shoved the necklace into his pocket as he raced out of the barn.

"Jesse...!"

# 34

They buried Jesse two days before his twelfth birthday. It was a difficult time for everyone. Collin's sleep was restless. He lived in constant fear of the princess' revenge. He wondered how long it would be before she came to him.

He returned to *The Great Trail* many times - day and night. "I've got to find it...I'm trying to find it...." He repeated his frantic mumbling over and over.

His body was exhausted. He shoved all thoughts of the princess from his mind. He was convinced that would only bring her wrath. He shuddered at the thought and again forced those feelings out.

With his face pressed close to the dark earth, he scanned the flashlight beam over the path where Julie Garret's body had been found. He'd spent too many hours to count in this area. He scrambled over the tree roots and stones that blocked his search praying for some luck. Fresh tears glistened on the hard ground. His body collapsed.

When he woke, it was dark. The batteries in his flashlight were dead. He shook it to restore its glow. The next thing he remembered was crawling into bed.

He woke in a pool of sweat. His heart raced, though he couldn't recall his dream. The face of the princess flashed in his mind. She called to him with out-stretched arms.

He jumped out of his bed. Dried mud caked his clothes. In a panic he threw his covers on the floor. The mud was ground to powder on his sheets.

Collin spent many hours alone in the barn after Jesse's funeral. He knew he had to get rid of this necklace once and for all. He couldn't count the number of spent tears. He wished he had never gone to 'Indian Hill' that day. So many people had died. Bill had lost everyone although it seemed in the midst of his anguish, he found Sharon. Their relationship had grown to a deep love--even Collin could see that.

He shivered at the thought of how his life had changed this summer. He was about to lose his home, the farm his father worked so hard to keep. The thirty days the bank had given them to satisfy the loan was nearing its term. Jack Hilbert, Liza, Julie Garrett, Greg Chardt, Samantha were gone and now he had lost his best friend, all from a stupid act of selfishness and greed. He cursed Jesse for the umpteenth time for stealing the pieces from the princess. He wiped the tears from his face.

Sharon walked into the barn. Collin heard her coming but didn't turn around. She stood beside him but was silent. The comfort of her arm around his shoulder brought tears to Collin's eyes again. He buried his face in the softness of her skin and sobbed. Sharon stared at the workbench covered with pieces of abalone, fishing line, and carving knives. She knew these things were precious to Mark and how they had brought him comfort in his final days. She was surprised how important they had become to Collin. She held him tightly until his whimpers stopped.

She felt Collin's shoulders relax. She lifted his chin toward her and kissed his forehead. She wiped the tears from his cheeks and smiled at him. She walked out of the barn without a word.

She stood on the back porch of Bill's home as she had done a thousand times before, but today was different. Her only task today was to clean Jesse's room. She swallowed the lump in her throat and walked into the house.

The smell of bleach from yesterday still lingered in the air. She set the newspaper on the kitchen counter. The headlines stared back at her:

### YOUTH'S DEATH RULED
### UNRELATED TO BRANDING GANG

She wiped the tears from her cheeks and walked up the stairs.

She silently swung Jesse's bedroom door open. She drew in a deep breath. Her eyes settled on his favorite pair of socks lying on his bed. One was turned inside out. She smiled at the super heroes' faces smiling back at her as she put them together in a sock ball. She sat on the edge of his bed and cried.

She took her time that morning in Jesse's room. She smelled each shirt as she re-hung them in his closet. The only thing missing was the belt, which was wrapped around Jesse's neck. The police had taken it weeks ago. She asked them not to return it.

255

The last thing Sharon did was smooth out the wrinkled bedspread. She fluffed the pillow and drew it to her nose. Her muffled voice couldn't be heard.

"Why, Jesse, why? You had your whole life ahead of you."

She placed the dampened pillow on top of the bed and rearranged it several times before finally walking out of the room. She drove home in a daze.

Bill walked into Sharon's kitchen freshly showered from work and threw his arms around her. He whispered, "Thank you," into her ear and she smiled. It had been three weeks since Jesse's death and thanks to Sharon his room was back to normal, whatever that was.

Sharon watched Bill read the paper in silence as he sat at her kitchen table. She stirred a pot of chili and smothered her face in the rising steam. He turned the front page over and put his head in his hands. Sharon wrapped her arms around him. They both cried.

Collin slipped into the kitchen without being noticed. He picked up the paper and read an article on the bottom right corner.

### TIM LORIE OFF TO NEW YORK

Two photographs of the now famous local reporter flanked the headlines. One photo showed Tim reporting from Mrs. Henderson's rose fence and the other was a photograph of Tim at his desk at The Daily View. His face was intense as he crouched over his computer keyboard. He had on a pair of black glasses that he never wore when he was in front of the camera. His pencil sat sideways in his mouth. The pictures had no captions under them.

The article continued with all of Tim's accomplishments and stated how his tenacity had been recognized by 'the big guys' and consequently resulted in two job offers. Tim was quoted as saying he would never forget his roots in Ohio. The editorial was written by the woman who would take Tim's place. It was her first article for The Daily View.

Her final comment was her own. "Good luck, Tim. You belong in New York." A thumbnail photo of a pretty blonde punctuated the article.

When Collin finished reading the piece, his mother and Bill were staring at him wide-eyed. He laid the newspaper down on the table and tapped the printed words.

"Tim's going to New York. How 'bout that?" No one answered.

Collin twirled his new creation around his fingers. He strung it onto the doubled moss-green microfilament fishing line. His carved spiral looked crude but was the best he could do with the materials and skill he had. The piece of abalone spun slowly as it dangled in front of him.

He gathered the rest of the pieces and strung them in their rightful place on the necklace. The final knot brought closure. He smiled at what he saw. He started to place the necklace over his head and then thought better of it. He carefully slid it into his pocket. He wrapped the rope from the haymow over his shoulder and walked toward *The Great Trail*.

The evening sun slid low into the western sky. The brilliance of its power added to the depth of the thickened breeze. The trees whispered of dark and lonely tales of the sinister summer. Hushed voices held their tongues as he slipped through the thicket at the wood edge. He walked uninhibited up the mound on Mr. Crafter's property.

Collin tied the rope round the tree and walked to the top. He peered down into the darkened hole. After patting his pocket for the necklace, he tossed the rope through the opening. He tugged on it for security one last time, drew in a deep breath, and disappeared from view.

The rope swayed gently as he shimmied to the floor. No longer afraid or intimidated, he stood in the darkness alone. The tomb was silent. He reached for his flashlight and filled the room with light.

He knelt beside the rummaged bones of the princess and pulled the necklace from his pocket. He swallowed hard.

"I...I...don't know what to say," he whispered. "We've been through a lot, you and I." He held up the necklace as if he was showing it to her. "I did the best I could." He pointed to the spiral. "It was a piece of abalone from my dad's tackle box, you know, fishin' stuff...anyway I carved it from the biggest piece I could find. I know it's smaller than yours, but I can't find that one." Shivers from thoughts of sure death ran through his body, "I hope no one has it...." He tried to smile.

"My dad loved abalone. He had lots of pieces, but this one was the biggest. I don't know what yours was made of, but this was the closest thing I had. I carved it myself. I remembered how it hung, with the large part on the bottom and winding around until it got smaller at the top." He held it up in the light, "See? That's how I did it." He sighed, "I hope it's ok." He dropped his voice, "It's the best I could do."

He rested back on his heels and touched each bead as he spoke, "When chute is opened, a helper will come." He felt the hair on the back of his neck rise when he realized that he was the helper. He sighed and continued to speak, "He will give you the light and show you the way. You will sing like a bird to announce your arrival. I will lift you toward the light and bring you to the gods."

It was then he remembered the dream. Those were the words spoken to the princess by the old man. Without another word he slipped the necklace over the princess' skull. He tried to arrange it to rest on the disheveled rib cage. He saw a vision of Jesse kicking the bones as he gathered the last piece of the necklace. Collin covered his mouth in horror.

He mouthed the word *sorry* as he stood. He moved the light over the skeleton to admire the necklace in its proper place. The spiral spun freely as it dangled through her dry bones. Collin smiled.

"You rest now. Your secret is safe with me. Your helper, me...I... have helped to restore your dignity." He moved a few bones to their proper position. "You have your necklace back, all together in one piece...as best as I could."

Collin felt a twinge of sadness as he stood over the young girl's remains. He knew this would be the last time he visited her. He knew he would never return to this place again. It was sacred to him, if only to him.

He walked to the rope and turned off the flashlight. He climbed up quietly in the dark and stopped a few feet from the opening of the chute to rest. He looked toward the dark floor and whispered, "Good bye, princess." His voice trailed to barely audible, "Good bye."

His hand touched the first of the climbing rocks in the chute when he heard her begin to sing. He stopped and closed his eyes. Contentment filled him as he listened to the sound of beauty. She sounded happy he thought. His chest swelled with pride. Pleasure streamed down his face as his suspended body swung in the center of the chute.

Suddenly the floor began to rumble and her voice grew louder and closer. He felt the rope swing wildly between his legs. He held his breath as cold air rushed from below him. His hands gripped the rocks with fear. He was frozen in place. He could feel her cold breath around him. He squeezed his eyes closed and tried to concentrate on the sweetness in her voice. He tried to dismiss the thought of death from his mind. He tried to relax and convince himself he would not be harmed.

Her voice was upon him now. The darkness below was flooded with a bright light. The sharp contrast from the gloom pierced his eyes like daggers. Once again he squeezed his eyes tight trying to ward off his certain fate.

He could feel the softness of her clothing as it brushed past his skin. He forced himself to open his eyes. He was startled to find two soft brown eyes smiling at him barely three inches from his own face. His fear melted as she pleaded to him for his help.

With renewed courage Collin moved his hands and feet from the rope and began to climb out of the chute. The princess waited for his guidance. He pulled himself through the opening and knelt on the ground. Instinctively, he lowered his hand through the hole. He felt the princess' frail hand grasp his, and he helped her through the final ascent.

When she appeared through the opening, the shadowed sun hid her shaded frame. The wind tossed her dress in a graceful twirl around her slender body. She began to sing again. Her face and hands were upturned. The breeze lifted her from the ground. She glanced back at Collin and brought her hand to her mouth, kissed it, and tossed it back to him. In a reaction that came as pure instinct, Collin's fist closed as if catching the kiss and drew it quickly to his chest. His heart warmed at the gesture. She smiled at him.

The sun behind her flashed in a bright burst of color. When the sunspots faded from his eyes, she was gone. Collin's upturned face stared into the clouds. The color turned to a brilliant orange. He was mesmerized as the color slowly faded to pink until the only shade left was a hint of purple. His eyes followed the fading hue as it settled to the edges of the clouds. Without moving, he watched until the sky grew dark.

He fumbled for the flashlight as he tripped. The rope lay coiled at his feet. The beam of the light skirted across the ground. The opening was closed. Not a single sign of the chute remained. Collin's smile was laced with amazement.

With the untied rope slung over his shoulder, he made his way through the edge of the woods. Not a sound rustled through The Whispering Trees. Even Dead Man's Lookout held its breath. His footsteps were silent as he moved down the trail.

He thought about the past few weeks——how the investigation seemed to die with the exit of Tim Lorie. There wasn't another reporter within the area that had the passion or skill to keep the newspapers flying off the shelves. The police seemed to keep all leads under a heavy blanket of silent submission. Not another word was printed about the Branding Gang and with no new incidents the story slipped to an unpleasant memory.

Collin swallowed the lump in his throat. Jesse was always on his mind especially when he was on the trail. He tried to shake his guilt, and it helped if he blamed Jesse for stealing the beads in the first place. Yet, he felt responsible.

Bill and Sharon walked hand in hand. They enjoyed their evening strolls these past few weeks. It seemed the frantic scare of the 'Branding Gang' died with Jesse. It probably had a lot to do with the fact that Tim was focused on his New York move and didn't want to continue a story that would keep him tied to the area. His dream of moving to New York City became a reality, so his coverage was quiet these past few weeks. And it was a good thing. It gave the town of Minerva a chance to recover from a story that should have never been told.

"Are you okay?" Sharon asked her silent walking partner.

"I'm with you," Bill toyed.

Sharon nudged him with her elbow. If the truth were told, she enjoyed his company. It reminded her of the old high school days, and lately reflection was a better place to live than in the future. Her bank countdown was rapidly approaching.

"You know I've been thinking, Sharon. You two can stay with me when the bank...," he swallowed the rest of his words.

Sharon expression never changed. She had been hoping for the invitation. She smiled, "...takes the house?" Bill coughed. "It's okay, Bill. I need to make plans. I keep hoping for a miracle, but..." she laughed at the sound of those words, "but I'll take you up on that offer."

Bill squeezed her hand. "Maybe that is *my* miracle." He lowered his head, "My house is not as nice as yours, but I swear if I could figure out a way to keep it for you, I would."

She patted the back of his hand, "I know you would and that's why you are so special to me. You've always had my back." She smiled at his flushed face.

Collin swung the beam of light over the path in front of him. He was relieved to have the necklace back with its rightful owner. He was proud of himself to have given it up so freely. He was more afraid of the consequences if he hadn't. It was hers. She wanted it. She should keep it.

His thoughts drifted to the princess and his last vision of her. He could feel his heart's burden lift as her feet moved from the ground. The spiral he carved pleased her. Her gratitude was obvious and he finally understood his role. He was her helper foretold hundreds of years before. *He was the helper.* That thought rocked him to the core. He couldn't comprehend it.

He tripped over a branch that covered the path. His face landed in a bed of fresh pine boughs. A fir tree had been uprooted from the last windstorm, and it blocked his passage. The root ball dripped with fresh dirt and pebbles and soared into the air nearly ten feet.

Collin moved his light over the exposed roots. Something glimmered in the beam. He moved closer and retraced the outline with his light. He saw it again. Dangling near the top of the roots was the spiral. He gasped.

He swung his legs over the tree and shimmied to its end. His arms were much too short to reach it and the unstable tree rocked. He was afraid to clamber over the exposed roots. The beam illuminated it again and he was mesmerized as it spun freely. It hung as though it were attached to something. He slid from the trunk and walked around the backside.

The hole from the pine tree left in the ground was huge. Nestled in the bottom were several large rocks and a small metal box. Attached to the box was a string. It wound its way through the tangled mass of roots, dirt, and moss. At the end of the string spun the spiral.

With one quick tug, the spiral broke free. It landed in Collin's hands. It was much larger than he remembered. His heart pumped from excitement. He was so happy to find it. His thoughts turned to the princess.

"She wanted me to find it!" he said in a loud voice.

He pulled a dead leaf from the spiral and wiped it on his pants. He was so preoccupied with the joy of discovery he forgot what was on the other end. He placed the spiral in his pocket and started to walk away. The fishing string pulled tight and yanked it from his pants. He traced the line to its end.

Deep in the hole was a metal box. Only the lid and one side were visible. Collin climbed under the root ball and tried to pick it up. It was stuck. With only his hands he dug through the mud. Finally, after fifteen minutes of digging by the light of the flashlight, it was free. He struggled to pick it up. It was small but extremely heavy.

His hands shook as he struggled with the lock. It opened with a loud crack. Collin fell backwards at the sight of what he saw. Gold coins spilled from the box. The coins were old, very old. His muddy hands moved through the loot. He had found a part of the lost French treasure. He thought that was just a legend. He shook his head in amazement.

Without thinking he began to gather the string. The spiral hopped along the bed of spent pine needles as Collin pulled it toward him. Gathered in his hands was the moss-green fishing line that strung the princess' necklace together. He sobbed uncontrollably.

"Thank you," was all he could muster.

He gathered his heavy box, which seemed oddly easy to carry. He placed a piece of the string and the spiral on the lid. He couldn't wait to go home. Did he have a story to tell his mother!

After he shook the mud cakes from his clothes, he started down the path toward home. His body stiffened in place as he remembered his promise. He promised to keep her secret. The trees swayed in hushed agreement. They seemed to echo the word *secret*. They whispered his promise the rest of the walk home.

Collin burst through the door with excitement. No one was home. Sharon's handwriting on a note simply stated:

*Went for a walk. We love you.*

Collin washed his hands, threw off his muddy clothes, and changed into clean shorts and a t-shirt. He placed the metal box on the kitchen table and opened it to face the kitchen door. He climbed up on the kitchen counter and pulled three stemmed glasses from the top shelf. He filled the champagne flutes with water. After a quick phone call, he turned out the light and sat at the kitchen table.

His heart raced with anticipation when he finally heard his mother and Bill talking to a young blonde who had just pulled into the driveway. The trio walked up to the back door; Bill and Sharon held hands while the young woman clutched her camera and tape recorder.

Breinigsville, PA USA
07 October 2010
246895BV00002B/1/P